I0629948

Winter is Past

by

Victoria C. Slotto

Lucky Bat Books

Winter is Past
Copyright 2011 Victoria C. Slotto
Cover Photography by David Slotto
Cover Design by Theresa Rose

All rights reserved.

Published by Lucky Bat Books
LuckyBatBooks.com

For, lo! The winter is past. The rains are over and gone.
Flowers appear in our fields.

Song of Solomon, 2:11-12

Dedication

To my mother, Brigid Ceretto, who gave me life,
To my friend and kidney donor, Paula Roukie Dinkins,
who saved my life.
And to my husband, David, who makes it so worth living.

Prologue

Fear has enveloped me like a subtle fragrance for as long as I can remember.

Not the Stephen King kind of horror, such as a corpse come back to place a moldy hand upon your shoulder, nor the wrenching terror you feel when a roller coaster crests to the summit before plunging off a precipice. This fear doesn't resemble a back-alley encounter with a rapist or the devastation of those who witnessed the tragedies of 9/11.

No, the fear I know is subtle and pervasive. It's more like a slow tug — the loss of control that takes over when you've been caught in the arms of a riptide — or like the blindness that surrounds your car when you creep your way through a heavy downpour, alone on a deserted stretch of highway. It's the growing sense of futility that unfolds in the pages of the daily news or that's spewed at us by talking heads and spin doctors.

I've never suffered the illusion that I'm in control of this unpleasant companion who's been with me from childhood. And it's only in the past year that I've accorded it a name.

That's how long it's been since the process of healing my fears began. I can recall it as though it happened yesterday.

One
A Year Ago, March
Mt. Rose, Nevada

We were standing on a hillside silken with fresh spring powder and I was nursing second thoughts about the wisdom of taking up a new sport at this point in my life. Fields of sparkling diamonds spanned the white slope in front of us.

Josh, my husband, slapped his gloved hands together and scattered snowflakes into the frosty breeze. "You're scared, aren't you?" he asked. "When we moved to Reno, you told me you wanted to learn to ski."

"That was a while back."

He pushed my sunglasses up my crooked nose. "So why should it be different now?"

When I reminded him that I was six years older and had Kathryn's kidney hitching a ride in my abdomen, he pooh-poohed my reluctance.

"You're not exactly an old lady," he said, "and a tumble in soft snow isn't going to hurt you or that kidney, honey. These are beginners' slopes."

I can still visualize every detail: my husband tucking a wayward strand of that chestnut hair of his beneath his hood; sunshine backlighting his angular profile while I cradled the life-giving organ I had received from my best friend and colleague, and the exact words I said. "Don't you think I owe it to Kathryn to take good care of myself?"

On cue, one of Reno's most caring healers propelled her way toward me. Kathryn Scott's cocoa brown skin stood out against the stark landscape.

"Hey, Claire, are you ready?" she hollered at me and I knew right away that she read my apprehension. It often seemed to me as if she knew what I was thinking before I did.

Her words confirmed my suspicions. "I didn't lend you my kidney so you could sit back and watch life go by, girlfriend." Then she saved my butt again. She grabbed my arm, and shuffled me across hard-packed snow to rent a pair of snowshoes. We left our guys to do their thing, with the promise of meeting up in a few hours.

As we trudged away, I tossed a warning over my shoulder in the general direction of our husbands. "You two be careful; don't forget, we're hospice docs, not orthopedists, and it's been a while since we played with broken bones."

That's how it's always been for me. What others might call fear, I would describe as an understated kind of trepidation masked as caution. That Saturday morning it hung in the air like the scent of the towering pine trees surrounding us on the exquisite Sierra slope. But this was only the beginning of a year that, for me, unraveled like a prescient dream.

A few hours later, clods of snow from my jacket formed puddles on the floor of the Mount Rose Urgent Care Center. A large digital clock above the admissions' counter announced that it was just after two o'clock. With my aching quads and calf muscles begging for reprieve, I watched the radiology tech disappear with my husband, whose splinted leg was propped on the wheel chair extension.

"What exactly happened?" I asked Michael, Kathryn's better half. I eased myself into a hard chair in the waiting room. "What'd you guys do this time? You took a shot at the advanced slopes, didn't you?"

I could picture the scene in my imagination.

Michael bowed his head and ran his fingers through black, nappy hair. His lips suppressed a guilty grin. "Well, yeah," he answered. "We were sure we could manage something more challenging. On the second run, Josh hollered at me, and before I knew it I saw his ski, sticking up at a right angle."

"Do you think he broke anything?" I peeled damp outerwear from my body.

The muscular black man shrugged his shoulders. "He could bear a little weight when the medics helped him off the slope."

"He knows how to fall — he used to ski every chance he got before he married me. Maybe it's only a sprain." My words were as optimistic as I could make them, but the knot in my gut tightened as I considered the possibilities. It hadn't been a week since some guy had smacked into a tree on that same run and died.

"You're both shivering," Michael said, looking from his wife to me. He sprang to his feet, searched his backpack, and extracted a wallet. "And Claire," he said to me, "you're as white as the snow outside. There's a vending machine down the hallway; I'll get the three of us something hot to drink."

"You sore?" Kathryn asked as she sank into the seat beside me.

"A little, but I can still move — it'll be worse tomorrow. How about you? Why'd you want to call it quits early?" I turned to study my companion.

"It got too cold when the wind kicked up, and I think I pulled a muscle," she admitted.

"A muscle — where?"

"My side," Kathryn said. "It'll go away."

"Show me."

Kathryn pointed to her right flank, which caused all kinds of alarms to sound in my head, but before I could say anything Michael walked up and handed us each a paper cup filled to the brim with piping-hot cocoa.

"What's the matter?" he asked Kathryn, whose expression now twisted in a grimace. She continued to brace her side.

"Just a tweaked muscle," she answered.

Michael sat beside her and drew his brows together. "We're in the right place; get it checked out."

"Please, Kathryn." I leaned toward her and saw a fine line of perspiration breaking across her upper lip.

"No. I'm okay." Kathryn dismissed me with a wave of her hand, but the hint of a frown stayed planted on her face.

At the end of the day, I rested Josh's crutches on the floor and then crawled into bed beside him. I had to lie on a diagonal to match him so he could hold me. His elevated leg protruded from beneath rumpled bed covers. I wove my fingers through his, squeezing tightly. "God, Josh, what if something serious had happened to you today? Why do you always have to take risks? You haven't been on skis for a couple of years."

"You're angry, aren't you?" he asked me.

"Damn right," I told him, "angry and scared. We've come through too much for you to take stupid chances." I have to confess that even as the words tumbled from my lips, I hated myself for nagging. There it was again, as always — fear — the nameless entity that marred this moment I could have shared with my husband, a moment of relief that his injury was no more than a sprain.

Josh ran his forefinger over the small scar that transected my upper lip and hushed me. "I'm not going anywhere, sweetheart," he promised. "We still have lots of living to do. You were given a second chance at life so we could enjoy it together, right?"

I took his other hand and kissed his fingertips. "I don't think I could survive without you — I don't know if I'd want to."

"You're stronger than that, Claire, but tonight, thank God, it's not an issue, is it?" Josh reached up and snapped off the light. The almost-full moon spilled through sheer curtains.

As my husband slipped into a medication-induced sleep, a different vision of loss jolted me back into full alertness. Like a waking nightmare, an image of Kathryn's face, distorted in pain, surfaced from my memory.

"Josh," I shook his shoulder.

"Huh?" he groaned.

"What if something's really wrong with Kathryn?"

"What do you mean?"

"The pain I told you about — it's over her right kidney — her only kidney."

Two
Reno, Nevada

The following day, Josh sprawled on our couch in the family room and fondled the remote, chasing scores for the beginning of the baseball season and the wind-up of pro basketball. His useless appendage reposed on a mountain of pillows piled on the coffee table. Beside him, our young terrier mix, Murphy, curled into a ball. Light streamed through the window and highlighted tufts of his white fuzz.

The Sunday paper, strewn in stacks about the hardwood floor, held my attention. I was busy searching for bargains and winter closeout sales. Benisse, my ancient Golden Retriever, sprawled on the rug at my feet.

I can't quite explain what it was like. A gnawing concern kept pushing its way into my consciousness and I kept shoving it back under. My heart fluttered off and on, and my breakfast threatened to come up on me. This nausea was compounded by the smell of bacon that still hung heavily in the family room.

"I've got to call Kathryn," I finally said to Josh. His reassurances the previous night hadn't been enough. I'd wakened frequently, disturbed by my wandering thoughts, until finally I abandoned the comfort of bed and retreated downstairs with a book.

"Michael told us they're having breakfast with his parents after church, remember?" Josh muted a commercial for beer. "Speaking of parents, did you call Helene yet?"

"Uh-oh! Didn't even think of it," I answered. "I'm going to be in trouble."

Here was another stressor I didn't need to think about right now. The controlling woman who raised me still made her presence known, even though hundreds of miles separated us. There were times when I continued to feel like a teenager returning home late from a date, and this usually happened during our weekly calls — Saturday, ten o'clock, or else.

I reached for the phone and scanned caller ID. "She tried to get us three times yesterday — I forgot to let her know we'd be out."

"Better do it now, Claire," Josh suggested. "Helene has you dead and buried if she doesn't hear from you."

"I know, but let me get a hold of Kathryn first. It's almost two o'clock — they should be home by now." I hit speed dial and headed to the study while Josh returned to the Oakland A's. I chewed at a hangnail — a really bad habit I'd recently acquired. Anxiety for Kathryn toyed with the resentment I felt toward my mother, although that anger, I suppose, should have been directed at myself for giving in to her every demand.

Kathryn answered right away without a greeting: "Yes, I went to urgent care first thing this morning, and yes, it still hurts." Her voice had a brittle edge to it. I wasn't sure if I heard anger or pain, so I listened as she continued. "They did some tests and tomorrow I'm going to see my own doc for follow up. That's what you wanted, isn't it? We didn't even get to church. My husband's a bigger nag than you, Claire."

"God, you do know me, don't you?" I said.

"What do you expect from your med school roommate? Sometimes I think I know you better than you know yourself. Not only that, you've got my kidney in you. You may have the white genes and I got the black ones, but no one can tell me we're not sisters."

A bit of relief at her humor fueled my laughter.

"So, how's Josh?" Kathryn asked.

"He's lost in the world of sports. I guess that's as good as pain meds for now. I finally talked him into taking a few days off of work. Homecare nursing isn't exactly sedentary, and he needs to stay off his feet. But tell me more about what's going on with you. What did they say?" I had to force the conversation back in her direction.

"Nothing more than what you already know. I pulled a muscle, it hurts, and I went to get it checked out — in self-defense. Listen, I'll call you tomorrow after my appointment. I promise. Now go and enjoy the rest of your day and stop dreaming up a crisis, okay?

After I call my mother, I told myself.

I can't say I felt any relief after talking to Kathryn, but somehow I managed to put it aside for the time being as I punched in Mother's number.

The phone rang four times before going to voice mail. By nine o'clock that evening, six attempts later, I stopped trying; I knew that she didn't want to talk to me.

Three

Bright light flooded through half-open blinds early the next morning. Josh and I still lay half asleep, cuddled under the comforter. The phone jarred me into full wakefulness with its shrill ring. Through half-closed eyes I saw Kathryn's number flash on caller ID.

Her voice sounded hoarse, as though she'd just rolled out of bed herself. "Can we get together for lunch today?" she asked me.

"Sure. Is something the matter? What time is it, anyway?" I sat up now, pulling the covers off of Josh by accident.

He stretched and peeked at me, his face screwed into a question mark.

"It's early — I'm sorry. Let's meet at your house — it's between our offices."

"Works for me. But, are you okay?"

"See ya later," was the only answer Kathryn gave me before the phone went dead.

"What was that about?" Josh asked. He shrugged his shoulders when I told him.

By noon, I had visited two patients in their residences, then dropped by the hospice office before returning home with an armful of paperwork that I hoped to polish off in the afternoon. I'd had a heck of a time concentrating and felt guilty, knowing how others depended on me for comfort in their last days. That didn't make me feel any better about myself or whatever was coming down.

Kathryn entered through the front door without knocking and without a greeting. She headed straight for the kitchen and pulled out plates and forks.

"What's going on?" I asked as she filled glasses with iced tea. Kathryn just shook her head and dished up the salad she'd picked up from a nearby deli.

The dread that had hounded me throughout the morning began to take on flesh. From vague disquiet — a form began to emerge and its shape was amorphous, but invasive. Something was about to happen that would change our lives. I felt it, and my premonitions weren't usually too far-fetched.

Once we settled on the deck, we ate without speaking. There was no way I could read Kathryn's expression with her eyes hidden behind her sunglasses. A brilliant spring day defied the mood hanging over us. The late season frost that had surprised us in the morning gave way to cerulean skies sprinkled with wisps of clouds and temperatures in the high sixties. I just ate and waited for Kathryn to take the lead.

When she finally set aside her half-eaten salad, I offered a plate of cookies. She took one, but just held it between her thumb and forefinger.

"Can I ask you a favor?" Kathryn said to me at last.

I nodded and watched a bee circling Kathryn's head; she swatted at the pest and it flew away. Sun reflected off of her dark glasses. "Are you free Thursday afternoon?" she asked. "I'd like you to go with me to see Brian Forrest."

Brian was a classmate of ours in med school. He's a surgeon specializing in diseases of the urinary tract and his father is my nephrologist, who monitors my kidney transplant. I just looked at her with what I imagine was the queerest expression. "Brian?" I finally asked.

Kathryn nodded, crinkling her brows.

A vision of Kathryn clutching her side popped onto the screen of my memory.

"I got a call from my internist, John Cormier, late yesterday afternoon — there's blood in my urine." Kathryn's voice cracked. "He made me come in to meet him at the Emergency Room. He doesn't want me to wait; he wants Brian to evaluate me for a tumor."

I stared at the tightened muscles in Kathryn's jaws. "It's probably an infection." I heard myself assuming Kathryn's role this time, trying to minimize the implications of what she'd just said to me.

"I wish — they tested, but it came back negative." Kathryn crunched the cookie that she held in her hand and it fell in crumbles on the table.

"It's got to be a mistake, Kathryn," I insisted. "Make them do it over."

"They did, Claire." Kathryn rose abruptly. "I'm sorry — I have to go. I have a meeting at one-thirty. I'll call you later." She stood and headed for the gate.

I trotted after Kathryn, who jogged along the brick path beside our house. My eye caught sight of a tiny wren, cowering in the dense foliage of a rambling juniper shrub. Overhead, a majestic red-tailed hawk circled, squawking a message of certain doom at the tiny bird. I felt tears well up in my eyes, then turned my attention back to Kathryn who now disappeared through the redwood gate.

When I caught up to her, I grabbed her by the shoulder and searched for words to soothe her and calm my own shattered nerves.

"I'm okay, Claire," Kathryn insisted, and pulled away from me.

"Things will work out. They always have," I said.

"I hope so," Kathryn said in a flat voice before getting into her car.

Oh, how the futility of that empty promise echoed in my brain as I watched Kathryn disappear around the bend. I loathed myself for letting her run away like that. That was when I remembered the day I had begged Kathryn not to take the risk of becoming my donor. My friend had laughed.

Josh arrived home late, still walking with a gimp, but without his crutches. He didn't say a word but just fetched a beer from the fridge, lumbered across the room, and fell onto the couch beside me. The dogs ran to him and hopped up, begging for attention, but he petted them without awareness.

"Where were you?" I asked. "You're supposed to be taking it easy."

"I went in to work to meet with my boss. Starting next week, they're gonna let me work the phone unless I can get around better before then. You know I'm not cut out for sitting around doing nothing." A smile hadn't crossed his face.

"What's wrong? Is being stuck inside that bad?"

"Michael got a hold of me this afternoon and told me why Kathryn had lunch with you. The guy's out-of-control, Claire."

A flush of horror overpowered me as I realized what Kathryn's husband must be thinking. "He blames me, doesn't he?" I asked Josh.

"If so, that's his problem — it's not your fault." He almost spat the words out, then went on. "We don't even know if it's serious; it could be something like a kidney stone or a blood disorder."

"Something like leukemia? That's comforting," I snapped.

"Whatever it is, they can treat it." Josh ignored my sarcasm. "You didn't know anything would happen when she gave you a kidney; nobody did. She had a thorough work-up, and the transplant team told you to leave everything to them, remember?"

I remembered, but couldn't accept what he was saying. "How would you react if you were me?" I said, crossing my arms about my chest, as though that would hold me together.

"There's nothing we can do about it right now, is there?" Josh stared straight ahead.

I reached for his beer and took a long draught, then handed it back to him. I swallowed and turned toward Josh, who leaned forward, shoulders stooped. He clenched the bottle in one hand while the fingers of the other were tensed into a fist. Josh worked the muscles of his jaw like he always did when he was about to say something he'd later apologize for.

"What?" I asked.

I dreaded Josh's dark moods. I always thought of him in the same sentence as sunshine and candy, but when things went wrong, shadows filled the spaces in my heart and I could find no sweetness.

"Nothing." Josh stood, strode across the room grasping the empty bottle, and tossed it with a clatter in the recycling can under the sink. "We can talk about it later. Let's go out to eat; I'm not up to cooking tonight."

We went to a nearby sports bar. Josh watched baseball in silence while I stared at a couple across the room. The younger people sat side-by-side, holding hands and laughing. I wondered how they could be so carefree.

Before heading up to bed, I tried to call my mother again. My attempts the previous day had gone unanswered. This time I decided to leave a message. "Mom, it's Claire. Sorry I missed your calls Saturday. We were . . ."

"Claire, you had me worried sick," my mother burst in. "Where were you?"

I couldn't help but think. What business is it of yours? But instead I explained where we had been and what we had been doing.

"Tell me you didn't do anything foolish." Her voice crackled with disapproval.

"Kathryn and I did a little snowshoeing, that's all." I hesitated and that's where I should have left it but, instead I told her, "Josh twisted his ankle; he's on crutches."

"Does that mean he won't be able to work?"

Just the kind of response I expected. I took a deep lungful of air before answering this time, then said in a steady voice, "He could, but I don't want him to — not yet."

"You let him off too easily," she snapped back.

Unlike you, I thought. "How was your week, Mom?" I closed my eyes and relaxed the hand I'd balled into a fist. Blood flowed back into my whitened knuckles. I hoped my question would redirect the conversation into a safer zone.

"Ugly," she answered. "Your brother is as inept as his wife is obnoxious."

"What happened?" I could picture Lauren, my brother André's wife. Short and forty pounds overweight, her face bore ravages of teenage acne and weathering from too much California sun. Her small eyes, closely placed and squinting out from behind thick glasses, gave her the appearance of a plump weasel.

"André told me we lost three store managers in as many days," Mother continued. "Lauren has the smarts, but no people skills. Claire, you should have been the one to take over the business."

"No, Mom. I'm right where I'm meant to be." Now I scooted forward in the chair and squared my shoulders as I prepared myself for the onslaught of her constant reproof about my career choice. I resolved not to take a plunge into guilt for escaping the woman's domination and the boredom of the world of business.

"Your father wanted you at the helm," she insisted.

"He'd want me to follow my dream, and that's working as a hospice physician. Don't forget, he's the one who taught me to think for myself." I felt a little smug that I had a comeback for a change, but she ignored me and continued to recount the problems that faced the supermarket chain founded by my father.

An image of André came to mind. When I'd visited Southern California last month, he'd sat in silence beside his wife, in crumpled clothes. The sparkle was gone from his eyes, and every time he'd try to speak, Lauren would shush him, or interrupt. He wore unhappiness like an oversized coat.

"I asked you a question, Claire. Are you listening?" Mother's voice pulled me out of my recollections.

"Sorry; what'd you say?" I answered but she just said "Never mind."

At the other end of the line, I could hear raspy breathing. "Mother, I said I'm sorry — I was distracted."

"You're always distracted when I talk to you about the markets." Iciness edged its way into her tone, then she announced that she was hanging up, which is exactly what she did without another word.

I sat in silence. The muscles in the back of my neck tensed and sent a wave of pain up my scalp until the clunking of my four-legged husband nabbed my attention.

"What's the matter?" Josh asked me.

"Same old thing," was all I could answer.

Josh eased himself into an empty chair and faced me. "Helene's pissed we weren't home?"

"Yeah, but more than that." I sucked in a deep breath and released it slowly.

Josh leaned forward on his crutches and listened as I recounted the conversation for him. I ran my fingers up and down the furrow between my brows as if to imprint my anger in my brain.

On the wall, behind Josh, hung a picture of my family. My brother's eyebrows, like untrimmed hedges, perched above hazel eyes, my father's eyes. Our mother stood tall, brunette hair streaked with silver piled atop her head. Perfectly formed lips held back a smile, but she glared at me from the photo, accusing me of some unknown crime.

A memory lingered on the fringe of my consciousness and conjured up a familiar image. I chased the chimera back into the darkness and spoke aloud to Josh. "Why's she so angry all the time?"

"Why don't you ask her?" Josh said. He dragged himself to his feet and hobbled back toward the family room.

I followed with outstretched arms, ready to catch him. "Damn," I said, as a moment of recognition flashed inside me.

"What's the matter?" Josh asked as he turned to face me.

I helped him back onto the couch and repositioned his leg. "Something weird happened just now."

"Tell me." Josh hit the mute button, silencing Bill O'Reilly.

"When we were sitting in the study, I was looking at the picture — the one of my family taken just before Dad died."

"Yeah?"

"It feels like someone's missing."

"What do you mean?" Josh asked.

"I don't know. I can't remember."

Four

uesday morning, I walked into my office and threw my jacket on the empty chair by the door. When I flipped through the calendar on my desk to the last day of April, I had to suppress a yawn. My concern for Kathryn had taken over the night and tossed aside all thoughts of my mother, as well as the fleeting memory of a missing someone, from my mind. Just when I'd begun to slip into a fitful sleep, the phone had rung and I'd grabbed it and listened to the on-call nurse who described a patient whose pain was out of control. I gave her the okay to up the dose of morphine, and then the worry began all over again.

My secretary, Connie, interrupted my lethargy.

I greeted the elderly woman whose blue frizzed hair matched the periwinkle of the sweater that hung loosely over her stooped shoulders.

"Are you okay, Dr. Bergano? Did I startle you?" Connie peeked at me over oblong reading glasses.

"I'm just a little tired, Connie, but I'm here." My scattered thoughts drifted back to Kathryn and I recalled how her brown eyes had sparkled that day almost six years previously when she offered me a kidney. It had been stormy, with thunder cracking in the background, lending even more drama to the scene.

She dropped a stack of medical records on my desk and said, "These are ready for your signature."

"I'll get them done this morning," I promised, and watched her waddle back to her cubicle, then I picked up the phone. I could no longer ignore the heaviness that nagged at me like the lingering dull ache of my leg muscles.

"St. Joseph's Hospice; Dr. Scott," a creamy voice at the other end informed me.

I announced myself and pushed aside the clutter in front of me to be able to listen carefully to Kathryn.

"I thought you'd call about now," Kathryn responded. "So, how's Josh?"

"Bored to death — but how about you?"

"I'm just waiting, girlfriend; you know how that is. Michael's being a piss-ant. As for myself, I'm dealing with it a minute at a time."

"Josh told me about Michael." I twirled an uneven strand of my mousy brunette hair between my thumb and index finger. I really needed a cut. "Is there anything I can do to help?"

"Not much, I'm afraid. He'll come to his senses; he's usually pretty level-headed."

"Kathryn, I'm so sorry."

"About what? It's not your fault." Kathryn hesitated. "Whatever happens, we'll deal with it — we're a team, you know."

After hanging up, I returned to the mountain of charts that teetered on the edge of my desk. I opened a thick folder with a death certificate protruding from it and reached for a pen when the harsh sound of the phone startled the crap out of me.

The Director's husky voice grunted, "I need to see you as soon as possible."

"Should I bring anything with me?" These meetings usually involved sticky money issues and I liked to come prepared to explain why I'd decided to treat a patient with whatever med Isabelle was going to tell me was too expensive.

"Grab me a Coke, will you?" she asked, then hung up.

The boss's abrupt manner didn't irritate me anymore. I'd learned to recognize the woman's façade and I knew that the director and owner of Comfort Care Hospice would do anything for our patients and staff.

"Take a seat," Isabelle said when I knocked at her open door. She took the chilled soda from my hand and motioned me to an empty chair. A grim expression accented her pudgy face, and red rims traced her lower lids. Isabelle pressed her fine lips into a straight, narrow line.

"What's the matter?" I asked. It was easy to see that this was going to be about more than spending too much of the agency's "non-profit," trying to manage someone's nausea.

"I've got bad news." Isabelle said straight-away as she picked up her soda and took a deep swallow.

A flicker of alarm flashed through me and I gripped the arms of the chair as if they were a life preserver tossed to me in the midst of a stormy sea.

"I sold the business," she told me. "A large, nationwide hospice made a good offer and I accepted. You already know we're barely breaking even." Then she told me that the new hospice was going to bring in their own medical director from Vegas. In effect, I was out of a job.

A roaring noise rushed into my head. When I closed my eyes, I saw tiny sparks of light that burst into my field of vision. My position as a hospice medical director had been my dream job since medical school. Since Kathryn held the same position for the only other hospice in town, I saw everything that I had worked for disintegrate in the space of a single sentence: I'm unemployed.

Isabelle came out from behind her desk and took the chair beside me.

"When?" I asked.

"Today's your last day," Isabelle told me. Up close, I could see new crevices between her brows, and the appearance of a wash of gray paint beneath puffy eyes. "Tomorrow at morning report I have to tell the staff," she continued, "then right after that, I'm gone as well. The new administration arrives the following day."

"Have you known this a long time?" Hurt swept over me — I couldn't believe that she had chosen to exclude me from whatever negotiations she'd been a part of. One thing I'd have to say about Isabelle — she'd always kept me in the loop and helped me to feel like a partner more than an employee.

"I knew, but the buyers demanded everything be kept confidential," she explained.

In the glare of Isabelle's thick glasses I saw a reflection of my fear and sadness mirrored in the lenses — a look not unlike those of a patient slowly absorbing the news that hospice care is for those who are about to lose everything.

"They didn't want people leaving for other jobs before they took over," the director continued. "Claire, I'm sorry I couldn't tell you sooner, but you will get six months severance — I did what I could."

Six months, I thought. What kind of irony is that? And I heard my own words, spoken to a frail woman just the previous Thursday. The hospice benefit is for those who, in the doctor's best estimate, have six months or less to live. But that doesn't mean..." But for me, this wasn't an estimate. It meant it is all over, and it's happening today.

Isabelle stood and I followed her implied direction. The boss gave me a clumsy hug and a handful of papers I had to sign, acknowledging that I accepted my fate. I choked back my feelings as Isabelle's stout body pulled away from me.

After the meeting, I snuck into my office, closed the door and buried my head in my arms for a few minutes. It'll be okay, I promised myself. I'd survived a heck of a lot worse than this. When I finally raised my head, I saw my surroundings as if for the first time. A picture of me with the hospice staff hung on the wall beside my desk. When the image began to blur, I grabbed a tissue and hurried to sign off on all the patient files waiting for my attention. This time I knew I couldn't put it off for the next day.

A little after two o'clock, I packed my personal items into an empty box that once contained gauze dressings. Before I left, I looked around the office, now devoid of my presence. A plaque proclaiming "Employee of the Month" still hung, taunting me, on the wall above the computer. I reached for it, but decided to leave it in place as a reminder to whomever chose to look. I locked the door and dropped the key and paperwork in Isabelle's in-box, then departed through the back door after slipping a note on Connie's empty desk: "Call me at home tomorrow." Nobody noticed my departure.

Mid-afternoon, I pulled into the garage. Josh's car was missing. I entered the chill of our empty house.

I waited for Josh in the family room, leaning against the French doors that opened onto the deck and watching Benisse muster up the energy to allow Murphy to chase her in the grass. They seemed oblivious of anything but emerging springtime. My breath fogged the windowpanes, but in amber light cast by late afternoon sun I saw tips of irises. Spent gold and purple crocuses spattered the flowerbed in between tulips that had tried to open, but had frozen, stunted in their voluminous leaves.

Yet again, I tried to dig deep inside myself for strength. I knew it was there, someplace deep in my core. Strength had gotten me this far in life. It wasn't that long ago that I'd faced the possibility of my own death. I'd spent hours in a dialysis unit, wondering if I would live long enough to find a matching donor.

Then I thought of Kathryn. Could it be, I wondered? Would my beautiful friend have to share the same fate?

Images of dying patients melded in my mind. Young people, along with those who had lived to the fullest. Those who accepted the inevitably of their approaching death and those whose expressions were etched with bitterness or denial.

The wind kicked up now, as it often did in the afternoon — blowing down off the Sierra, following the Truckee River along the I-80 corridor. Blossoms from our ornamental pear and cherry trees swirled around the yard like soft snow.

When I opened the door for the dogs, Murphy bounded in, flew onto the couch, and crashed on his red blanket. Benisse dragged her now-weary body onto the area rug and collapsed. The energy she'd gathered for playtime was spent. I hunkered down beside her and nuzzled my head into thick fur.

The grinding sound of the garage door announced Josh's arrival. He entered the family room and tossed a quick greeting my way. Wrestling with one crutch and a paper bag overflowing with feathery leaves of parsley, Josh pitched his keys on the wet bar and struggled toward the kitchen.

"Why didn't you call me?" I asked as I rushed to help him.

"I got along okay, but it's a good thing I didn't have to go too far. My ankle's still pretty sore." He looked at me, stopped short, then plunked the bag on the floor and reached out to me. "You're home awful early and you look like hell; what's the matter? More news about Kathryn?"

"Not yet; not till Thursday. I got laid off, Josh." The story tumbled from my mouth.

"Did you have any suspicions at all?" Josh asked when I'd finished speaking.

"I didn't see it coming, but when I look back I understand why Isabelle's been so aloof."

"You said something about that last week." He stood there, in silence, facing me for a few moments until a smile broke out across his face.

"What? Why are you smiling?"

"Maybe this is a blessing," he said.

I stepped back, bewildered by his response. "A blessing? How the hell can you say that, Josh?" I heard my voice. It was strident. It was anger, vomited out into the air.

He raised his hand as though to fend off a mad dog. "Think about it," he said to me, "you barely took a break after your surgery." He moved forward tentatively, reached for my hand, and dragged me to the couch. "You were so close to dying, but you just kept plugging along. You never even thought about taking time off. Maybe it's time you did."

I shook my head. "I worked too hard and too long to become a doctor, Josh. Medicine is my life — I can't not practice my profession."

"I'm not saying retire. But, just listen to me for a minute. Maybe there's something else you're supposed to do for a while? Or be? You're so much more than a doctor."

There was no way I could accept that. I knew myself, and just the thought of not working terrified me. I felt like a lump of dough, kneaded by forces outside of myself. This man I loved could be such a fool-dreamer, and at times like this it pissed me off. I stood and stomped across the room, looking out at the sun, now a red orb sinking into the mountains.

"We can reverse roles for a while," Josh continued. He limped over to where I stood. His bright eyes signaled his willingness. "You know I've always wanted to be the one to provide for you. I think you should at least take a sabbatical and see what happens."

The clean smell of his aftershave swept over me. "I've never doubted you, honey. This is about me." Who would I be without my job? I wondered.

"There're lots of things you've always wanted more time for; think about it, Claire."

"But I'm a doctor." I let my head fall on his shoulder.

"You can still be a doctor, damn it. I'm just saying you should take some time for yourself, okay?"

The band of resistance that encircled me snapped right then and I heard my voice at a distance. "Okay. I'll give it a couple of months, and then we'll see."

Josh planted a kiss on my lips. "I picked up something I planned on cooking for us next weekend, but I'm gonna fix a special dinner tonight instead. We're gonna celebrate."

Celebrate getting laid off? I thought. Only he would think of that.

I followed him as he limped around the kitchen. The scent of the spices he used filled my senses and distracted me from my troubles for the moment. I tasted perfectly seasoned sauce from his finger and then tasted his lips until the pasta boiled over.

Later that evening, Josh lumbered upstairs and I followed. He removed his shirt then unbuttoned my blouse slowly. The heat of his skin rubbed against my bare flesh.

Our lovemaking was tender and lingering. The dogs interrupted our afterglow, roused by their need to be a part of any family play. Murphy jumped up on the bed, while Benisse shocked my naked shoulder with her cold nose.

"I don't know if I can do it, Josh. I can't not work — I'm not so sure about this idea," I said.

He placed his finger on my lips. "Let it be for now, okay?"

In my dream, I stood in a damp place. I crept along a dim pathway and clung to walls that crumbled at my touch. The smell of mold filled the musty space. Breathless, I inched forward, reaching for a young woman. Someone I didn't recognize swept me into his arms and carried me to safety. I relaxed then, until loneliness overtook me — the man had disappeared. So had the girl. A miniscule light glimmered in the distance, as though somebody had lit a match. A breeze caused the flame to falter, but it didn't go out. I awoke, naked and bathed in cold sweat. I lay still and didn't move.

Who's the girl? I wondered. Why do I want to know, and why can't I remember?

Five

I arose before Josh, and stood to watch him as he slept. A few minutes later, dogs in tow, I slipped out of the bedroom and shut the door.

After I started the coffee, I settled with a glass of orange juice, retrieved my journal, and jotted down the date. The dogs curled up and plunged back into a stupor.

Feelings, stirred up from the memory of my dream, pummeled me. I closed my eyes and tried to picture the girl who'd stood on a ledge, just beyond my reach.

The young woman looked like a picture of me as a teenager: long stringy hair, blond-almost-brown; startling blue eyes punctuated by heavy brows and lashes. Even those damn freckles dotted the bridge of her nose and spread over her cheekbones. But there was a difference: sadness had spilled from the teenager's eyes; her full lips had been down-turned.

There was someone familiar in my dream, last night, I wrote. I don't know where she came from, but I felt afraid. Why would I fear a young person like that? I wanted to hold her close, to keep her from getting away.

I paused, gazed out the half-moon window over the front door. Light stole in through the panes and spilled into the entryway of our home. It wasn't really the girl who scared me, I added. It was that I didn't want to lose her.

Before I could scribble off the next sentence, I heard Josh hobbling down the stairs.

"'Morning, sweetheart! Coffee smells good; it woke me up." He kissed me. "'Morning, dogs!" He bent over and roughed them up.

"Where're your crutches, Josh? It's too soon to begin full weight-bearing." First thing in the morning, and already I was hounding him.

"I'm okay; the walking brace keeps me steady," he told me, and then he asked me how I'd slept.

"Off and on — mostly off. I dreamed a lot." I set aside my notebook, pulled myself to my feet and headed for the kitchen. "You know how I told you about the feeling I had the other day — that someone's missing from the portrait of my family?"

"Yeah, sort of. A lot has come down since then, though. Remind me."

"It's probably nothing, but it won't go away."

Mid-morning, a sharp ring startled me. I was perched on my gardening bench, pulling weeds from the rose garden. I expected it to be Josh, checking-in, but, instead, Kathryn's voice greeted me. "Why didn't you tell me?"

"I didn't mean to hold back, but you don't need anything else to deal with right now." A light breeze swirled through the tops of the trees, scattering leaves that had hung on through the winter. Our wind chimes tinkled in the background. "Besides, they vowed me to secrecy until they had a chance to tell the staff. I should've known the gossip would make its way to you before I could."

"Are you okay?" Kathryn asked.

"It's not a big deal — not compared to what you're facing." I propped my feet on a gnarly root of the nearby oak and looked on as Murphy plunked down beneath the branches of the old tree.

"You must be heartbroken."

"Sure, I'm sad," I admitted, "but let's talk about it when we're together. Do you want to have lunch tomorrow before your appointment?"

"How about today? I can clear my schedule. Will you meet me at Brick's?"

"I'd love it — I need to feel like I have somewhere to go." I tossed my gardening gloves in the bucket and headed toward the house.

I arrived at the restaurant before Kathryn and requested seating on the upper tier. I soaked in the atmosphere, cooled by walls of brick that cached recessed wine cellars, but it wasn't long before I saw Kathryn walking in my direction. Heads turned to follow the tall African American woman with ebony hair hanging in a thick braid down her back.

"How's Michael?" I asked as I stood and hugged my friend.

Kathryn just shook her head.

"He's still angry?"

"Claire, he's not angry — he's scared, just like we all are. We've been there before, you know."

Kathryn reached for the menu and waved her hand to dismiss the subject. A soft glow of indirect lighting hit her face. Thirty-five years had been kind to her. Kathryn's dark skin showed no wrinkles, I noted as she scanned the menu.

"How're you doing?" I asked.

"I don't know." Kathryn laid aside the menu. "I need to find out what I'm dealing with."

"How can I help? You've supported me through so much." I reached over and placed my hand on skin the texture of satin. I ached to comfort, to sooth, but felt so helpless. "Now it's my turn, and I can't even find the right thing to say."

"Maybe there's a reason you're not supposed to be working, did you think of that?" Kathryn said.

Just then the waiter approached us and began reciting the specials. I didn't hear him. A chill enveloped me and worked its way through my body. Is there a bigger purpose in my life right now? Maybe Josh is right.

After we ordered, Kathryn shifted and faced me. "Now, tell me about you."

In that moment I understood that we were there for each other. Would be, I prayed, for a long, long time, just as we had been since pre-med.

While we waited for our meal, I told Kathryn about the events of the previous day and she gave me her full attention, as usual. "So, it looks as though I'm going to have a sabbatical," I concluded.

"I love it, girl! You deserve some time for yourself."

I still couldn't buy it, and told her as much. "I know it doesn't make sense, but I feel like I'm losing control of my life. This is the first time ever I've had time to do some things I've always wanted to do, but I don't feel like I have a sense of direction."

"What do you mean?" Kathryn lifted one eyebrow.

"It's about losing my job, but I know it's not just about money," I admitted. "Josh works part time and we both know that nurses don't have a problem getting more hours. But, somehow my identity is tied up in being a doctor. There's a reason I ended up in a healing profession then drifted into hospice, of all fields, dealing every single day with death and dying and loss. It has something to do with my own life, and that's what I wanted to bounce off of you."

My friend's expression encouraged me to keep talking.

"There's something in my past — something that makes me want to fix people. It's almost as though focusing on someone else's problems keeps me from dealing with my own." I leaned back in the booth and closed my eyes to stop the room from whirling around me before I continued.

"But it's more than that. I have such a horrible dread of losing someone I love — right now of losing you. When we were at the urgent-care center on Saturday and you had a twinge of pain I panicked; right away my mind flew to the worse-case scenario. I've got a hunch that something happened a long time ago — something I don't remember. Where do you suppose that comes from?"

"If you don't remember anything, how do you know about it?" Kathryn took a hunk of bread from the basket on the table and handed it to me.

"I don't, really, but this is what happened: a few days ago Josh and I were in the study discussing my mother. The family portrait — the one with my father in it — caught my eye. A gut feeling came over me that someone was missing. Then I had this dream." I pulled my journal from my purse and handed it to Kathryn, then watched her while she read slowly.

Goose bumps covered Kathryn's arms. She closed the cloth-bound book and handed it back to me. "What does Helene have to say about it? Have you ever asked her?"

"Oh, my God! My mother. That's another topic. We got into an argument the last time we spoke, on Monday. She's upset that I told Josh to take time off; can you imagine what she'll say when she hears I'm unemployed?"

Kathryn handed me my glass of water.

I took a gulp and continued. "God, Kathryn, she'll be livid. And if there's something behind my suspicion, she's never told me about it; that means she doesn't want me to know."

"For heaven's sake. First of all, why would she care about you taking time off?"

"My mother sees life as work, you know that. She judges people on what they produce. That's one reason I'm so uptight — I'm not used to not doing."

Visions of my mother, overseeing homework and Girl Scout projects, invaded my memory. I could hear her chiding voice in a distant recollection, when I took second place in a science fair.

"Come on, Claire," Kathryn insisted. "Listen to what you're saying!"

"Maybe she'll surprise me, who knows?" I pulled a tissue from my purse.

"I don't know Helene like you do," Kathryn said, "but I can't imagine any mother reacting like that."

"Can't you just hear our next conversation? 'Gee, Mom. What huge family secret are you keeping from me? And, by the way, I got fired.'" I grinned.

Kathryn's infectious laugh escaped full force. "Well, then, what would make it easier for her to take? What would make her happy?" she asked me.

I took another sip of water and considered the question. "She'd love for me to work in the family business, but that's not going to happen. I won't let it. I don't like working with numbers and I couldn't stand reporting to my mother."

"What do you mean?" Kathryn asked.

"I could never live up to her expectations."

"Could that have something to do with your mystery girl? Could she be the person your mother wants you to be?" Kathryn continued to prod me.

"Who knows?" I looked into her eyes. "You should have gone into psychiatry, you and your probing questions."

"That's what friends are for." Kathryn stopped and stared off into space before continuing. "Isn't there anything else that would please her? Not that you should give a damn about it."

"Grandchildren. I can't envision my brother and his wife giving them to her, and I won't get pregnant because of my health." As soon as I said it, desire flared up inside me. It was familiar — the longing to be a mother. An aching pressure swelled in my chest. A vision of the first birth I'd assisted as an intern came to mind. Back then, the slippery baby I'd handed to the nurse had stirred something in my gut, a yearning I'd squashed so many times in recent years.

"People with transplants can have children, you know, with careful oversight," Kathryn reminded me. "Would you want that?"

I couldn't answer. I'd put off motherhood, at first because of my career, and then my condition. I took a peek at that empty place inside me, but slammed the door shut, afraid to deal with the tangle of emotions that lay inside.

As we ate, I tried hard to turn the focus of our conversation back to Kathryn, who volleyed it back in my direction. It went on like that until, at last, we talked about our work. Her work, that is.

Forty-five minutes later, we divided the change and laid a five-dollar bill on the table.

Kathryn admonished me, "When you do talk to your mother, I wish, for once, you'd think about yourself and not lose sleep over her or anyone else. Remember to pay attention to what you want."

I nodded, digesting her advice.

"Let me know what happens, okay?" Kathryn rose and brushed the crumbs off her lap. "I need to get going. I'm late, as always."

Then I experienced an unexpected and unwelcome tinge of envy: Kathryn had things to do and people who needed her. I didn't.

After I hugged Kathryn goodbye, I drove west on Plumb Lane. A bank of threatening clouds shrouded the Sierra Nevada, but a sliver of light shot through the gray sky.

Late that evening, Josh sat on the floor next to Benisse, holding the printout of exercises from the doctor. "Why don't you wait till you talk on Saturday? If Helene doesn't phone, you call her. Just act like nothing happened last Sunday."

My knitting needles flew across a row of the purple scarf I was creating. "I'll feel like I'm badgering her. She'll think…oh, I don't know what she'll think."

"Does it matter?" Josh stood, balanced himself by holding the mantle, and pulled his foot against his rear end to extend his quads. Murphy stood facing him then began to whine.

I shook my head. "There's nothing I can do about it, is there?"

"Nope." Josh stretched the other leg, then swiveled his ankle. A grimace crossed his face. "Let's go, dogs," he said. He headed for the door.

"You know what would make my mother really happy?" I wrapped up the yarn and slipped it into my bag.

"What's that, honey?"

"If one of her children gave her grandchildren."

"I can't imagine that'll ever happen." Josh opened the door to the back-yard and escaped with the dogs into the night.

Six

uried in a bulky orange sweater, Kathryn leaned against the white railing of the porch surrounding the old Victorian that housed her office at St. Joseph's Hospice. It was the second of May and cool for the season, even for Reno.

I knew she hadn't seen me pull up to the curb so I followed her stare. Beside us, the Truckee's flowing water tumbled over smooth rocks; white caps curled into the air, spraying a fine mist.

"Hey, Kathryn," I finally shouted through the open window.

"Oh. Hi." She got in the car and exhaled deeply, sinking her head back on the seat.

I reached over, and squeezed her forearm, then slipped the car into gear, hung a U-turn and headed east.

"I got a lot done the last couple of days," Kathryn told me. "My paper work's caught up, just in case."

"It's tough waiting for results, isn't it?" A lump formed in my throat. I couldn't help but think of the months of uncertainty that I'd gone through before my transplant — things put on hold while I wondered if I'd even be there to enjoy them. Things like the vacation to Europe that never did make it on our agenda.

"If something happens to me, you'll take my job, won't you?" Kathryn asked me. "It'd be perfect for you."

"Please don't say that," I whispered, "don't even think it."

We kept quiet the rest of the trip as I drove through light traffic. An array of spring colors taunted us as we passed through an old residential neighborhood that flaunted the change of seasons and arrived at Brian Forrest's office early.

I skimmed through an old edition of Field and Stream, unable to concentrate. Words and images of outdoorsy men hauling in rainbow-sparkled trout blurred on the page.

Kathryn sat like a statue until someone called her name. She stood, looked at me and asked, "Come back with me?" She turned toward the medical assistant for approval. When the woman in floral printed scrubs nodded okay, I grabbed my purse and followed.

While I helped her into an open gown, I brushed Kathryn's arm and touched skin frigid as a corpse. I wished at that moment that I could turn back time. If I'd known this would happen, I would have waited my turn for a donor. Before I could take a seat, the doctor knocked and entered the examination room.

Brian Forrest had aged a bit since I last saw him, but he still commanded attention. Auburn hair fell loosely over his forehead and his green eyes scanned us. We glanced at each other when he flashed us a broad smile.

"Hey, it's the hospice dream-team! You both look wonderful — to die for," he said in greeting.

We laughed but I felt like howling. Then an expression came over his face — he must have realized that our nerves were on edge.

"Are you okay with Claire being in here?" Brian asked Kathryn.

"I need her, Brian, because I might not grasp everything you tell me."

"I can identify with that," he said. Brian paused, opened Kathryn's thin chart, and got down to business. "I reviewed the notes John Cormier sent. You've got red blood cells in your urine but no infection — same results with the repeat test, but there's no palpable mass."

Kathryn nodded. "That's as much as I know so far."

"As I see it, the possibilities are wide open right now. I hope you haven't let your imaginations go wild." Brian glanced at me and I wondered how well he really had known me back in the day. Had my constant worry been that apparent?

"We both have — it's hard not to," I admitted. I sat upright in the vinyl chair, twisting my fingers in my lap like the uncertain intern I used to be.

"It's tough being a doctor because we tend to assume the worst, and under the circumstances..." Brian left the sentence dangling. He cleared his throat, thumbed through a stack of papers, then grabbed his pen and scribbled a brief note.

"Kathryn, hop up on the table; I want to poke around. Your remaining kidney's on the right?"

"Yes."

I watched Brian prod Kathryn's abdomen. "It's enlarged," he said, "but, as you know, that's normal — it's doing double duty."

When I heard those words, I turned away and inspected my hands as if trying to decide whether red nail polish clashed with my lavender slacks. Blood pounded in my temples. The implications of his statement screamed at me.

"Here's what I want to do," Brian continued. "Let's skip x-rays and go straight to a sonogram. I want to scope your bladder, too. Can you stay? We can do both exams today."

Kathryn looked at me and I nodded.

"The sooner the better." Kathryn echoed my thoughts.

Brian gazed intently at us. "Odds are that it's not serious, but if it is, I'm sure it's very early."

"Kathryn only has one kidney," I blurted out. I have the other, but then you already know that, don't you? A blend of embarrassment and guilt set my heart racing, and the pulse in my neck bound into sprint mode.

"So do a lot of people — you included," Brian answered. "God gave you Kathryn when you needed her; don't you think He'll take care of her now?"

A flush spread over my face as I took in a side of Brian he'd never revealed before.

"Women don't have a corner on the God-market, you know." The physician gave the two of us a crooked smile.

Brian stood, snapped off his latex gloves, and dumped them on the tray of used instruments. "There's nothing abnormal in the bladder," he announced, confirming what we'd seen for ourselves on the screen.

"Darn," we said in unison.

"Normally people would be happy for that news, but you're too smart, aren't you?" Brian said.

"It's the kidney, isn't it?" Kathryn asked.

"I'm going to re-test this sample I took to see if it's still positive for blood. Wait here, okay?" Brian squeezed Kathryn's shoulder as he left, but avoided answering her question.

I browsed anatomical charts and pamphlets littering a counter in the far corner of the room without learning anything new. Kathryn lay unmoving, face up on the table.

When Brian returned, his face remained a blank. "The blood's still there, so I'm going to send in the ultrasound tech. Leave your cell number with my receptionist, Kathryn." He turned before opening the door. "I'll give you a call as soon as I get results. If there's a problem, I need to schedule a C-T scan. I'll try for a weekend appointment if that works for you."

"Yeah," Kathryn answered. "Michael and I don't have plans, and if we did, I'd change them." She turned her face to the wall, away from me.

Kathryn's high cheek bones accented the strength of her features, but my imagination propelled me into a future of emaciation and pain. I found my-self picturing Kathryn wrapped in a tangle of dialysis tubes, or wasting into nothingness like I had while waiting for someone to die and give me a kidney. In this scenario, however, I wouldn't be able to ride up on a white steed and pluck her from certain death the way she had done for me. I didn't have anything to give her, except my time. The power of my helplessness crushed me.

When we were alone Kathryn said, "He won't need to call — he knows we'll both be watching the monitor."

During the test, I saw a spot the size of a pea. The tech blocked my view of Kathryn and prevented me from reading her reaction. At the end of the procedure Kathryn's eyes remained closed. Because I wasn't sure of what she'd seen, I said nothing. I handed my friend her clothes and helped her to her feet.

"Are you okay?" I asked as I turned the Lexus left onto Kathryn's street. The digital clock in my car read 4:31.

"I guess." She unfastened her seatbelt, leaned forward, and covered her face in her hands. "Did you see the sonogram?"

"A little." I kept my answer vague. "The tech was in and out of my line of vision. Did you watch?"

"Yes." Kathryn replied, without further comment. "Thanks, Claire. I'll let you know when Brian calls about the C-T scan. Michael will take me." She lifted her angular body from the seat, closed the door and walked away without looking back.

I sat and watched Kathryn disappear behind the heavy oak door that opened into her house. A few moments later, I drove down the hill into our neighborhood by the river. Clouds covered the bright sun that struggled in vain to burst out of its prison.

When I arrived home, smells of burnt sugar emanated from the kitchen.

"I'm making a pie — strawberry-rhubarb — just in case you need comfort food."

I ran into Josh's arms, and it was there that I found a moment's solace. He cradled me for a while, then opened the oven door and removed his creation. Murphy and Benisse trotted up to me and I squatted in greeting and allowed Murphy to lick salty tears from my face.

While Josh peeled potatoes, I filled him in on the details of Kathryn's visit to Brian Forrest. Pensive furrows lined his brow. I followed him outside to the grill and handed him a topped-off glass of wine. We stood together and watched the cloud cover defeat the sinking sun.

"What's the plan?" Josh asked me when I'd finished and we both plopped onto deck chairs.

"Brian's supposed to call Kathryn and schedule a scan if the sonogram's positive, which I'm certain it is," I reported. "I hope she hears something before the weekend."

"I wonder how Michael's handling it. Do you think I should I call him?" Josh asked me.

"Will it help?" Based on Kathryn's assessment, I had my doubts.

Josh shook his head and fixed his eyes on a quail eating seeds he'd planted in the flower garden. "Maybe not, but I can try; I'll call after we eat. Honey, why did Kathryn ask you to take her to her appointments instead of Michael?" Josh grabbed the meat with tongs, slid it onto a plate and headed back into the kitchen.

"I don't know — I didn't even think about it — I just thought she wanted another pair of trained eyes and ears. Why?" I served myself and followed Josh into the dining room.

"His response to this whole thing just made me wonder. Maybe he had to make some sales calls."

"Or maybe he's still out-of-control? What'll you say when you call?"

"I have no idea," Josh answered.

While I cleared the table, Josh dialed the Scott's number. After discussing the Wolf Pack's baseball team, he stood up and went to his office. Less than five minutes had passed when he trudged back into the room and slammed the phone on the charger. I knew not to ask questions, but a dull pain gathered at the base of my skull as I watched my husband disappear into a shadow of his own making.

Seven

Mid-morning the following day, I hooked the dogs to their leashes and set off for a walk. Forty minutes later, I reentered the house and caught the phone on its third ring.

"Claire, it's me, Kathryn." A tone of panic tinged her voice. "Brian wants to see me now; can you come with me? Michael had to go to Sacramento."

No one occupied the reception desk when we entered the waiting room and took a seat. It was ten to one.

"The staff must still be at lunch," I squeezed Kathryn's frozen hand, but she drew back, away from my attempt to comfort. I couldn't do anything at that moment — I had to let her go away, to go within.

At one o'clock the front desk remained unattended. I studied my watch as the second hand rotated around the periphery. Within a few orbits, Brian opened the door to the hallway that led back to his office. "Kathryn, Claire."

We rose and followed him. The smell of pastrami and mustard from his half-eaten deli sandwich attacked me when we entered the room.

Brian motioned to two oversized green chairs in front of his desk. Soft leather enveloped us. Kathryn's purse dangled from her shoulder, neglected, and she sat erect with her arms wrapped around her body as though she were forcing herself not to fall apart.

We watched as Brian opened a file. "Kathryn, I'm sorry, but things aren't what I'd hoped." He handed her a printout of the ultrasound and I looked over her shoulder to see what I already knew would be there.

"I saw it during the procedure," Kathryn admitted, gulping air.

A tight band squeezed my chest. Oh God, don't let this be happening. Tense silence hung in the room like steam in a sauna.

"It looks like it's confined to a small nodule." Brian tapped his finger on the spot. "We're working on an appointment for the scan on Saturday, but I want to go ahead and schedule you for a needle biopsy ASAP. Monday, if I can arrange it." Brian's pale skin blanched under the white light.

Kathryn closed her eyes.

I answered for her. "We'll make it, Brian — the sooner, the better."

Brian paused then looked at Kathryn, who met his glance and nodded in agreement.

"We've got several options." He spoke slowly and directed his comments to his patient while she stared off into space. "We can do the biopsy at an outpatient surgery center. Depending on the results, we'll schedule our next step." He waited. "Or we could go ahead and schedule it at St. Joe's. That way, if I need to, I'll get you into surgery right away."

Before Kathryn could react, Brian said, "Since you only have one kidney, if you do need surgery, I hope to remove just the affected portion."

"What then?" I asked. Pressure began to build up deep in my gut, but escaped through my hands in a fine tremor.

Brian's eyes didn't leave Kathryn. "We'll evaluate your kidney function immediately post-op, and if necessary, I'll put you on the transplant list and start dialysis."

Wrinkles crisscrossed Kathryn's forehead and her shoulders began to shake.

I rose and put an arm around my friend and this time she let me. Brian walked toward a narrow window filled with views of an adjacent office building, and looked out at the bland architecture.

When Kathryn regained control, she assumed a professional persona. In a detached voice, she began to pummel Brian with questions, as though seeking information from a specialist while considering treatment choices for one of her own patients.

At the conclusion of the Q & A session, she spoke in a hushed tone: "I want the biopsy as soon as possible, then go ahead and schedule surgery when you know exactly what's going on. I need time to get Claire into my position and hand off my patients."

My head jerked up, but Kathryn continued.

"And I have to deal with my husband, who's not doing well with all of this, Brian. Now that there's a possibility of…" she hesitated, "of cancer, I need to make sure he gets help."

Brian nodded and swallowed hard. "Okay, let's get things in motion. I'll call you as soon as I line up the procedures." The physician crumbled paper around the remains of his lunch and tossed it in the garbage. "Stay in here as long as you need to," he said, glancing at his watch, then at the two of us. "I'm so sorry — I have a patient waiting."

I got out of the car when we arrived at the Scott's.

Kathryn took me by the shoulders. "Do you mind if I suggest you to be my backup?"

"I'll do whatever you need me to do," I answered. That's what I promised, isn't it? I asked myself.

After we parted, I parked my car up the street, in the shade of ancient elm trees, and wept.

That evening, Josh and I bundled up and sat on the deck. The days were lengthening. As shadows deepened we chatted about redecorating my office and creating a space for me to do art. A sunset, painted in hues of orange and mauve, streaked an indigo sky.

When we stood to go inside, Josh put his arm around me and pulled me close. "Honey, when you had your transplant, I was a match. Kathryn reminded us that I needed to be here for you and work to support us, remember?"

"I know that," I said. "Why are you bringing it up now?"

"If Kathryn needs a kidney, I want to be tested as a donor. We both matched you, so I'm sure I'll match her. Is that okay with you?"

Josh let go of me and waited.

The evening air turned chilly in an instant. A coyote's howl pierced the stillness. In the open land down by the river, a predator searched for its prey.

"What if something happens to you?" I asked.

"What if something had happened to Kathryn when she gave you her kidney?" Josh said.

I lowered my head. The words I'd allowed to escape lingered in my mouth like sour wine, but I couldn't help but relive the terrors of the previous Saturday — the fear I'd tasted when I realized what could have happened to my reckless husband who thought he was an Olympic skier.

Another cry escaped the coyote, and in the distance I heard the squawking of a goose.

"I knew you'd be the one to offer," I finally said.

I listened to the words I'd just spoken as if they'd come from someone else. "I don't know how, but I knew."

Josh pulled me back into his arms.

"So did I, Claire."

We stood together in complete darkness. The silence was absolute now.

Eight

The next morning, Saturday, I snuggled up to Josh's warm body and allowed a cocoon of comfort to surround me. Murphy jumped on the bed at the very moment the phone rang.

"Hi, Claire." Kathryn's voice sounded taut, like a guitar string wound too tightly. "Thought I'd better let you know — I'm going for my scan in an hour."

"Can I drive you?" I offered.

"Michael will — he's right here." Kathryn sighed. "Brian called late last night and told me he'll call tomorrow with the results. Sounds like he spends Sundays catching up on medical records; all that man does is work. What a waste of a gorgeous hunk of humanity. Anyway, girl, relax today and don't give me a thought."

"Call as soon as you know something, okay?" I hung up and fell back onto the pillow.

"I heard." Josh rolled over and stretched. "How are you handling all this, honey? Are you all right?"

"I don't have much choice, do I?" I brushed a strand of hair out of his eyes. "I have to be all right."

"What about last night?" Josh asked. "Are you still comfortable with what we talked about?"

"About you being a donor? I don't know, Josh — can we sit on it for a while?"

"What do you mean?"

"Let's not say anything to Kathryn or Michael, okay? Can we wait?"

"Wait?" Josh leaned on his elbow and stared down at me.

"Until we're sure." I put my hand on his scratchy cheek. "I need to absorb it. We can tell them after the biopsy, when we know exactly what's she's dealing with."

"I think it's what I need to do, but it's okay with me. We can hold off for now." Josh swung his legs over the side of the bed and pulled himself to a sitting position. "I guess I should talk it over with my folks first, so you're probably right."

"Good. What do you have planned for this morning?"

"Tell you what — I'll feed these monsters," Josh said and pulled on his sweats, "then we're gonna play. You need a change of pace. It's been one heck of a week."

As I dressed, my thoughts and emotions bounced around like a ping-pong ball. The simple task of preparing for a day of play evoked a tingle of excitement but then sadness slinked in, propelled by the thought that Kathryn would spend the morning on a hard table while a machine scanned her body a layer at a time. The next moment, I breathed a sigh of relief that I wasn't the one who was ill this time. Then guilt entered, center-stage. Seconds later, anger joined the tableau: anger toward Michael, whose response to me had teased out even more guilt. And anger toward my mother, toward my sister-in law Lauren, and above all, myself. As a finale, fear for Josh left all the other feelings standing in the wings. Nausea climbed from the pit of my stomach, and my hand flew to my throat in an effort to stanch it.

By the time I met Josh downstairs, that dull ache had returned to the back of my head. I faked a smile that made me feel like a clown hidden behind makeup. "Let's go," I said, trying to squash the emotions still raging inside.

At Starbuck's, Josh pulled out the classifieds and turned to garage sales. "Here's the plan," he said and began marking the stops we'd make.

After breakfast, we scoped out a few of the listings, not looking for anything in particular, but catching peeks of lifestyles and histories while imagining the missing pieces. At the fourth stop, I dug through dog-eared paperbacks until Josh nuzzled his way into my space. I abandoned him to his treasure hunt so I could browse for other items. Something about the house seemed familiar.

The elderly woman running the garage sale came over to me. "I remember you, Dr. Bergano. You took care of my husband when he had hospice. Most of this is his stuff."

"Tom Hardin. Of course! You're Emily." I remembered the woman now — a woman I thought I could have confided in, who could have been a friend. The type of person I would've chosen for a mother, if I'd had a choice. "How are you, Emily? It's been over a year, hasn't it?"

"Almost sixteen months, and it's still tough. The pain doesn't go away. I'm just getting around to this," Emily said, sweeping her hand across the cluttered yard.

"It's got to be hard for you. Are your children helping you?" I took the woman's wrinkled hand.

Emily's eyes began to tear up. "My son moved to California and I don't see much of my daughter, so I'm alone most of the time."

"Do you still have Fluffy?" I asked, remembering the furry mutt who'd parked itself on the dying man's bed.

The older woman shook her head and swallowed. "He died a few weeks after Tom."

"I'd really like someone to talk to, Dr. Bergano, and I've always wanted to show you my thanks somehow. Do you ever find time for lunch, or even tea?"

"That'd be fun, Emily." I rummaged in my purse. "Here's how to reach me — give me a call and we'll get together." I offered an old business card on which I'd scratched out the number, and written in my cell.

Emily squeezed my hand and ran off to help a lady with a pile of men's polo shirts as Josh approached with a stash of adventure novels. "I gotta pay for these then we can head for home."

"It's been a good morning, Josh. You're a brilliant therapist, you know that? Today's a perfect spring day, and I ran into someone I know." I told him about Emily.

"Now you have time to start making some friends outside of work."

Yeah, I do, don't I? I realized. "Let's get going, honey. I've still got to face up to my mother."

When we returned home, the sun shone directly overhead.

"I'm gonna tackle the garden," Josh said, scrounging for his work gloves in the garage. "You want to join me?"

"I need to make that call first. What do you think — should I tell Mother about Kathryn?"

"Not today; the fact that you're not working will be enough of a crisis. We don't need Helene stroking out on us now."

"Josh!" I held in a laugh.

"Sorry. But it's true. Good luck. You'll come outside when you're finished, won't you?" He seemed so eager, standing in vintage jeans and scuffed up, torn sneakers.

"Maybe — it depends." I couldn't think beyond the task at hand.

"The sooner you get the weeds, the easier it'll be," Josh reminded me. He grabbed a pitchfork leaning against the side of the house and headed toward the plot of earth that would become his vegetable garden.

"Okay, I'll be out as soon as I can," I promised. I popped a cup of water in the microwave and fixed tea before I headed into the study and my rocking chair.

After I've told her what's going on, should I ask about the young woman in my dream? I rocked back and forth, but decided to do some research first, remembering a box of old pictures in the garage — I bet I can find an answer there.

I punched in the numbers and held my hand on my chest as though to slow down my racing heart. Maybe she won't be home, I hoped.

She answered on the second ring.

"Hello, darling. Happy Saturday!" my mother greeted me. "Did you have a good week?" Not a word about our recent confrontation.

"I lost my job, Mom — I'm going to take some time off." I blurted out the words without a preamble.

A deep intake of air, followed by lingering silence at the other end of the line informed me that astonishment or displeasure, probably both, had overtaken her.

"I don't know what to say," she said to me. "You sound happy about it." My mother's words hung like icicles.

"They eliminated my position," I explained. The window across the room was open a crack and allowed a breeze to ripple through the curtains, bringing with it the scent of sweet peas.

"They don't eliminate doctors' jobs." Mother blew out her breath in a huff.

I spoke again with a faltering voice and tried to explain the details behind my layoff. I wiped a sweaty palm on my jeans and switched the phone to my other ear.

"You won't have any problem finding another position," she said to me.

"It's not that I can't get another job," I rebutted. "I don't want to for a while."

"You don't want to." She stretched out the sentence, one word at a time, slowly. It was a statement, not a question. "How nice. Did I raise you to only do what you wanted? Laziness is not how you make something of yourself, Claire."

"I'm not lazy — I'm doing what's right for me now. I may or may not return to medicine. I have to think about it. I haven't decided." The boldness of my words — an attitude that was alien to me — shocked me.

"Most people don't enjoy that luxury," she interrupted. "You made your choice when you left home and told us what we could do with the business. You've already decided, don't you think?"

Can I really do this? Am I ready to step away from my career? I ignored the doubts shrieking inside my head. I couldn't afford to let my mother see my confusion.

"Claire, think about what you're doing."

"I have. I've worked hard these ten years. You know I kept on going when I was sick, when I should have taken time off." I pressed the fingers of my right hand on taut muscles in my neck, then continued, "I need some time for myself, and I'm surprised you don't understand."

Silence prevailed for an eternal moment. Finally Mother said, "I thought you were more dedicated than that. How do you expect to live in the manner to which you're accustomed when your husband can't hold down a job and makes a mere pittance of the money you're able to earn?"

"Josh is going full time as soon as there's an opening," I shouted. The anger inside me uncurled like a viper ready to strike.

Mother ignored me and her tone of voice rose as she continued to hammer home her disapproval, but I tuned her out. I'm doing this for Josh, I reminded myself. I'd felt his need to prove himself as if it were my own. I'd even retire, if he asked me to.

And for Kathryn. I wanted to be available for my friend.

And for myself. That I wasn't so sure of.

Finally I interrupted her tirade. "I'm sorry you don't agree, but I've got to hang up now — we can discuss it later."

Once I'd disconnected, I glared at the phone and waited for it to continue the conversation. I wondered if I'd ever understand the woman who raised me, or even if I wanted to. I stared into the tepid cup of tea cradled in my hand until Josh tapped lightly on the door and entered to find me curled in the large rocking chair, gently swaying back and forth.

"It didn't go well, did it?" He stooped in front of me and grasped my hand. An earthy aroma clung to his clothes, along with tiny clods of dirt that rimmed a tear in his shirt.

I studied the man I loved. The insinuations my mother had made about him echoed in my mind. I could never tell him about that, never. I looked at Josh and shook my head slowly. "Thank God I've got you."

Josh touched me on the cheek. "Anything I can do?"

"No." I pulled my hand from his, stood, and walked to the window. Afternoon sun poured in and dissipated the gloominess. "I can face anything as long as we're together. I didn't expect her to understand — you do — that's all that matters." I finally allowed a smile to emerge. "I held my ground."

Josh put his arms around me. "Helene doesn't mean to hurt you, Claire. I don't think she understands you because you're not like her. You defy her control."

I knew he was right.

"Let's get on with the day," I said. "The weeds are waiting for me."

"They'll be there tomorrow. To be honest, my energy's zapped and my ankle's killing me. Let's go watch golf." He most likely knew I would fall asleep in front of the TV and I didn't let him down.

That night I lay awake for a long time and listened to Josh's rhythmic breathing. The conversation with Mother replayed itself like the tune of a catchy commercial. Vacillating between confidence and doubt, I spent the night in slow motion until I finally fell into a light, restless sleep.

In my dream I rode up an escalator. As it neared the top, it suddenly went into reverse. Try as I could, I wasn't able to outpace the momentum of the descent, and eventually just rode it down to the starting place. After a while I fell into a brief, but deep, slumber. I woke up before Josh and realized that I didn't need to take the escalator. I could go up the stairs.

With the rising sun, another light dawned on me. Something else was out there, waiting to lend meaning to my life.

Nine

A hummingbird fed in the garden just outside her window, causing Helene to shift in her plush easy chair to get a better view.

She referred to the closed-in porch attached to her bedroom as her serenity room. It was here that she came to do battle with her pride, to wage her war for perfection. Soothing tones of peach and celadon green clashed with a blur of red satin: her bathrobe. Helene's emotions simmered. She closed her eyes and waited for her thoughts to settle.

After a few moments she leaned forward, struck a match and lit a candle, setting the stage for prayer. Helene closed her eyes, drew in a deep breath, held it for the count of four, then released it. She visualized negative thoughts flowing from her body through her fingertips and toes, then sucked in another lungful of air. At last, sun broke through coastal fog. Helene exhaled and willed to rid herself of resentment.

Another breath. It didn't help. A taut band squeezed her chest.

Claire's always done things her way, Helene reflected. Yet sometimes she seems afraid of me.

Helene dredged up a conversation that took place when Claire was fifteen. The family was at the dinner table.

André toyed with his broccoli, as if wishing it to disappear. She had reprimanded him — he'd deserved it — but Claire had come to his defense.

The scene reran in Helene's memory.

"Mom, he'll never eat broccoli — you make too big a deal of it," Claire told her.

"Don't interrupt, Claire; this isn't about you."

"He'll put it in his cheek and go spit it in the toilet," her daughter countered.

"She wouldn't let it go," Helene said aloud to her cat, who stretched out, belly up.

The meal had proceeded in silence for a while. André ate a couple of bites of the dreaded vegetable and Helene didn't say another word.

During dessert her daughter announced she wanted to apply to some university in Nevada. "I'm going to medical school — I want to be a doctor."

"A doctor? Where'd that idea come from?" Helene had asked.

"I've thought about it for years, ever since that first hospitalization for my kidney problems."

Claire's father spoke for the first time. "You're taking my place in the business — that's been the plan from day one."

"No way, Dad. You want to bore me to death? André can have it."

André slurped his ice cream and ignored the rest of them.

Turning to her father, Claire had said, "You've always told me to follow my dreams — that I'd be a success. Well, this is what I want."

Claire was right. But she wasn't supposed to want to be a doctor, and definitely not in small-town redneck Reno, Nevada. Southern California offered so many more opportunities. Where had that come from? And now, was her daughter throwing it all away?

Returning to meditation, Helene forced another deep breath. An instant of peacefulness came as the influx of salty ocean air filled her lungs. Helene released her breath into the humid atmosphere then breathed in yet again.

She meditated daily. Each morning she dragged herself out of bed early and prayed her rosary. Did mindfulness meditation. Wrestled her demons. Analyzed and brooded.

Another unwanted memory filtered in, as it often did when she tried to quiet her mind. Crushed by the weight of her remorse, Helene emitted a low wail.

The image of Stephanie on her First Communion Day appeared in her mind, as crisp as the white dress Helene had starched and ironed for the occasion. Helene gulped air, returned to her breathing exercise, and tried to shoo away her bitter secret.

When calm continued to evade her, Helene reached for the basket that held her journal and prayer books. She grabbed a small silver flask buried beneath her Bible. Just a sip was all she took. She worked hard to maintain a façade of control, and didn't think anyone knew about her drinking.

Not that she drank all the time. It was just that when she did . . . But certainly nobody knows.

Then André came to mind. Where'd he come from? With all his degrees, he's basically useless, a figurehead.

Her hands curled into fists, clenched and unclenched. She tried to squeeze anger from her soul. Finally, Helene reached for the phone, entered Claire's area code and prefix, but could go no further.

A flash of rage overwhelmed her and she slammed the phone back on the charger. Her cat, Scruff, leaped off the back of the sofa and glared at Helene. She glowered back.

Then she changed her mind. I'll call Lauren. Maybe she'll understand.

Ten

André squinted at his wife over his reading glasses. The cluttered table beside him held piles of work he'd brought home. He always filled his free time, to avoid being with Lauren.

He stared when she hung up the phone, smacked the desk, and left the room. What is her problem? Why are Lauren and Mother meddling with Claire? What did my sister do to provoke them? André was puzzled, but instead of asking questions, he snatched his briefcase and retreated to the library. Lauren's brittle energy agitated him.

I don't get it. He slipped into his easy chair, reclined, and reached for his book. Why can't they mind their own business?

A call to Claire was in order — he hadn't touched base with her in ages — but he'd put it off for now because he couldn't afford to get caught in the middle of whatever mess his wife and mother had whipped up. Besides, he was in an exciting part of a James Patterson novel.

Banging in the kitchen caused André to cringe. He knew she'd binge now — she always did when she didn't get her way.

Lauren doesn't care about Claire or, for that matter, anyone but herself. But Claire s effect on Mother really gets to her. She's so sure Claire could take her place someday.

The day he'd met Lauren remained clearly etched in André's brain. He'd seen his dull brown hair, slicked back and already beginning to thin, reflected in her thick glasses. She stood, squat like him, built like a mailbox. People mistook them for brother and sister, but he was the one with the gap between his teeth.

The class was statistical analysis. Their professor assigned them to share a computer. Both students approached their work seriously, spoke little, and spent their free time studying.

"You want to cram together?" Lauren suggested at the end of the semester, before finals.

"Sure — at the library?" he suggested.

She'd known what she wanted and went after it. I handed her the ticket to her dreams and she grabbed hold of it. All I wanted was to teach, and all she wanted was to run our family business.

Lauren had courted Helene as much as André. His mother recognized the younger woman's skills immediately. No doubt, they had plotted in the determination of André's fate.

André set his novel aside. A familiar ache fanned through his body. I traded love for convenience. He swallowed hard. My marriage is nothing but a sham, a business transaction. He rose and walked into the kitchen.

Lauren sat at the table, slurping clam chowder. Beside the bowl sat a sandwich, oozing grilled cheese. She grunted in greeting and wiped her mouth. "Claire got fired," she told André.

"So? She can get a job anywhere." He inventoried the fridge and settled on leftover pasta.

"She doesn't want to — she's taking time off."

"Good for her. She works hard." André popped the plastic container in the microwave.

"Your mother wants her to come and work with us," Lauren wiped her mouth with the sleeve of her sweater.

"That's never going to happen — Claire won't consent to it. Besides, it's none of our business what she decides."

"I don't like it." Lauren helped herself to three of the oatmeal cookies she'd baked that morning.

André changed the subject. "I'm going to the office this afternoon. I need to run some spread sheets."

"I'm going out, too. I've got something to do." His wife stood, left her dishes in the sink and disappeared into her home office.

André stood in the doorway of the kitchen to listen.

"Mom, it's Lauren. I've been thinking about a few things. We need to talk. Can you meet me for tea at Chloe's?"

After Lauren hung up, André heard her say in a loud voice, to no one in particular, "I know what I have to do."

Eleven

A china teapot snuggled inside its floral-print cozy. Helene sipped Earl Gray tea as she eyed André's wife. Lauren wasn't pretty, but she became downright ugly when she spewed criticism.

"I think we need to make sure Claire earns a steady income — she can't afford to be without insurance." Lauren leaned back in her chair.

The older woman added another sugar cube to her cup and stirred. She kept her eyes on Lauren but remained quiet.

"If something happens, she'd expect us to help her," Lauren continued. "There's no reason for her to become dependent on us." Lauren's strident voice became too loud for the small room.

"Claire told me Josh will work full time," Helene answered in a gruff voice. All of a sudden, she felt like a bitch protecting her puppy. She knew her daughter would never allow, let alone expect them to support her.

Hot tea burned Helene's tongue. She swallowed quickly and propelled a wave of fire down her esophagus. All the while she gawked at the younger woman, who'd ordered scones and clotted cream with her latte.

"What kind of money can a nurse make?"

Helene didn't reply.

Shifting in her chair, Lauren took a big bite of food. Goop stuck on her chin. She wiped it off and dusted crumbs from her ample bosom, then glanced furtively at Helene. Lauren squirmed beneath her mother-in-law's gaze.

"Mom, don't you understand my concern?" Lauren gulped her latte noisily. "Couldn't you get her a chair at UCLA? After all, you've given lots of money to the University over the years."

No response.

Sweat beaded on Lauren's forehead and betrayed her discomfort. She ate faster. "Well, what do you think?" Lauren prodded.

Helene stood up and pushed in her chair, which scrapped across the tile floor. She looked at her daughter-in-law without expression and didn't offer to pick up the tab. "I think it's time for me to leave; I'm going to evening Mass."

Helene left without saying goodbye.

Taking her usual place, in her usual pew toward the front of the church, Helene knelt briefly and felt her sinfulness oppress her. She glanced at the statue of the Little Flower in the alcove beside her. Votive lights flickered in the near-darkness. She wished she'd died at a young age like the saint, escaping the complexities of life.

Her breathing became short and quick. She struggled to take in enough oxygen to fill her lungs, but came up short. A sharp pain hit her behind the eyes, and Helene sucked in more air in an attempt to relieve a sense of suffocation. She exhaled with a quiet moan that, for the moment, seemed to satisfy her need for air.

A woman sitting behind her leaned forward and asked: "Are you okay? Do you need help?"

"No, thanks. I'm just a little winded. I'll be okay in a minute — this happens to me sometimes."

"Keep an eye on her," Helene heard the woman's husband whisper. "She looks like she's going to pass out."

Oh God, I'm sorry. A heavy weight, a lifetime of regret pressed down on her.

She watched an altar girl trying to light a candle. The flame faltered and went out and the girl had to summon help.

In the dim light, the church, clothed in red, marked the joyous season of Pentecost. The altar was covered in an abundance of flowers — gold, yellow, orange, and red gladioli — tongues of flame marking the climax of the Pascal season. Helene's mood, however, was somber, spiraling into blackness. The red surrounding her spoke to her of blood and death — the death of her spirit. She suppressed a sob lest the woman butt in again.

I should have supported Claire and André in their decisions. I should have, should have, should have... I should never have borne children.

Guilt throbbed with her pulse, and a familiar ripple of self-hatred swept over Helene, burrowed itself in the nooks and crannies of her consciousness, and obscured the peacefulness of the sacred space in which she knelt. She opened her eyes and noticed that no sun filtered through the stained glass windows. The rank odor of sulfur replaced the sweet scent of the blessed candles and incense as the young altar girl continued to struggle with the candle. Everything converged as a sign of God's displeasure, and Helene realized how poorly she'd succeeded in her quest for perfection.

Dizziness and nausea swept through her. Helene rose and grasped the pew to steady herself. When she regained her balance she left the church before Mass began. She didn't even genuflect.

Helene knew she wasn't worthy to partake of communion before making amends to God and her children. She felt as inadequate as anytime she could remember, and decided to stop off at the lounge for a Martini before going home. She hoped this might help her to relax and to evaluate her situation with more clarity.

Twelve

Birdsong erupted outside our bedroom window on Sunday morning as soon as daylight made its appearance.

Josh buttoned an orange plaid shirt and topped his tousled hair with a San Francisco Giants baseball cap and leaned over me, running his finger down my crooked nose. "I'm gonna garden first thing — how about it?"

"I'll be with you in a little while — I need some time to myself." I propped myself up in bed and accepted the cup of coffee he handed me. "I want to have a little quiet time, then research some stuff about transplants before I go outside."

"Wear a hat," Josh cautioned. "It's gonna be bright out there today."

Forty minutes later I entered my office, opened the blinds, and flipped on my computer. The box of old pictures I'd found in the garage sat, tucked away, on a shelf of my bookcase. I dragged a finger through the layer of dust that covered it and drew a question mark. These will wait till tomorrow, when Josh is at work. The young girl of my dream still haunted me.

I checked e-mail, then logged onto the Internet and entered the key words, "pregnancy and kidney transplant." Dozens of references popped up. I clicked on the first website and scanned it. A warm feeling stirred in the pit of my stomach and fanned throughout my body. I dragged the mouse to the printer icon, clicked and waited for it to spit out two pages.

"Pregnancy is common…" As I read, my pulse began to race. "The effects of pregnancy . . ." No warning bells went off and I continued to skim the article. "…increased incidence of premature births." I folded the papers in half and stuck them in my desk drawer under a medical dictionary.

After shutting down the computer, I just sat there awhile and allowed desire for motherhood to deluge me. I'd opened the floodgates and yearning, dammed in for too long, poured through my body. I had to clutch the edge of the desk to steady myself. Women with transplants can become mothers! I'd known that, of course, but had chosen to let my old companion, fear, hold me back.

Benisse lay on the floor, her tail whooshing gently from side to side. Murphy curled under the worktable. "Don't get excited yet," I told the dogs. "I need to talk to daddy and consult with my doctors."

Downstairs in the mudroom, I armed myself for gardening. I fetched work gloves that were stiff with mud from my last digging expedition and headed toward the back door. I still heard my heart thumping inside me. Would Josh feel the electricity of my excitement? I wasn't prepared to discuss it with him — not yet.

On the way out the door, the phone interrupted my reverie. I raced across the family room and hit "Talk" before the call could transfer to the answering machine.

Lauren's shrill voice pierced the silence. My sister-in-law barked, "What the hell are you doing to your mother? You're so damn selfish."

"What are you talking about?" I had to balance myself against the cool stone of the kitchen counter.

"You call Helene, drop a bombshell, and then hang up on her. You have no idea how every little thing you do affects your mother, do you, Claire?"

Is it true that Lauren's envious of me? I wondered. Her words stung like venom.

"Do you know how much your mother worries about you? It's obvious that she doubts if you and Josh can even make it on your own and I, for one, agree with her."

"Lauren, I . . ."

But she ranted on, screeching like an angry crow. "You're so ungrateful. Helene's proud that you're a doctor, and now you're just going to ditch it all for some stupid pipe dream that pleases you?"

I winced.

Without stopping for a breath, Lauren continued. "She helped support you through medical school — think about all she does for you. Your mother should disown you."

That's when I snapped under the pressure that was building up inside me like a volcano on the edge of eruption. "I didn't know she owned me, Lauren."

"Don't forget about the rest of us," she babbled on. "Your selfish choices impact us, too." Lauren raised her voice a few notes.

"Be quiet for a minute, Lauren, and listen to me. I don't need to defend myself to you. How the heck do my decisions affect the family? What I do has no bearing on you."

"You're clueless, aren't you?" Lauren said.

"That's enough," I yelled. I'd had it. "When you cool down, call me. I don't have to take your abuse. Josh and I manage fine on our own."

"We'll see," Lauren said. "But don't expect any of us to give you money." The line went dead.

Stunned, I stared out the door. Josh was bent over in the rose garden, scooping up debris left over from autumn. I opened the door and stepped onto the deck, and felt the warmth of the sun licking my skin. When he stood up and saw me, he beckoned at me before he squatted and swept up another handful of spent leaves.

As I walked toward him, my spirit, so recently elated with thoughts of creating new life, felt trampled. I flinched at the thought of interrupting his obvious serenity. With a catch in my voice, I said, "I'll start on the weeds, but we need to talk first."

Josh didn't hear me. Engrossed with digging, he used only his gloved hand. "Come and look at this."

When I approached the patch of soil where Josh worked, I stood over him and looked. Ground, still wet from the snowmelt, teamed with worms that wove their way through the dirt and aerated clay that would harden with the force of summer sun. Pungent earthy aromas engulfed me.

Josh stood, put his hands on his hips, and leaned backward to stretch the muscles in his lower back that had tightened over the winter months.

I held out a bottle of Samuel Adams that I'd fetched from the cooler on the deck and pleaded, "You want to take a break? You'd better. You're pushing your luck with that ankle. Besides, I really need you to listen to something."

"Sure. Thanks, honey." He reached for the frosty bottle after removing his gloves and dropping them on the damp turf. "What's going on?" He drew his forehead into a frown.

"Lauren called," I told him as we sank into the deck chairs, and then I related my sister-in-law's allegations, blow-by-blow. Fury coursed anew though my veins as though I were considering the words for the first time.

Josh pulled himself to the edge of his chair and seemed to study the amber bottle he'd emptied. "Here's what I think: Lauren sees you as a threat to her — I bet she thinks Helene will offer you an important position in the company."

"She didn't call me out of concern, I can promise you that." I scrutinized the pattern on my floral shirt and asked him if he thought I should talk to my brother.

Josh shook his head. "Leave it alone. If you react, Lauren will have the satisfaction of knowing she's pushed your buttons."

"And André will feel more helpless than he already is. You're right." I stood abruptly, and headed for the yard. "Let's get to work."

I ripped weeds from damp earth, and that helped my anger to cool to a simmer. I focused on tugging at relentless roots, but that didn't dull the hurt I felt, a nagging pain just below the surface of my awareness. When I wielded the hand rake and plunged it into the ground with a bit more force than needed, it struck something solid and I withdrew it. Attached to a claw, I discovered a small tulip bulb that had just begun to sprout. I replanted it carefully into the moist soil and prayed it would survive.

When I entered the house hours later, scents of garlic and rosemary wafted from the kitchen. "Smells wonderful, honey. I'm going to call Kathryn," I said, as dirt from my hands swirled down the drain. "She must've heard from Brian by now."

"Invite them over for a glass of wine," Josh suggested, "or even dinner if you want — we'll have plenty."

"What about Michael?" I asked. The thought of having to meet him head-on repelled me, and the tips of my fingers turned icy.

"He needs to consider Kathryn for a change. It'd be good for her to get out, don't you think? And maybe I'll have a better chance of getting him to talk to me when we meet face-to-face."

The Scotts arrived early. Rays of light from the open door bounced off the wine rack in the entryway and set the rich hues of merlots and cabernets aglow. Dust motes rose from the stored bottles and danced in unsettled patterns. When I hugged my friend, her body trembled. I looked her in the eye and saw her dilated pupils.

Michael muttered a greeting. I waited for his usual bear hug, but he slipped past me and greeted Josh, who threw an arm around his shoulder.

"Come on, man," Josh invited. "Let's get us a cold one — they're in the cooler on the deck. I wanna show you my plans for this year's vegetable garden."

Kathryn and I stood watching our husbands through the panes of the French door.

"I don't know what to say." Kathryn folded her arms across her chest as though shielding herself from a blast of arctic air. "I never thought he'd act like this."

"Maybe Josh can help him talk it out." I heard a warning whisper in my head. And maybe not. I handed Kathryn a glass of Pinot Grigio and we took seats beside one another but remained silent for a long while, still watching the men through windows.

Standing posed with his hands on his hips, I saw Michael, focused on Josh, who gesticulated with a fork from the grill.

"Tell me how you're doing," I asked Kathryn without taking my eyes off of Josh's wrinkled brow.

"There's not much to say. Brian still hasn't confirmed the time for the biopsy, and hasn't called about the C-T scan either. Now Michael's mad at him." Kathryn's voice faded. "It's like he's built an armor of steel around himself, Claire."

A vision of Michael, blaming me, persisted in its race through my mind and I choked on the sip of wine I'd just swallowed.

"By the way, did you call Helene yesterday?" Kathryn asked me.

"Yeah."

The question snapped me out of the world my imagination had created, and I cringed when recalling the sound of Mother's reproach. "It didn't go well."

When Kathryn opened her mouth to respond, Josh stuck his head in the door. "Two minute warning!"

"This can wait, Kathryn." I was relieved at the timing and reached for our almost-empty glasses. "I'm not ready to talk about her now — there's too much else to worry about." I stood and retreated to the kitchen, followed by my friend.

While we filled goblets with ice water and lit candles on the table, Kathryn admitted: "I'm scared — I feel like everything's whirling out of control."

I itched to tell her about Josh offering to become her donor, but his parents hadn't been at home when we tried calling earlier and I wasn't quite ready to give life to the idea by putting it into words. Instead, I walked over, took Kathryn's hand and gave it a squeeze.

As we took our places at the table, Michael gazed into space, still not talking.

"I started back to work already," Josh told him, but Michael merely nodded and forked a mouthful of green beans. Michael's lips were drawn in a straight, tense line and he gave me the impression that he wanted to be anywhere — anywhere but here with us.

"How's your job going?" I tried asking him.

Without taking his eyes from his plate Michael answered in a monotone voice, "Same as always." He worked the muscles in his jaw, causing tension to ripple across his dark face, and pressed his full lips together in a scowl.

Kathryn pushed food around on her plate and I struggled to swallow, my mouth as dry as a wad of cotton. When the bite I'd forced down hit my stomach, I felt like the gates had clamped shut and dispatched the food on a journey back up my esophagus. I gave up trying and pushed my plate to the side.

Josh caught my eye and opened his mouth to speak but I placed my hand on his knee, which brushed against me under the table. With my lips I formed the word No, in an attempt to restrain the anger that seemed to gain momentum within him and hovered on the verge of explosion.

After dinner, Josh and Michael migrated to the family room. Josh popped channels until he came to Sports Center. The two men sat without speaking while Kathryn and I did dishes and served dessert. When I took a seat beside my husband, he slipped his arm around me. Michael sprawled at the far end of the couch and studied catalogues during commercials. Beside him, Kathryn kept her head down, studying each bite of pie.

As soon as we finished, Michael rose and walked out of the room. "We need to go — we might have an early day tomorrow."

Kathryn stood and glanced over her shoulder at me and raised her eyebrows in a look of helplessness.

I nodded my understanding, but felt like crying for her. "Call me when you hear from Brian," I said.

Josh took my hand and we accompanied the couple to the door. Michael walked briskly ahead of his wife, mumbled his thanks, and left without turning back. After Josh closed the door he slammed it with his fist.

I cringed, stunned at the intensity of his reaction.

"That son-of-a-bitch!" Josh grimaced. "It took all my willpower not to punch him out." He bent at the waist and buried his face in his hands. "I'm sorry, Claire," he said, pulling me into his arms. "I couldn't do a thing — he's an asshole."

"No, Josh. Remember what you told me?" I said. "He's afraid — he's scared he's going to lose his wife."

I am, too.

As I was undressing, my head spun. A whirlwind of passion caught me in its vortex and I couldn't control my trembling.

Josh came up behind me and encircled me in his arms. His soothing voice enfolded me in comfort. "I know I lost it, honey, but we gotta let it go for tonight," he said, brushing my bare neck with his lips. "There's something else I want to think about for the moment."

I turned, and pressed my body against his. The desire for motherhood I'd entertained long hours earlier scurried back into my consciousness. We fell onto the bed and Josh's muscular body engulfed me, when the piercing sound of the phone interrupted us.

Kathryn's voice sounded tiny at the other end of the line.

Thirteen

At six-thirty Monday morning, Josh dropped me off at the entrance to the outpatient surgery center while he parked the car.

Michael and Kathryn waited for us, slouched in cushioned chairs. They held hands but didn't speak to one another. Kathryn stood and hugged me, while Michael nodded without smiling.

When Josh arrived a moment later, Michael acknowledged him with half a wave, but continued to study the floor.

The four of us sat facing each other. A medical assistant swept across the near-empty waiting room and handed Kathryn a clipboard. Kathryn began to write quickly, scrawling information like a robot.

It was almost seven o'clock when the door to the OR area swung open. I looked up and saw Brian Forrest stride toward us and pull up an empty chair. He leaned into the group, propped his elbows on his knees, and braced his chin in his hands. Speaking in hushed tones, he outlined the procedure once again.

Kathryn sat on the edge of her chair but Michael's face remained expressionless.

"If it does turn out to be malignant, I'm hopeful it'll be contained to one small area," Brian said, midway into his explanation.

"How long can a person hang on with a partial kidney?" Michael interrupted. In an instant, his forehead creased and mouth turned down.

"Michael, you're jumping to conclusions — we don't know what we'll find yet." Brian spoke in a firm tone of voice.

"So, can you re-transplant Kathryn's kidney back into her?" Michael asked. He stood and barged out the door without listening for an answer.

Josh's face turned red as he shot up to follow.

"Don't, honey. Just leave him alone," I pleaded.

Josh fell into a chair by the exit and buried his head in his hands, like a turtle withdrawing into its shell.

Brian stretched out his arm and touched Kathryn's shoulder. "Do you want me to try to talk to your husband?"

"Not now." Kathryn shook her head and reached for a tissue. "Not yet."

I moved into the chair Michael had abandoned.

"I've got to scrub," Brian told us. "There's a short procedure before yours, Kathryn. They'll come for you in a few minutes."

When he'd left I turned to Kathryn, who was in tears. "This must make it so much harder."

"I'll just be glad when it's over." Kathryn leaned forward in the chair, shaking her head from side-to-side. "I'm so sorry, Claire — and so disappointed in him." Kathryn said, a weary smile crossing her lips.

"Don't, Kathryn. Don't do this to yourself."

"Looks like it's time." Kathryn clenched the arms of her chair and nodded toward the pre-op nurse who headed our way, a hospital gown hanging over her arm.

I rose, gave her a hug, then followed her with my eyes as she trailed behind the woman in blue scrubs. She stopped and looked out the glass door at Michael, who stood, slumped against a tree.

When the swinging door closed behind Kathryn, I reached into my purse for the rosary I hadn't prayed in years. I sat, closed my eyes, and began my vigil.

The vibration of my cell phone, attached through routine to the waistband of my slacks, jarred me back into the present. I glanced at my watch and noted that barely ten minutes had passed since Kathryn left me.

"Dr. Bergano," I answered, as though anyone cared these days.

"Claire, where are you? I thought you'd be home." My mother sounded old, frail.

"Mom, what's the matter? Are you sick?" My concern squashed the rancor of our last conversation.

"Where are you, anyway?" Mother acted as though she hadn't heard my question.

"Kathryn's having some health problems," I answered, knowing I couldn't keep this a secret from her forever. "I didn't get to tell you sooner. She's in surgery now; they're doing a biopsy."

"A biopsy. Of what?" she asked.

"The kidney." Anxiety skulked through my nerve endings and prickled my skin like a bolt of electricity.

"Oh, my God! Oh, no." Mother's voice shook. "That can't happen; she's only got one kidney."

Mother's words fanned an ember of terror that exploded in my hammering heart. "Maybe it's not serious; we won't know anything for sure until after the procedure." I choked on the words in an attempt to convince myself as well as my mother.

"Do you want me to come up?" she asked.

"Not yet," I answered. Not at all, I thought. The bitter aftertaste of my mother's condemnation still loitered in my mind.

"What'll they do? Will she die?"

"We don't even know what we're dealing with," I said. "Are you okay?"

Mother cleared her throat. "I told Lauren about your plans when we met for tea on Saturday."

"She called me." Muscles in my shoulder blades tightened and pain seared down my back.

"Lauren wants me to get a teaching position for you at UCLA. Because of our endowment, she thinks I can tell them what to do. I'll try if you want me to."

"I don't know what to say." I remembered what Josh had said. "Maybe Lauren is afraid I'll join the business. Let it go for now, Mom. I'm looking forward to some time for myself — besides, I need to be here for Kathryn."

"What have I done?" Mother released a long, audible sigh. "Can't you move down here? I'll take care of you."

I heard a sob, then her speech thickened, and she began to babble. "I'll find a place for you," she promised. "It's all my fault — everything's my fault."

As I struggled to control the blend of anger and worry that swelled inside me, I realized something enormous had happened to Mother over the weekend. Something I knew too well. Memories played on the screen of my mind: days when I'd come home from school to find her slouched in a chair, the scent of gin filling the air, the bottle hidden from view.

"Are you drinking again?" I asked, in a whisper, aware that the chairs around me were filling with curious ears. Mother didn't hear or else chose not to answer.

"Oh, God," she sighed before she regained control. Now she spoke clearly, in a forceful tone. "Call me later; I'll be waiting to hear about Kathryn." She disconnected.

"What was that all about?" Josh squatted in front of me.

"That was my mother — something's really off kilter. To start with, it's not like her to let our arguments drop. She drifted off in the middle of the conversation like she used to when . . ."

Josh shook his head and took me by the elbow. "Let's get some coffee."

"Someday I've got to talk to her, adult-to-adult," I promised Josh. "Someday when the timing's right." And when she's sober, I thought.

I followed my husband out the door.

I looked for Michael as we exited the glass entryway.

"He's gone," Josh uttered in a coarse whisper, putting an arm around me.

"I don't know what to think, Josh. If I could give the kidney back to Kathryn, I would." I wanted to wail. An aura of sadness stifled me.

"Michael's not thinking straight, honey."

"Why are we all taking turns explaining his behavior, then in the next breath reacting to it, personalizing it? Oh, Josh, this is so bewildering. We're all in pain here."

Josh just took my hand, and it felt like his strength touched my weakness.

Patients and their families weaved through the parking lot toward the medical building. Anxious energy crowded me and I fought to get a breath to fill my lungs, but came up empty.

"How long do you think it'll take?" Josh asked.

"Not too long, but we've got time to go across the street. I need a break." I wiped my eyes with the edge of a sleeve and glanced in the direction of Michael's car. It was empty.

"Maybe he's walking off his anger," Josh said.

"You'd think he'd want to stay close. Come on — let's get our coffee so we can get back in case Brian's looking for us." I started out ahead of him.

We discovered Michael, slouched at the counter at Java 'n Jazz. He handed a five to the clerk, grabbed his cup, and left without waiting for change. When he passed alongside us, he turned his gaze in the opposite direction.

"He's going back," I said, following him with my eyes.

"That's where he should be. Why don't you get a table while I order something to eat." Josh took his place at the end of the line.

Hunger and fatigue filled me, competing with fear for my attention. When Josh returned bearing coffee and toasted bagels, we ate slowly to prolong our reentry into the world of crisis.

We returned to the waiting room and found Michael buried in a magazine. He set it down and motioned for us to sit across from him. He reached out as I drew near and gave my hand a little squeeze before returning to reading.

I grappled with confusion. I understood Michael's struggles, but that didn't soothe the wound he'd opened earlier. The memory of his words still bruised me.

Josh sat with his arms shoved in his pockets. Michael leaned forward, elbows on his knees, face pressed into his strong, black hands. We waited like that for another thirty-five minutes.

When Brian emerged from the surgical suite, a surgical mask dangled around his neck but his face remained unreadable. He led the three of us into a small conference room and motioned for us to sit around a polished mahogany table in chairs designed to keep conversation short.

"The tumor's confined to a small area." Brian struck at the heart of the matter. "We need a pathologist's confirmation, but it's highly suspicious. I'm going to schedule surgery for a week from today — does that work for you?" he asked, looking at Michael, who nodded and allowed tears to flow unchecked now.

Josh got up, stood behind Michael and put his hands on Michael's shoulders, which began to heave in grief.

"I'm sorry," Brian continued. "I promise we'll do all we can. I'll ask a colleague to scrub in with me when we remove the tumor. He's the best, and doesn't know any of you. I need someone who can guide me, who can stay objective."

Numbness spread throughout me; I stood and went to Josh's side.

Brian rose, gave me a quick hug and tapped the two men on the shoulder. "I'll be in touch as soon as I get more details and confirmation of the biopsy reports. You three stay in here as long as you need to." He crept into the hallway and closed the door behind him.

"Don't get up, Michael," Josh commanded in an unfaltering voice.

Without a word, Michael obeyed.

"We can't go on like this." Josh began. "We gotta support one another, no matter what happens. None of us expected anything like this when Kathryn gave a kidney to Claire."

Michael's sobs subsided but pain continued to distort his features. He looked older, and exhausted. His brow creased and wrinkles framed his lips.

My hurt waned as concern for Michael took its place.

Josh continued. "I need to let you know something." He glanced at me, and I nodded, then stood and grabbed his hand. "Claire and I have already discussed it — if needed, and if I'm a match, I'm going to give a kidney to Kathryn. I know we're the same blood type because Claire and I are both A positive and Kathryn matched Claire."

"It takes more than blood type," Michael answered.

"I know that, but it's a start."

Michael's dark eyes registered bewilderment. He looked at Josh, then me.

"It's the only thing we know to do, Michael." I spoke with confidence now, even as the pounding of my heart caused me to sway. "The only way I got through my illness was trust — trust that God would care for me, and trust in the people who love me. This is all we can offer right now."

Michael shook his head, then stood and hugged Josh.

I watched the man shed layers of angst. He began to relax and light returned to his eyes. No one said a word, but the change was visible. Michael released Josh and approached me, holding me at arms' length. He looked into my eyes and spoke in a coarse voice. "Claire, I'm sorry — I'm so sorry. I've felt so hopeless. I should be the one to give a kidney, but I can't. Kathryn and I aren't even the same blood type."

"I know. We've been where you are, too, remember?" I added, loosening my grasp a bit on the ache that had gnawed at me for days.

Brian stuck his head back in. "I forgot to tell you that Kathryn should be ready to go home within the hour. When she's awake, do you want me to tell her what we found?"

Michael spoke up, "No, I'll do it myself. Thanks, Dr. Forrest."

The surgeon looked at me with a puzzled expression, shrugged his shoulders, and left.

Josh said, "Hey, doc, wait a minute." He turned and took my hand and we followed Brian into the corridor.

"Sure, what's up?" Brian stopped and faced us. The fluorescent lighting threw the two men into relief.

"I want to start the process so I can donate a kidney to Kathryn?" Josh said.

"You'd do that?" Brian asked, eyes wide open.

"Kathryn did it for Claire, didn't she? It's logical, and I'm healthy. We're the same blood type. Why wouldn't I want to help the woman who saved my wife's life?" Josh put his arm around me.

"Okay, here's the deal." Brian said. "After the surgery, we'll evaluate Kathryn's kidney function. My guess is that she'll need dialysis. If so, I'll set her up with the transplant center right away. Once she's evaluated, they'll test anyone who offers to be a donor."

"Make it happen, Brian." Josh reached out and took the physician by the arm. "I want to be tested as soon as possible. We can't live like this much longer. I talked to Michael. It's important to all of us, and I need to do it for Claire." Josh looked at me. "She can't help being upset by all of this — she feels guilty." He turned toward me, now. "And I can help."

"I know," Brian said, looking straight at me. "This has got to be your worst nightmare. The transplant team's due to visit Reno at the end of the month, so I'll make a tentative appointment for Kathryn." He cleared his throat then continued. "They can draw your blood at the same time, if you want. But there's no guarantee you'll match, you know."

"Let's hope we don't have to deal with that," Josh said. "Thanks, Brian. Don't tell Kathryn yet, okay? Michael needs to do that. He's got some distance to make up with her — they've been through a rough time."

"You're quite a man." Brian's jade eyes glistened as he shook Josh's hand. "I feel privileged to know you. Now, you take care of your beautiful wife."

Josh pulled me even closer and smiled. We looked at one another as Brian walked away.

"What's his story, honey?" Josh asked me.

"I don't know. He seems to be working all the time. He's wearing a wedding ring, but somehow I think he's lonely."

We took leave of Michael and exited the surgery center, walking into a gust of fresh air. The bright sunshine made me squint. Nature tossed its beauty in my face, taunting the heaviness of my mood. It's out in the open, now. Josh made his promise — there's no way to take it back.

He dropped me off at home. I stood on the curb and threw him a kiss as he hung a U-turn in the cul-de-sac and headed out to visit patients.

Shedding slacks and sweater in favor of jeans and a tee shirt, I snagged leashes from a hook by the backdoor. Murphy galloped across the yard to greet me; Benisse tagged along behind him. I fastened them up and set off toward the river.

My steps slowed, weighed down by ponderous thoughts. I entered the river walk at the end of our street. Water rushed east, toward the city.

An elderly neighbor who had just lost his wife ambled in my direction, an ancient dog in tow. The man's body, bent like a comma, spoke of grief. I halted and eked out a smile as he passed and greeted me. I reached into my heart for words of comfort, but they failed me. On the bank of the Truckee, moldy leaves and the smell of loss engulfed me, and dread seeped into me.

At the end of an hour's walk, the three of us returned home. Murphy and Benisse took off for their water dishes. I headed up to my office — I was anxious to talk to Kathryn. When I reached for the phone I noticed the blinking light. I hit play and Michael's voice boomed out. "Hey, Claire, call me at home when you can."

He answered before the end of the first ring.

"Everything okay, Michael?"

"Yeah, we're home, but Kathryn's out cold and I'm afraid to leave her. I need to go in to work for a while. Is there any possibility…?"

"I'm on my way. I have no idea what to do with myself this afternoon, anyway."

The door opened as soon as I reached the front porch. Michael greeted me with a hug, but a troubled expression lingered in his dark eyes. "I won't be long; I have to stop by the office and then call on a couple of accounts."

"Take your time. Is Kathryn still asleep?"

"I brought her a glass of juice right after we spoke. She's in and out but wants to talk to you. She knows about everything — I told her about Josh."

"You go ahead and do what you need to," I said. "I'll be here."

Michael pecked me on the cheek and headed off to his car, still parked in the driveway.

As he drove away, I wondered how things would be if Josh hadn't offered to be Kathryn's donor. I shut the door and tried to erase the thought before I headed to the bedroom.

Kathryn sat on the edge of the bed, sipping apple juice from a cardboard container. The curtains were drawn, blocking the light.

"What time is it?" Kathryn asked.

"Just after one. You okay?"

"I've got to be — I plan to go in to the office tomorrow. There're only a few days to get things squared away. Brian scheduled my surgery for next Monday."

"Good — the sooner the better, don't you think?"

"Yeah," Kathryn nodded. "I talked to my boss and she wants to meet with you."

"Did she say when?"

"Pop in anytime, but call ahead to make sure she's free. Michael told me about Josh — I don't know." Kathryn shook her head.

"He's going to be tested. No one, but no one, can talk him out of that." I placed a hand beneath Kathryn's knees and helped her lie back on the bed.

Kathryn let out a deep sigh and sank into the pillows. "Why did it have to take this to turn Michael around, Claire? What if Josh isn't a match? Will he go into a rage again?" She handed me the juice and pulled the blanket up to her chin.

"Let's just get through today, okay?" I struggled to mask my own misgivings. "Besides, Josh is going to be a match — I know he is. Now, try to get some rest."

I watched Kathryn drift off into a drugged fog. I propped my feet on the edge of a stuffed ottoman and circled my arms around my legs. From my erect fetal position, I pondered Kathryn's doubt.

Josh and I pulled into the garage in tandem.

"Where've you been?" he asked, closing the car door behind him. "I tried calling — you don't have your cell phone, do you?" Josh planted his lips on mine as I patted my waistband.

"Guess I left it on my slacks again." I took a bag of groceries from the trunk and he unloaded the rest. "I went over to stay with Kathryn so Michael could get some work done."

"How'd she do?" Josh pulled spices from the rack and began to season pork chops as I related the details of the afternoon, but omitted my on-going uneasiness about Michael.

"I finally got a hold of Mom and Dad," Josh said. "They're fine with everything — I expected they would be. Said they'd drive up from Half Moon Bay to be with you while I'm laid up."

"I love your parents."

In the distance, I heard my cell playing Für Elise. I bounded up the stairs, two at a time, and discovered it in the laundry basket, along with my clothes from the morning. As soon as I grabbed hold of the phone, the ringing stopped. I retreated back down to the kitchen where I retrieved my messages — there were four from Mother. I listened to the most recent.

"I can't count on you to call me, can I?" I heard reproach in my mother's words.

"Oh boy! I messed up again." I said to Josh.

"Call now, honey. We've got half an hour till dinner's done."

"I'm so sorry, Mom," I responded to her greeting. I cradled the phone in the crook of my neck and scooped up food for the dogs.

"You know how I worry; I've been so anxious. What happened?" she asked.

"Kathryn's scheduled for surgery next Monday."

"What're you telling me?" Mother raised her voice a pitch.

"They suspect a malignancy, but Josh has offered to give Kathryn a kidney if he's a match — and if she needs it."

"Oh. Mon Dieu! Ce n'est pas possible. It just can't be."

"He'll be okay." Another warning sounded inside me when my mother spoke French, the language of my grandparents, the language she used to slip into when she drank.

"Now I've got two of them to worry about," she moaned.

"Are you okay?" I sat on a bar stool at the counter and watched Josh add a handful of green beans to a pot of steaming water.

"Nothing's okay — I'm not okay at all," Mother answered with a sharp cry.

"What's going on? You don't sound like yourself."

"Je ne le suis pas. Pas de tout. I'm not. Not at all."

"Are you drinking again?" I asked. "Is that what's happening?"

"Pas maintenant. Not now. But..."

I waited for her to continue, but only heard sniffling.

"Can I help, Mom? Do you want me to come down, or call André?"

"Non!"

I ran my hand through Benisse's soft fur. "What happened? It's been years."

She ignored the question again. "Please don't call André."

"What are you going to do? I mean, right now?"

Mother blew her nose.

"Shall I check in with you later?" I asked.

"No. I'm going to bed." She sniffled again.

"Let me know how you're doing in the morning, will you?" I asked.

"I will, Claire. Je t'aime, ma fille."

Startled at the admission, I answered, "I love you, too."

"What was that all about?" Josh asked as he took the phone and handed me a glass of wine.

"She's drinking, Josh. I'm sure of it, now. But she wouldn't talk to me about it. I wonder what brought that on."

"Maybe she feels guilty about the way she treated you."

"I think there's more to it than that." I followed Josh out on the deck. The evening breeze blew my hair into my face. I held up the glass of Pinot Noir and studied the deep burgundy color, but hesitated before taking a sip.

Fourteen

"*You've reached the home of . . .*" A detached voice completed the standard message. For the second time that morning, a flicker of anxiety struck me. When I'd phoned earlier, I assumed my mother was still in bed. Now it was ten-thirty. This time I spoke to the machine, asking for a call back.

Where was she, and when would Kathryn return the call I made just after Josh left for work? Muscles in my back tensed as I vacuumed the same spot over and over. The next two hours, spent housekeeping, progressed in slow motion.

Josh called during his lunch break. I listened to chewing and related my concerns.

"You know what I'd do?" Josh crunched on a stalk of celery. "I'd go to hospice today. Have your meeting with the director, then drop in on Kathryn. You'll have a better chance of sizing her up if you see her face-to-face."

After spending time with Kathryn's boss, I poked my head into my friend's office and cleared my throat. "You look exhausted."

"Yeah. I am." Kathryn rubbed her bloodshot eyes and stretched. "Michael tossed and turned all night — he's back in the worry mode."

"Would he talk about it?"

"Not really. He's shrink-wrapped, and I can't get through to him." Kathryn sighed. "Sorry I didn't call back this morning, but I needed time to wade through my emotions before talking about them."

I sat and tossed my purse on an empty chair, then leaned toward Kathryn, propping my head in my hands, which rested on the desk that formed a barrier between us. A burning sensation crept up the back of my throat. My eyes fixed on an abstract painting hanging behind Kathryn's head. Brilliant streaks of red ripped across the canvas: the artist's rage unfurled for all to see. Or was it fear? Splashes of black and indigo hid behind the anger. I'd never noticed that piece before, or, at least, had never felt it so deeply.

"Later this week I need to review these patients with you," Kathryn said, gesturing at a pile of charts. She spoke in a restrained, measured voice, like a vocalist practicing scales.

"I'm all yours," I said, still staring at the acrylic. "That picture, how long have you had it?"

"About a year. A young man, a patient dying from AIDS, painted it for me." Kathryn swiveled her chair around and faced the painting. "He named it Helpless." When she turned back toward me, tears rimmed her eyes.

"Is that what you feel?"

Kathryn nodded and reached for a tissue. "At least Brian has offered an intervention for the tumor, but there's nothing I can do about Michael, is there?"

In my mind, I searched for an answer to her question. "I wish it were as easy as writing a prescription. Do you think counseling would help him?"

"I suggested it — he won't even consider it." Kathryn turned and looked at the painting again. "We'll just have to wait and see what happens."

"How about your procedure Monday? Do you know what time it'll be?" I asked.

"I'm still waiting to hear from Brian." Kathryn folded her hands on the edge of the desk.

"Whenever it is, I'll be there — and don't tell me Michael doesn't want me to come."

Kathryn stood, walked around the desk, and took the chair next to me. "It's not his decision."

"Dr. Scott, line one," a voice from the intercom announced.

"I better run, Kathryn. You're busy." I reached for my purse.

Kathryn took my face into her long slender hands and planted a kiss in the middle of my forehead. "Thanks, girl. I'll call you later. There's something else we need to talk about."

"I'll be late getting home today."

I played the message a second time just to hear the sound of Josh's soothing voice.

"I'll explain later. Let's go out to dinner," the message broadcasted in conclusion.

The door to the pantry stood open a few inches. I eyed a box of lasagna noodles and decided to surprise Josh, so I gathered the ingredients and set about building one of the few dishes for which I was famous. As I spread ricotta between layers of sauce and noodles, my thoughts flitted from Kathryn to my mother. A thread of anguish wove them into one piece of fabric.

When he returned home, Josh's eyes danced. His off-centered grin spoke of mischief. "You cooked! How'd you know I didn't really want to leave home tonight?"

The fragrance of garlic filled the house. "You've had a long day, honey, and I was in the mood."

"I'm in the mood, too!" He laughed and grabbed me by the waist and whirled me around the kitchen till we stumbled on the dogs.

The heavy energy surrounding me diffused. "Something's lurking behind your exuberance, Mr. Bergano."

"Maybe." He squeezed me and I gasped for air.

Josh waltzed over to the oven, turned it down to its lowest setting, then led me to the guestroom and began to remove my clothing, beginning with the apron and working his way through the rest.

"What's this?" I asked breathlessly.

Josh placed his fingers on my lips then covered them with his own. A soft down comforter cushioned us; dim light streamed through drawn blinds.

"We usually eat first," I mumbled

Josh ignored me and drew my body against his own until we moved as one.

After, we lay together in silence, spent and satisfied.

"I love surprises," I whispered.

"So do I. And I've got more."

"This is delicious," Josh said, after his first bite of lasagna. "Maybe it's time for you to take over cooking."

"Please! You don't need to lose weight." I laughed at the thought.

"I mean it, honey." Josh sat up straight and leaned across the table toward me. "I might not have much time, except for weekends."

"What're you talking about? It's never been a problem before." I pursed my lips.

"Well, that's the rest of my surprise," Josh said.

I set my fork on the plate, gave him my full attention, and waited for him to explain.

"When I went to the office this morning to get supplies, I saw a posting for a full time position," Josh said, not taking his eyes off of me. "I went straight to the director's office and it's mine! We'll get benefits, and the pay will do just fine."

"Oh, Josh!" I reached for his hand.

"Now you don't have to work if you don't want to, once this stint filling in for Kathryn is over."

I studied him. A grin took over his face, echoing the eagerness in his voice.

"Promise you'll let me in the kitchen whenever I have time," Josh added.

"I'm happy, honey," I said, trying to convince myself as well as Josh.

"I feel pretty good about it, too," Josh concurred.

In spite of the warmth I felt, I pulled my robe tighter about my body. A nagging ache lingered between my shoulder blades — the threat of losing my identity that was still so tied in to being a doctor.

Josh tossed a crumb of bread in the air for Murphy, who leaped high to catch it.

In the back of my mind, an unwelcome image gnawed at me. I thought of the painting in Kathryn's office and couldn't quite abandon myself to joy.

I smoothed lotion on my naked body. "Honey, can I talk to you about something?" I asked Josh, who stood across the room.

"Anytime, Claire — you know that," he glanced in my direction.

"I have an idea and can't hold it in anymore. It's really important to me — to both of us," I added.

"You scare me when you talk like that!"

I slipped a silk gown over my head. "Just hear me out."

"Go ahead. I'm listening." Josh rummaged through a drawer looking for pajamas.

I walked over to him and put my hand on his arm to command his full attention.

"Okay." He grinned sheepishly, abandoned his quest, and followed me to the bed.

"Now that I'm a housewife, can we try to have a baby?" I asked.

"You're kidding, right?" Josh drew back and stared into my eyes.

"No, I'm very serious." My heart pounded in my ears.

"I've always wanted children — I have," Josh said. "With you. But there's no way I'd allow anything that could jeopardize your health." Josh's voice crackled, rough with emotion. "Just being with you is enough of a reason to sacrifice being a dad. It's too risky — I'd be afraid."

I reached into the top drawer of my bedside table and pulled out the folder of articles I'd printed from the Internet. "Here, read these when you find time. I promise you, I wouldn't consider it if it were dangerous, and not without the approval of the transplant center. Will you just look at these before saying 'No'?"

"Okay." He paused, staring up at the ceiling. "Wouldn't that really be something?"

Josh studied the papers for a moment, then set them aside. "You know, in the meantime, we could practice."

"We could do that."

Josh's craving was intense. I quivered as every instinct to nurture became aroused within me. I prayed for the time he would leave new life within my womb. A burst of pure, explosive pleasure followed, and a gentle promise filled me.

"Oh God, Claire, we could do it, we could. But only . . ."

I covered his mouth with mine to prevent him from verbalizing doubt.

Fifteen

Helene turned the phone's ringer back on. She'd been drinking since Saturday in an attempt to drown the myriad causes of her overwhelming guilt. It was Wednesday morning.

The room closed in about her and she hadn't opened the drapes. Wastebaskets overflowed, and odor from Scruff's litter box competed with empty gin bottles. When she opened the faucets in the shower, steam obscured the mirrors. She reeked of body odor and booze.

She'd have to do something about her problem as soon as things settled down. There was Claire and Lauren. And now, Kathryn. There were too many things to deal with at once.

Hot water beat her flesh as she mulled over her disintegrating relationship with Lauren. She'd managed to steer clear of her daughter-in-law since Sunday, and tried to avoid people in general. What if they figured out she was drinking again?

Helene made essential phone calls early in the day, every day, so her words wouldn't slur. She hoped Claire would call again. She regretted that she'd ignored her daughter's message, but now she wanted an update on Kathryn. Until she spoke with Claire, she'd need to be cautious about her alcohol consumption.

The situation in Reno rattled her. Helene considered making a novena for Kathryn but that brought to mind her standing in the Catholic Church.

She couldn't live up to such expectations anymore. Or was it her own expectations?

Water washed over her. Helene prayed the psalm, "Miserere mei, Domine, Miserere. Have mercy on me, Oh Lord, have mercy. Cleanse me from my sins." Forgiveness eluded her. She wasn't worthy yet. She'd hurt too many people and damaged too many lives — lives of people she loved.

Twisting a small towel around her soaked hair, Helene enfolded herself in a velvety purple bath sheet. As the fog cleared from the mirror she saw her face, etched with anger and remorse. Clarity rushed in upon her. "I need to make up for what I've done to my children," she spoke aloud. "I need to put them first for a change. Before the business."

After dressing, she mixed a martini. Just one drink would be fine. It would sustain her through the angst of waiting for Claire's call.

She dozed a bit after a second martini, then fell into a deep, dreamless slumber. The ring of her telephone snapped her awake. Helene looked around the room, unsure of her whereabouts when she remembered the call from Claire and fumbled for the receiver.

"Mom, is that you?"

"Claire?"

"No, it's Lauren."

"Oh." Helene fell back into her chair and waited for her daughter-in-law to state her purpose.

"Where've you been?" Lauren asked in a shrill voice. "We haven't heard a peep out of you all week. Are you okay?"

"I'm fine, Lauren. Perfect."

"What's going on? You don't sound like yourself."

"I was taking a nap. You woke me up." Helene allowed bitterness to lace her words. "I'm waiting for a call from Claire. Her friend Kathryn is having health problems."

"You're talking to Claire?"

"I'd like to leave the line open." Helene ignored the question. "Stop fussing over me — I'm fine. I'll talk to you soon. Say 'hello' to André for me." She hung up the phone, but distaste for her daughter-in-law lingered in her mind. Why hadn't she seen the woman's deception before this?

Helene rose and pulled the blinds shut. She sat in the shadow of dark thoughts that continued to harass her. She poured a third martini, and blamed it on her son's wife.

Walls of pretense that she'd carefully constructed crumbled about her. Helene couldn't permit Lauren to manipulate her or her family again.

The embryo of an idea began to take form within her.

Sixteen

he doorbell rang, followed by a knock. I uncurled from my chair in the library and peeked out the window. A cab idled in front of our house.

Puzzled, I raced down the stairs, peeked through the side window, and caught a glimpse of my mother. I sucked in a deep breath and ran my fingers through my disheveled hair, then opened the door.

Before wrapping her arms around me, my mother motioned to the driver, who stood on the curb with a carry-on.

My emotions were in turmoil.

Mother released her grip and held me at arms' length, studying me like she used to when I was a kid. "I didn't call ahead of time. I was afraid you'd say 'No.'"

"I'm so glad you're here." I was astonished when I realized I really meant it.

"I thought it would be good for me to get away for a couple of days. I can stay in a hotel if you want."

"Of course not. I'll just change the bed in the guestroom."

My thoughts flew back to the crazy love-making Josh and I had enjoyed there so recently.

"I'm really happy you're here, Mom."

I couldn't help but focus on Mother's eyes, which were ringed with black circles as though sleep had evaded her for days. I saw slightly stooped shoulders, visible beneath a gray knit dress that hung loosely on her medium frame. From beneath arched brows, my mother stared back at me, then she handed a large bill to the cabbie, who deposited the bag at the door. Mother dismissed him with a wave of her hand.

Grabbing the suitcase, I stood aside as she entered.

"Thank you. Thank you, Claire." There was an almost-apologetic expression on her face. "I don't want to be a burden — I promise I'll keep out of your way."

"You won't be a burden. I'm glad to see for myself how you're doing — I've been worried, Mom." I headed toward the guest room in the back of the house.

"Now you won't need to wonder if I'm sober or not." she said, with a slight chuckle.

I swiveled on my heel, faced her, and let the suitcase tumble to the tile floor.

"You knew, didn't you?" she asked.

"I suspected." I took her by the arm. "Come on — let's get something hot to drink. Does André know you're here?"

"I called him from the airport when I landed. He doesn't know about my . . . my problem. That's part of the reason I'm here. I have an idea, and I need your advice."

As the coffee brewed, we huddled over the breakfast room table.

"What happened? You've been sober for years. What got you started again?"

"Sometimes reality wallops you, dear. Everything happened at once. You. André. It's all so clear now."

"What's clear?" I poured the coffee and watched my mother stir sugar into hers.

"How I've meddled in your lives. I'm so sorry. It came home to me Saturday afternoon when I met with Lauren — I saw her for what she is."

I choked on the first sip of coffee. "But I thought you were close to her. You've always told me she's a lifesaver for the business."

"Damn the business. I should have sold it when your father died. Lauren doesn't love your brother. Their marriage is nothing more than a wise investment for her, and I sealed the deal. I'm the one who gave her the position of chief operating officer. God forgive me."

Her words caught me off guard. "She's got operations expertise, Mom. André has the smarts but . . ."

"But he's so unhappy. I should have encouraged him to go on with his studies like he wanted," she interrupted. "He hates what he's doing and I'm the one who put him into that miserable position. I would have done the same to you if you hadn't held your own. Is there a way to undo what I've done?"

The taste of java mingled with uncertainty in my mouth. I couldn't remember my mother ever asking my opinion on anything.

She grabbed a tissue. "Is it too late, do you think?"

Too late for what, I wondered, but asked, "Why didn't you tell André about your drinking?"

"I don't want Lauren to know." She faltered, then explained, "She came to the house on Monday; I didn't answer the door. I was only on my second martini, but it was just ten-thirty in the morning. Then she called me, wanting to meet with me. She accused me of not caring about her and André or the business."

"Why'd she come to see you in the first place?" I pushed the creamer toward her empty mug and went for the pot of coffee. "Do you know what she wanted?"

Her shoulders slumped. "She wants to control me and André — of that I'm sure. And the business. She wants to control everything. Oh Claire, if only . . ." She paused. "A couple of weeks ago she gave André a ridiculous project. Data collection, or some such thing."

"But that's what he's good at."

"She gave it to him at noon and wanted it early the next day. He didn't get home until three in the morning. Those are the kinds of things she does."

"What was that all about?" I refilled my cup with steaming liquid and offered some more to Mother, but she shook her head.

"She wants to expand further north. André told me the data doesn't support her decision but she wasn't going to pay attention to his advice. He said that's why she stopped by — to sell me on the project using her own interpretation of the figures."

"Sounds desperate."

"I bet she knows I'm on to her. André visited me the day after he'd pulled the all-nighter and could hardly keep his head up. He told me Lauren banished him to the guestroom. The guestroom of his own house."

"You said you had a plan."

"I do. I want your permission to put the stores on the market. You're an equal shareholder, so you have a say."

I stood and carried our empty mugs to the sink. Through the window I saw a female quail disappear beneath the leaves of a hardy geranium, the same place where it'd nested last year. The bird's mate sat on the fence, protectively.

Mother joined me and watched.

I faced her and burst into a smile. "Sell it. You know I support your decision. Now, what do you suppose Lauren will do about that?"

"Josh, it's me. Are you sitting?" Mother was napping and it was my first chance to call him since she had arrived.

"Yeah, I just pulled up to the office. Why are you whispering? What's the matter?"

"Mother's resting."

"What?"

"She's here, honey. She showed up at the door this morning."

Josh's voice sounded raspy. "She just showed up? That's not like her at all."

"I told her she could stay with us — it's only till Sunday morning."

"Great. Just great." Sarcasm dripped from Josh's words. "Did she tell you why she came?"

"There're lots of reasons. We'll talk tonight, okay? I'm going to pick up something for dinner."

"I'll be home in time to cook. Listen, Claire, I'm sorry if I came across as upset — you caught me by surprise."

About an hour after, my mother walked out of the guest room and found me with my purse dangling from my shoulder as I opened the back door to let the dogs outside.

"Going somewhere?" she asked.

"I was just going to leave you a note. I'm running to get some groceries — do you want to come?" I dug into my bag for the car keys.

We headed up McCarran Boulevard when I took an unplanned right turn. The car snaked along the Truckee toward St. Joseph's Hospice. "Let's drop in on Kathryn. Is that okay with you?" I asked her, like she had a choice.

"That's another reason I came — I had to see her for myself. Is it possible the tumor's not cancer?" Mother tapped her fingers on her knee.

"It's possible, but unlikely. Brian was adamant about scheduling surgery quickly — maybe she's heard something by now."

Kathryn met us on the porch. "I was in the reception area and saw you pull up. What a surprise! A double surprise." She hugged my mother, then took me by the arm.

"I wanted to check up on you." Mother raised her eyebrows and scrutinized my donor. "I'm so upset — is there anything I can do?"

Kathryn shook her head and opened her mouth to speak, but nothing came out. "I'm sorry. I just got off the phone with Brian. I was heading to call you, Claire. Let's go to my office; I'll grab us some soda."

We followed Kathryn down the narrow corridor and waited in silence till she returned with a liter of Diet Coke and glasses of ice.

"I'm Brian's first case on Monday at seven thirty," Kathryn said, as she poured our drinks. "I'm glad it's early."

The room spun when I heard the news, even though I knew it was coming.

"How's Michael?" I asked.

"Honey, today he's fine. But he's worse than a woman going through the change. His moods have been all over the place."

Taking a long draught of the fizzy liquid, I shot a look at my mother.

"Is Michael sick too?" she asked.

"He's having a hard time accepting what's happening." Kathryn paused to take in a deep breath. "Why don't the three of you come for dinner Friday? It'll be a good distraction for us all."

I nodded. "That's the day you wanted to orient me, anyway. I'm going to fill in for Kathryn, Mom; I forgot to tell you."

"You're going back to work already?" Mother's eyes widened, accenting her surprise.

"Only if Kathryn has to take time off — and only on a temporary basis," I said.

"There's something else you need to know. Brian called to confirm that the biopsy was malignant." She leaned back in her chair and closed her eyes.

I felt my jaw muscles stiffen and looked at Kathryn, whose mouth was frozen into a straight line.

"It's okay," Kathryn said in a whisper. "It's renal cell carcinoma. Very small, he told me."

Mother bowed her head and pressed her forefingers against her temples. "I was hoping it was all a mistake," she said.

I stood, walked around the large desk, and held out my arms to Kathryn, who rose to accept my embrace. "Why do you have to go through this?" I asked. "Why you, of all people? I'm so sorry."

From the corner of my eye, I saw my mother — her head bent, her face covered by hands with swollen joints.

I released Kathryn and handed my mother another tissue from the box on the corner of the desk. "We better not take up too much of your time. Call me when you get home, okay?" I gulped down the rest of the soda.

Charts lay sprawled over Kathryn's desk and stacked on the floor. "I don't want to leave all this for you," Kathryn said, sweeping her arm across the clutter. "Can you give me about four hours on Friday? Around ten o'clock?"

"Do you mind having some time to yourself?" I asked my mother. "You can drop me off and take the car if you want."

"I won't need the car — I already found a dozen books in your library I want to borrow, and by then, I'll need some quiet time." She picked up her purse and hugged Kathryn, who followed us to the door.

As I walked beside Kathryn, I said in a low voice, "You said you needed to talk to me."

"It's okay, friend. There's nothing left to say," Kathryn told me. "Spend as much time as you can with Helene."

"But what can I do to help?" I asked. "Yesterday, you told me we had something else to discuss."

"I wanted to hear how your mother was doing," Kathryn said in a whisper. "And she's here. Michael's better — for the moment, anyway. The surgery will be over Monday. I know you're there for me and would be here in an instant. What else can anyone do? I'll see you Friday, okay?" Kathryn waved before vanishing back inside the building.

Thoughts of helplessness battered me. A gust of wind rose from nowhere, a blast of warm air. But I shivered and led my mother to the car.

"I've never seen your mother this open before. She just laid bare her soul, put it all on the table. She even thanked me for taking care of you." Josh threw back the covers as I crawled in and slipped into his arms. "How do you feel about her selling the business?"

"Happy. Very, very happy. She's going to call André in the morning. I wish I could hear his reaction." I traced the outline of Josh's profile with my finger. "I called the transplant center this morning."

"About?" Josh asked.

"How quickly you forget — about getting pregnant, silly."

Josh bolted upright in bed. "What'd they say?"

"They haven't gotten back to me yet. Come here." I reached up and cupped my hands about Josh's jaw and pulled his face to mine.

"Do you think your mother can hear us?"

"Hmmmmm. That's an exciting thought. I love you, Joshua Bergano. And I don't care who knows it."

He slid back down under the covers and his hands explored the curves of my body.

Forgetting the churning emotions of the day, I focused on giving myself to the man I loved. I savored his taste, the scent of his aftershave mingling with the sweat of our bodies, undulating like the waves of the ocean.

I was about to surrender when a crashing noise from downstairs shattered our bliss.

I flew down the stairs behind Josh, expecting to find my mother sprawled on the floor.

"She's not in the bedroom," Josh called, so I headed for the family room.

We found Mother sitting at the breakfast table with her head buried in her hands, sobbing. In front of her was an empty glass. On the floor, an overturned bottle of gin spilled its contents into a widening puddle.

In a swoop, Josh turned the bottle upright and carried it into the kitchen. I stepped across the pool of alcohol and stood beside my mother, who pounded clenched fists aimlessly in the air.

I ran my hands up and down her back and cooed in a soothing voice, "It's okay; it's okay."

She pulled away from me and spoke, her words broken by weeping. "I don't know what happened. I opened the pantry to look for a graham cracker to take with my pills."

I handed her a tissue.

"I saw the Tangueray, then the next thing I knew, I had the bottle open and was about to pour it."

"It's okay," I muttered again.

"No. No, it's not. I threw the bottle — I hate myself for this."

I caught Josh's eye. He stood at the kitchen counter with his mouth agape and shook his head.

"I didn't drink any, but I almost did."

"It's been a long day — go easy on yourself. Do you want to call one of your friends from AA?"

Mother sat and stared ahead without answering.

"Josh will take care of this. Let me help you to bed — I'll stay with you a while."

Josh grabbed a wad of paper towels and squatted to soak up the mess.

"Get rid of the booze," I mouthed to him.

Once she was in bed, I settled into the easy chair at the foot of her bed.

Mother folded into her pillow like a child, waiting for someone to tuck her in. Slowly her tears subsided and she slipped into a restless sleep.

Memories of recent phone exchanges with my mother swirled through my head. Was this the same woman, now moaning in her sleep and curled into a fetal position? Nothing that I saw here conjured up strength, let alone combativeness. What unknown enigma rendered her so fragile?

I remained with her until she snored noisily.

"I love you," Josh mumbled, when I crawled back into bed. I curved my body to his shape and wove my arm around his chest. The strong rhythm of his heart calmed me. When he didn't fully awaken, I lay motionless, absorbing his warmth and the solace he radiated. Finally, I drifted into a dream that I couldn't remember in the morning. It left me with a longing to protect, to be a mother.

Seventeen

About nine-thirty the following morning Mother walked in to the family room. Her full hair, streaked with silver, hung loosely. She held her head erect, shoulders back, masking the vulnerability that had engulfed her the previous evening. She breezed past me with a brief good morning and went into the kitchen, then returned with a glass of juice and took a seat adjacent to me.

I held my breath.

"I apologize for last night. I can't explain what happened," she said.

"Would you like me to help you find an AA meeting?" I put down my journal and pulled my sweater around me. "I have a friend who can help."

"No more AA. It's the same old, same old. Same people, same sad stories. They depress me — I'm not like them. I don't want to go and hear them moaning about all the bad luck they've had." My mother shook her head. "I believe in controlling my own fate, while they like feeling powerless."

"Isn't admitting that part of the program?"

"I'd rather do it on my own. Angelique, she used to be my sponsor, can help me when I get home. I don't need to go to those damn meetings." She dismissed the subject with a toss of the head and buried herself in the paper. "I was over-tired last night, that's all."

"I'm scared for you," I told her. "Why'd you start drinking again, after all these years?"

Mother folded the paper and looked back at me. She remained silent for a while, then spoke in a hoarse voice. "I never really stopped, Claire, but I'm not ready to talk about it yet."

Stunned, I rose to fix breakfast.

The ring of the phone blared through the quiet that hung between us as we ate. On the other end, I heard my brother's voice. "André!"

Mother's head shot up.

"She's here," I said. "We're just starting breakfast. Are you at the office? Can she call you back after we eat?"

Mother looked up and let out a deep sigh.

"Okay, we'll talk to you soon. Love you," I said as I disconnected and looked into my mother's piercing eyes.

She dissolved into tears. "I can't call him back — I can't do it, Claire. The business is all I have left of your father."

"No, Mother. You've got more than that." I took a sip of coffee without looking away from her. "You've got his children. You've got us."

When Mother emerged from the guest room, her lips curved into the bare hint of a smile. She handed me the phone. "Here — your brother asked to talk to you. I'm going to get dressed."

I held the phone to my chest and watched her disappear around the corner into the guest room.

"Hi." An audible sigh chased my greeting.

"What's going on with Mom?" André asked me in a voice laced with excitement.

"What'd she tell you?"

"She wants to sell the business. What the heck happened to bring that on? Why now?"

"What else did she say?" I stood to let the dogs outside, and followed them onto the deck. A strong scent of honeysuckle welcomed me.

"She told me to go for my doctorate," André said. "I don't get it, Sis. She's been so evasive lately. God, she never allowed me to even bring up the subject of what I wanted to do in life. I'm really confused — why the sudden change? And what made her fly up to see you at the last minute. Have you ever known her to do anything this impulsive?"

"She hasn't let me in on her secret, little brother. At least, not all of it. You must be ecstatic — what happens next?"

"We're going to meet when she gets back Sunday and start planning," André said. "I've got till then to digest it. What's your thought — are you okay with selling?"

"You know how I feel about the stores. Go for it, André. This is what you've always dreamed about." I bent over and reached out to the dogs, who hovered at my feet. "How's Lauren going to take it?"

"It'll show her true colors, won't it? I'm sorry about that phone call you got from her. I should've gotten back to you sooner."

"You're not responsible for Lauren," I reassured him. "Do you think she'll want a divorce?"

"Nope — I'm not giving her a chance. I plan on preempting her. It's something I've mulled over for months."

"Wow! I had no idea." I stooped to nab a clump of dog hair off the redwood deck.

"She never loved me, sis. We all know that," André continued. "I'll treat her fairly. When we sell, maybe the buyer will hire her back. But I'm not going to make it my worry."

I looked up to see the neighbor's cat scurry across the lawn. Murphy sat at my feet, whining. I gave him a tap on the butt, and followed as the dog raced to the corner where his quarry disappeared over the fence.

"I guess I've been waiting for something to knock me off my duff," André said.

In the garden, withered daffodils bent to touch the wet soil. Beside them, buds unfurled their petals in a brilliant array of colors. Sadness and joy mirrored the feelings conflicting inside me. "I wish we'd spoken more often, little brother. I always suspected you weren't happy — I'm sorry I let you go through this alone."

"I probably wouldn't have admitted anything to you anyway, sis. You don't think Mother will change her mind about selling, do you?"

"Did she say something that makes you think she would?" I asked.

"She told me she's been drinking," my brother responded. "I wasn't surprised."

"André, does it seem to you like there's some kind of huge albatross hanging around her neck?" I asked. "Something weighs on her; I hope she can let go of it, whatever it is."

"She's taking a big step," he sighed.

"We all are," I answered. I headed toward the house and saw my mother watching me through the window.

Eighteen

Friday evening, when Josh pulled the car into the Scott's driveway, we found them waiting. The scent of beef on the barbeque jump-started my appetite as I opened the passenger side door for my mother.

Worry lines zigzagged across Michael's face, but he welcomed us with a friendly hug and a smile. "It'll be a while before the roast is ready; come on in," Michael motioned. He brushed a kiss on my cheek, shook Mother's hand, and clapped Josh on the shoulder. "You want beer or wine?" The two men disappeared to raid the refrigerator in the garage.

"How is he?" I asked Kathryn, while I sized her up. She looked even thinner and wore a weary smile. In the background, a solo saxophone filled the room with tones in a minor key.

"At least we're talking more." Kathryn pulled out a stool at the kitchen counter for my mother. "I'm opening a bottle of red — can I get some for you?"

"Just water," Mother answered.

"I'll help," I said and traced Kathryn's steps to the wine cellar.

"Michael's driving me crazy, Claire. One minute he's full of optimism — the next he just simmers rage. I feel so overwhelmed." Kathryn pulled two wine glasses from a rack and set them on a table.

I put my hand on hers. "Josh is going to be your donor. He's a match — I'm sure of it. Worry about yourself for now, and let Michael deal with Michael."

Kathryn removed a bottle of Australian Shiraz from its cubby and circled her arms around it. Her body trembled. "Why can't he understand that this is all beyond our control? Why can't he just accept it and help me move on?"

In a corner of the dimly lit room, a tiny spider worked diligently, spinning an intricate web. I knew how it must feel to fall victim to its hunt, to become tangled in its snare. As each delicate filament wrapped around its victim, I felt a sense of suffocation, of helplessness. Without a word, I picked up the glasses from the table and followed Kathryn up the stairs.

When we returned to the kitchen, we found Mother studying a cookbook. While Kathryn stirred molasses into homemade baked beans, I watched Josh and Michael, who were glued to the TV, flipping channels and sharing a bag of chips with a dip that reeked of garlic. Frosted glasses of amber ale sat beside empty bottles.

"Psst, you two, there's something I want to share with you," I whispered to my mother and friend. "Josh and I have already talked about it a little, now I want your opinions."

"What's that, dear?" Mother asked.

"I want to try to get pregnant."

Kathryn held a wooden spoon in mid-air. Syrupy liquid dripped onto the open flame of the gas stove and sizzled. Her jaw dropped open.

"You gave me the idea after I lost my job, Kathryn, remember?"

"Oh, my God!" Mother's eyes bulged.

"Holy shit!" Kathryn wiped up splatter from the baked beans and set the spoon on a saucer. She turned the flame on low and abandoned the stove. "Are you serious?"

"I did some research," I explained, "and consulted my doctors. They're doing some checking of their own, and they're supposed to get back to me in a few days."

"Sweet Mother of God!" Mother stood and faced me, eye-to-eye.

"What does Josh say?" Kathryn asked.

"He admitted he's always wanted children but he never told me that before. He didn't want to hurt me and never guessed we could have a baby. I gave him literature about pregnancy in transplant patients."

Kathryn wiped her hands on a paper towel and approached us.

"I want to go off the pill as soon as I get the okay," I continued.

"Don't you think you should hold off for now?" Mother said, sweeping her hand toward Kathryn then Josh, who sat in the next room, enrapt in a Budweiser commercial.

"I don't suppose it'll be easy for you to get pregnant right away," Kathryn said. "But I agree with your mother — you've got enough stress in your life these days."

"You're right," I admitted. "It's probably going to take a few months and, who knows? I might not even be able to conceive. That's why I want to start trying if they give me the okay."

"I don't know, Claire." My mother sat back down, propped her elbows on the counter, and covered her face with her hands. "How can something make me this happy, and scare me to death, all at the same time?"

A feeling of déjà-vu surfaced. Mother doesn't want to lose another child, I realized.

Nineteen

Michael and I sat in the hospital lobby. I had never noticed how much the waiting area — decorated in steel gray and white — withheld comfort. In the background, CNN anchors blathered as headlines ran across the bottom of the screen in an endless blur.

"Can I get you a coffee?" I asked my companion, stooping to reach for my purse.

"No," Michael said. He slammed shut a Newsweek bearing last year's date that had been open to the same page for over an hour.

"How much longer?" he asked without looking in my direction. Then he stood, bulleted across the room, and hit the mute button on the television.

"Hey, I'm listening to that!" a fifty-something man barked at him.

Michael ignored the complainant and walked back to me. "So, what the hell's going to happen next? What if Kathryn doesn't make it?" He grabbed my shoulder and pinched until the pain caused me to squeeze my eyes shut. The throbbing lingered when he finally let go. I struggled to understand the intensity of his assault.

"I'm sorry," he said, and fell back into the seat beside me. "God." He swayed back and forth. "Oh, God."

I reached over and touched his hand, but he pulled away from me. Across the room, the previously disgruntled TV viewer stood and shook the hand of a woman with a stethoscope hanging around her neck. The man wore relief in his smile.

When the doctor breezed by, a draft drifted in and forced me to shiver.

Moments unraveled in strained silence until Michael jumped to attention. "Here comes Dr. Forrest."

Brian threw a half-smile in my direction, then turned to Michael. "The procedure went well; we took less than a quarter of Kathryn's kidney. The tumor was contained; I think we got it all."

"Will she need dialysis?" Michael asked straightaway.

"It's probable, Michael. We inserted a central line so we can begin as soon as we need to."

"How long before you'll know?" I asked.

"We drew labs, and I'll repeat them till we know what direction things are going." Brian took the mask hanging around his neck and crumpled it in a ball.

"I operated through a laparoscope so this should be an easy recovery for her." Sweat beaded on the surgeon's forehead. He swiped the sleeve of the surgical gown over his face. "You can wait in her room, if you want — she'll be up in an hour or so, and I'll come by with the results of her kidney function tests as soon as I've finished my next procedure."

As Brian and Michael shook hands, I noticed that Michael was shaking. "Let's pick up some lunch on the way up," I suggested, then took a firm hold on his elbow and propelled him toward the cafeteria.

"I'm scared," Michael said. He scooped a ladle of soup into the bowl sitting on a cafeteria tray that reeked of chlorine.

"Me, too." At a distance I saw an old friend, one of the hospital's chaplains. I wished he'd notice me and come by to absolve me of the guilt that surrounded me like a cloud of smoke — the guilt I still felt for accepting Kathryn's kidney. I wished he'd fix Michael, too. But, instead, he hurried down the hallway to the elevator without seeing us.

"I'm sorry if I hurt you, Claire," Michael said to me as he slid across a vinyl bench at a booth in the cafeteria.

I blew out a lungful of air and grappled with my own fear and anger. "I'm sorry you did, too." The unyielding tone of my voice surprised me.

"Michael, I don't care about myself. Oh, I feel awful all the time, but deep down, I know I didn't do this to Kathryn." I wished I could convince myself of this, too. "Don't you understand what you're doing to her? She needs you more than ever."

He hung his head, and I watched him stare into a sea of tomato soup with croutons floating on the surface.

A moment later, he sat up straight and caught my eye. "I've hurt her?" he asked.

"Let's just say you haven't been there for her. She knows you're scared — we all do, and we all share your fear." I swirled a glass of ice tea as though it were an expensive cabernet. "But it's time to move beyond your own feelings, Michael. You've got to, for Kathryn's sake."

So do I, I realized. So do I.

After lunch, as we approached the nurses' station from the visitors' elevator, an attendant pushed a gurney from the service elevator and headed toward Kathryn's assigned room number.

Kathryn was drowsy, but awake. She mumbled inaudible words, laced with the effects of morphine.

We sat with her as she dozed all afternoon, then that evening watched as the staff hooked Kathryn to a machine.

Josh joined us, congregating in the all-too-familiar environment of the hospital's dialysis unit. Of the four of us, Kathryn acted the most upbeat, chattering endlessly at first. She took on the task of explaining the procedure to Michael.

As soon as she began to doze, Michael withdrew again and buried himself in an orange and white pamphlet that outlined the dietary requirements and restrictions of dialysis patients.

I caught him peeping at Kathryn over the rim of the booklet. Finally he dropped his prop and took a seat beside his wife. His large hand rested on the crown of her head, while he leaned his own head on the edge of the stretcher beside her shoulder.

Josh took my hand and we exited the unit, leaving Michael with Kathryn and his thoughts. We stood and watched the couple from the doorway.

A flashback swamped me and I broke out in a sweat. Memories of hours bound to a recliner poured in: claret red blood cycling in and out of my body; chemicals dispensed by a machine that beeped and groaned; nausea, weakness, restless legs and insomnia; the thought that someone would have to die in order that I might live.

Back then, it was Kathryn who rescued me.

Twenty

"We worked hard today," *Josh said* as I rinsed dirt from my spade, late in the afternoon on the Saturday following Kathryn's surgery. "Okay if we order in a pizza?" He pulled a beer from the cooler and handed me a bottle of water.

I was checking out the pansies, verbena, and petunias I'd planted. A quilt of color unfolded before us: yellow, purple, and scarlet settled on a bed of green. The perfume of sweet peas mingled with the pungent aroma of marigolds. Pleasure filtered in and I surrendered to its offer.

Josh dragged a bag of twigs he'd pruned from the butterfly bush and hollered over his shoulder, "Let me get rid of these and I'll call for a Combo."

When he returned, I joined him on the deck.

"I looked at that stuff you gave me to read about us having a baby," he said. "I think we could consider it after everything's behind us."

"Everything?"

"My surgery, if I do become a donor. Plus you need to get the okay from the transplant center."

I hadn't told Josh that the transplant specialist had called back the previous morning. To my surprise, Dr. Cantor didn't hesitate: "If you want to, sure, go ahead," he'd told me. "But be quick about it — I don't want you getting pregnant after forty. You've done well, Claire. I'll help guide your nephrologist and obstetrician through it if you're able to conceive."

My heart pounded. I'd already stopped the pill, knowing I wasn't fertile. But tonight, could I be? The thought was arousing.

When we climbed the stairs late that night, Josh leading the way, I ran a fingernail up the back of his leg, then worked my way up his inner thigh.

He wobbled. "What're you trying to do? Catch me off guard?"

"Not me." I felt like the temptress and pulled him down on the top step. The dogs hopped over us and ran into the bedroom. My hands glided down the buttons of his shirt. I slipped them inside, lightly touched his chest, and ran my fingertips over the sides of his rib cage.

Josh reached for me and kissed me gently behind the ear, then nibbled on the lobe.

I had him. "Remember that time, under the Christmas tree?"

"Yeah," was all he said as the dogs lay at a distance, watching.

"Not bad for a couple of old folk," I whispered as we crawled into bed a half hour later.

"Speak for yourself," Josh sighed.

"We could be starting something new," I said.

"Okay, where are we going next?"

"No, I don't mean that; I mean that I got the okay to get pregnant."

Josh sat upright, startled. In the background, David Benoit played When You Wish Upon a Star. "You stopped the pill?" he asked me.

"Yep." I pulled him back on the pillow beside me.

He enclosed my face in his rugged hands.

We fell asleep entwined in one another. The duvet fell on the floor, so the dogs nested in the folds. That's how we were when I woke up about one thirty. I wasn't chilly. In fact, warmth throbbed throughout my body.

Twenty-One

Scruff scratched at the screen door leading out to Helene's garden.

"Go back to bed." The woman pulled a cover above her head and tried to burrow back into sleep, but the cat persisted. Bright sunshine filtered through the skylight in her bathroom. She pulled herself into a sitting position and ran her fingers through long thick hair, sweeping it away from her face.

The animal pounced on the bed and wove about Helene's body, purring.

Eleven o'clock popped on the digital clock sitting on her nightstand. Helene slipped her feet into a pair of moccasins and scuffed her way into the bathroom. She threw water on her face, then sat on the toilet in a daze.

Lethargy had replaced the comfort of alcohol, she realized. Anything would do as long as it didn't require her to think about what she'd done to her family — what she'd done to Stephanie.

Helene leaned on the kitchen counter and watched coffee dribble through the filter of the Mr. Coffee machine. In the background, three landscape architects on HGTV presented plans to improve the curb appeal of a Beverly Hills mansion. She silenced the tube and sat with her brew and her thoughts.

When the doorbell sounded, her coffee sloshed from the mug as she hurled herself into a standing position. The gate hadn't called, so it had to be a neighbor or André. Or, God forbid, Lauren. She'd have to remember to remove her daughter-in-law from the visitors' access list.

Peeking through the curtain in the dining room, she discovered her son, staring right back at her. Smiling.

"God, André, I just got out of bed. Can you believe it?"

"You're not sick, are you?" He walked in and gave her a hasty peck on the cheek.

"No, I'm okay. It's Saturday — I like to sleep in on the weekend. You want some coffee? I just brewed it."

"Smells good, but I'll pass." He walked to the fridge, helped himself to a Diet Coke and sat in the recliner that had belonged to his father.

After she wiped up the spilled coffee, Helene took her seat and reached for her mug. "What brings you here?"

"I spent last night at the Hilton," her son answered.

She jolted forward in the chair. "What?"

"I couldn't get in the house."

"What do you mean, you couldn't get in the house? It's your house."

"Lauren had the locks changed."

Helene leaned back and closed her eyes. Pain shot up from between her shoulder blades and settled at the base of her cranium. "What happened?"

"Well, I told you I met with our corporate lawyers on Wednesday, right?" He took a slug of his soda and set it on the coaster beside him.

Helene nodded. Her breath escaped in short spurts. "Go on."

"Yesterday morning Johnston came to the office early and we met Lauren at the door. We took her in the conference room and gave her a notice of termination. I told her we were selling the business."

"Did she react?"

Andre's brow wrinkled. "No. She signed the papers, stood, and walked out of the office without a word."

"You just let her go?"

"What else could I do?" Andre rose and crossed the room to the window. "I thought I'd gotten off easy."

Helene joined him and put a shaking hand on her son's shoulder.

He stared straight ahead, his facial expression as blank as a newly erased blackboard. "You can figure out the rest. I spent the day with the lawyer and a commercial real estate agent. We did what we had to in order to move things forward. I didn't hear a word from Lauren but when I got home . . ."

"The house is in your name, son. She signed a quitclaim."

He nodded. "I'm going to let her have it. It's worth it to me to get her out of my life."

"Are you sure about that? Are you okay?"

"I'm better than I've been in a long time." He turned and took Helene by the shoulders.

"Does Lauren know about the divorce?" Helene asked.

"She will, on Monday — they'll serve her papers first thing."

"Stay here with me, André. The guest room's always ready."

"How about you, Mom? Are you all right?"

"I'm sober, if that's what you mean."

"Are you sure you don't mind me invading your space?"

"I'll be glad not to be alone right now," Helene admitted.

And to have someone else to focus on she acknowledged to herself.

Twenty-Two

Wednesday arrived in tones of brown. I peeled myself out of bed. Smoke from an early season wildfire cast an orange hue throughout the Truckee Meadows, and the scent of burning sagebrush filled the valley.

Josh made coffee and dumped grounds on the floor that I had scrubbed the prior evening.

"Damn it, Josh, I just did that by hand." I grabbed the paper towels from him and stooped to clean up the mess myself.

He ignored me and continued to stir a pot of oatmeal.

"I don't want oatmeal," I snapped.

"This isn't for you."

I opened a can of dog food and slammed the dog's dishes on the counter as I mixed the meat with kibbles.

"Why don't you go back to bed, Claire?" Josh said in a subdued tone of voice. "I don't want to start my day like this."

Blinking back tears, I left the room. The atmosphere weighed heavily on me, as though a storm would creep in within the hour. I fell into the rocking chair and swayed back and forth in darkness, but Josh didn't follow to comfort me.

Once I was alone in the dim room, I searched myself to uncover the reason for my foul mood. I felt as hormonal as I used to when I was a teenager, when crabbiness would descend on me without warning, but worse. In the background, the buzz of Josh's electric razor preceded the running water in the shower. At seven thirty, the back door closed. Josh had left me without a goodbye kiss.

My irritability dissipated like the steam in the bathroom when cool air poured in through an opened door, but wisps of sadness still surrounded me. I felt like a strange character had usurped my persona and I had no idea who it was or why I couldn't control my feelings. I hated myself for it.

When the phone rang mid-morning, I ignored it. I stayed in my robe and watched Fox News repeat the same breaking stories over and over, while crunching on a bag of potato chips.

Around noon, the dogs became restless and Murphy made little whining noises. I finally forced myself to uncurl my legs, silenced the TV, and pulled myself up the staircase. When I stooped to tie the laces of my walking shoes, the two crazy dogs danced about the bedroom, emitting eager whimpers.

During our brisk walk, I began to emerge from the funk. The smoke from the fire had cleared and I breathed deeply. By the time I arrived home, a smile threatened my face. When I released Benisse and Murphy from their leashes, they raced to lap water from their dishes. The phone rang.

My mother's voice greeted me. "Claire, where've you been? I tried to get you earlier."

"I took the dogs for a walk and didn't remember to check for messages or missed calls." I choked on the half-truth. "Sorry, Mother. Are you okay?"

"Fine, but I want an update on Kathryn. You haven't called me since Saturday."

"I didn't hear anything yet this morning." I didn't even think about Kathryn, I realized in shame. "The doctor said she can work on days when she doesn't have dialysis, if she feels up to it."

"Is that wise?" Mother asked.

I filled a glass with water and took a gulp. "As long as we share the load. I'll visit patients at home for her while she stays in the office and reviews charts."

"But is that safe for you? What if you get pregnant? Is that still on your agenda?"

"Oh, it's an active item on our 'To Do' list. God, I've been so crazy this morning; my emotions are all over the board, and poor Josh got the brunt of it."

"So, he gets to practice for what you'll be like when you do become pregnant," Mother said. "Do you know you could make me a grandmother? However, for the record, I still believe you should wait."

"Well, don't get your expectations up."

"I need to have something to hope for, Claire. You're giving me another reason to stop drinking."

A moment of tenderness overwhelmed me. My mother was talking to me like an adult, like a friend. This seemed like a good time to raise the question that had been rumbling about in my head. "Mom, there's something I've been wondering about — something from when I was a little girl."

"What's that, dear?"

"I've been thinking a lot about family lately," I said. "Last week, I was looking through an old album and I found a picture."

"A picture? Of what?" My mother's voice broke.

"Of our family," I continued, wondering now if I was pushing it, but not sure of how to turn back. "There's someone else in it — someone I don't remember or even recognize." The pulse in my temple pounded.

"Someone else?" she questioned.

"A young woman."

Mother said nothing for several moments then spoke in a whisper: "I can't imagine who that would be." She'd constructed a distance between us that was almost palpable.

"Oh, never mind." Now I knew for sure that I'd gone too far. "I'll show the photo to you sometime when we're together."

"Well, take care of yourself, dear, and give Josh a hug for me, will you?" Mother's voice sounded far away. "And, please, keep me posted about Kathryn."

"I will — I promise. I held the phone to my body. I felt sure now that Mother was keeping a secret of some sort — she'd shifted gears too quickly.

When I returned to the kitchen to rinse the breakfast dishes, I couldn't keep thoughts of Josh from pouring in. I felt horrible about how I'd treated him that morning. Never before had he left for work without a kiss. I started the dish washer then dialed his cell phone.

"Joshua Bergano," he answered on the fourth ring.

Through the window, I watched a blue jay scare off a couple of wrens picking seeds from our flower garden. "Are you in the middle of something?" I asked.

"Claire. No, I'm driving to a patient's house. What's up? Are you better?"

"Sorry about this morning," I said.

"Me too. I should have come to you before I left." The noise of traffic rushed by in the background.

"I don't know what made me so moody." I trekked over to the stove and started boiling water for a cup of tea.

"You've got a lot to handle right now, honey," Josh said. "I was serious when I told you to go back to bed. You tossed and turned all night."

"My mother called a few minutes ago."

"Is she okay?" Josh asked.

"She wants to be a grandmother." I turned off the burner and poured steaming liquid into my cup. A pungent citrus aroma drifted up and soothed my senses.

"I'm happy to oblige. Hey, I'm only a couple of miles away. How about I come home for lunch after I see this patient?"

"Making love in the middle of the day seems illicit, doesn't it?" Josh asked as he buttoned his shirt.

"It felt just right to me," I answered. I'd sprawled back on the bed after we'd showered. "But I don't know if I'll get much done this afternoon."

"Good thing there's only one more patient on my schedule."

I sat up. "Honey, I think there's another house call you and I should make tonight, don't you?"

"Kathryn! You're right," Josh agreed. "Call and tell them I'll pick up some dinner to bring with us." He leaned over and planted a kiss on my forehead. "That's all you're getting for now. Otherwise, I'll never get my work done."

I followed Josh to the door, watching until his car disappeared around the curve, then I went inside to call Kathryn. I wanted to know how she was, but also wanted to ask her what she remembered about mood changes in early pregnancy.

We arrived home early that night.

"Kathryn's in good spirits, isn't she?" Josh said. "She doesn't seem to mind the delay in meeting with the transplant team."

"Wish we could say the same for Michael," I said. "He's pissed at Brian Forrest again."

"I can understand he's frustrated, but it's not the doctor's fault. Too bad the transplant team only comes to Reno once a month." Josh followed the dogs up the stairs in front of me. "And we just missed them."

A memory from my days as an intern popped into my awareness. It was a simple gallbladder surgery that had claimed the life of one of our patients, a man about Josh's age.

"It'll be here soon enough," I said. Too soon.

Fear of loss covered me like the comforter I pulled up around my shoulders.

Twenty-Three

Stumbling into her bathroom, Helene threw open the medicine cabinet and snatched the bottle of nitroglycerin. Panic surged through her as hot fire rushed down her left arm and up into her jaw. She popped the small tablet under her tongue and sat on the edge of the tub, breathing deeply. The angina subsided within a minute, but relief didn't come with the absence of pain.

After a few moments, Helene wobbled to her chaise lounge and rummaged in her basket. She gulped a slug from the silver flask and eased back into the chair, waiting for comfort to settle in.

How would she handle this situation with Claire? She'd known that someday the truth would emerge. She was only kidding herself all those years she'd hidden it from herself and her children.

Recollections of her husband, Robert, filled the slate of her mind. He'd raged, blamed her and then colluded. Days had passed, then months, years. They'd carefully packed up boxes of Stephanie's life — her clothes, school books, toys — and sent them to St. Vincent's. They'd even torn up the child-like drawings from grammar school that had filled the cork bulletin board. Why had they wanted to erase her so completely from their lives?

Helene retrieved the bottle again, promising herself that only one more sip would be okay. After swallowing the gin, bilious liquid slipped back into her throat — the taste of remorse.

Why did this secret have to emerge now, of all times? Maybe Claire wouldn't think of it again. Her daughter would put the picture away and by the time Helene visited, the photo would be long forgotten.

The next time she reached for the alcohol, the bottle was empty. Flinging the vial across the room, she pushed herself to the edge of the seat and stood. As the room swirled about her, she steadied herself on the tall bureau that used to hold her husband's clothes.

Helene drove slowly out of the gated community and passed André as he entered the complex. She smiled and signaled a greeting, realizing she couldn't bring a bottle home with her as she'd intended — not while he was living with her. She flicked on her left turn signal and executed the maneuver from the right hand lane, heading toward the bar instead of the liquor store.

She'd have to stay out late that night. If she got home after ten, André would be in bed. He had an early morning appointment with his divorce lawyer.

Twenty-Four

André pursed his lips. *His mother hadn't told him* she was going out. Or had she?

The last week had passed in a blur. All the hoopla with Lauren and the business. Lawyers invading his personal life and his office. Meetings with real estate agents.

He'd always felt lonely, but had never been so alone. His mother was wrapped up in trying to stay sober and he couldn't bother Claire, not while her friend was sick.

Letting himself in the back door, he threw his briefcase on the bed in the guestroom — his room for now. André wandered up to the front of the house and searched the kitchen, hoping for a note from his mother. Her calendar hung above the desk she used to pay her bills. Every Wednesday night she'd penciled in AA — maybe she'd changed her mind and was going to meetings after all.

On the way back to his quarters, he stopped at the double door leading into the master suite. It was slightly ajar. When he poked his head in, the scent of gin overtook him. André felt his heart skip a beat. A familiar sense of dread fanned throughout his body in a swell of heat. He fled down the hall to the den, picked up the phone, and punched in Claire's number.

"We can't do anything about it André — she's got to figure it out herself." That's what Claire had told him, and the words echoed in his ears.

André tossed and turned in the muggy beach atmosphere. Images of the girl Claire described rolled through his mind as he scratched for memories. Claire seemed sure that she'd pushed her mother too far.

It was after midnight when he heard Helene enter through the front door. Warped because of humidity, she had to slam it with a thud. Soon after, the sound of a dead bolt sealed her in the master bedroom.

Light poured in the following morning and chased away a dream that he couldn't remember, but one that left him with a heavy feeling in his chest. He hurried to shower and shave. When he left for work, Helene's room was still dark. No sound emanated from within.

He recalled that, as a child, he'd been afraid to leave each morning for school. And when he came home, his fear was that he'd find his mother hanging in the bathroom from a nylon stocking. That's what had happened to his friend, Timmy Blaire, when they were in second grade.

Twenty-Five

The month of May crawled along like a semi going over Donner Summit. Each day lasted forty-eight hours, or so it seemed. Kathryn went to the outpatient center three times a week for treatment. When possible, I stayed with her, remembering boredom, chills, and the helplessness of it all.

The days she didn't have dialysis and was strong enough to drive, Kathryn joined me at the hospice office for a couple of hours.

"When we get through all of this, maybe we could job share," Kathryn suggested to me one day.

I didn't reply — I hadn't told anyone I suspected I was pregnant.

Kathryn studied the chart of a young woman dying of cancer, then handed it to me. "At least I have an option," she sighed.

"I saw her last week," I told Kathryn. "She's my age."

An unwanted, recurring thought caused me to squirm. What if Josh can't be Kathryn's donor?

As though reading my thoughts, Kathryn reminded me of next week's appointment with the transplant team. "Are you sure, Claire? Are you and Josh sure that you want to go through with it?

How could I be? I wondered, but said: "Josh is convinced he'll be a match, and already spoke to his boss about needing time off."

"I understand now, Claire. I get how you felt when I offered you a kidney. You freaked, remember? You were sure something would happen to me.

God, girl, I lie awake at night thinking of that. I think about it while I'm having dialysis — it haunts me. I worry about Josh the way you did about me."

"I can't talk you out of that one," I admitted.

"Are you afraid something will happen?"

"I can't be. Today's all we have, isn't it?" As I spoke the words, I only wished I felt the strength that they implied.

We worked in silence for another hour without interruption. The mood oppressed us as we read reports, signed orders, and pondered. At three o'clock we locked the door to Kathryn's office and headed out for hot fudge sundaes.

That night in bed, I clung to Josh, who fell asleep in my arms as my imagination sparred with common sense.

Fear about Josh mingled with uneasiness about my mother who, according to my brother, left the house at night several times a week, sometimes after he'd retired to his room. In his call the previous day, André told me that mother had become reclusive again, leaving the details of closing out the business to him and avoiding her friends from church.

I toyed with the idea of confronting her, but the thought of deepening the crisis overwhelmed me. During our weekly conversations, Mother plied me with questions about Kathryn and my work, but steered clear of topics that could turn in her direction.

Oftentimes, after hanging up, I'd find myself staring out the window at nothing in particular. If I caught a glimpse of my reflection, my mind would wander to the girl who continued to visit my thoughts every so often. If it were true — what Kathryn had suggested — that she was only a symbol of the expectations I couldn't live up to, then who the heck was that in the picture I kept upstairs, hidden under the blotter on my desk?

Twenty-Six

"Claire, it's late. We've got to get it in gear!"

"What's the hurry?" I mumbled into my pillow.

"It's seven-thirty and our appointment's at nine."

"What appointment?" I surfaced from a deep sleep that left me clouded by confusion.

"Claire, hello! We're meeting with the transplant team in two hours."

I sprung into a sitting position. "Oh, my God, it's already morning?"

"I'll feed the dogs and make some breakfast. Don't fall back to sleep," Josh warned.

Fully alert now, I hopped out of bed. I opened the blinds and leaned on the windowsill. In the garden, mid-June greeted me. Bearded irises smiled, and pink buds of climbing roses splayed across the back fence.

By the time I descended the stairs, energized from a shower, the scent of roasted coffee and frying bacon launched my appetite. I leaned over Josh and brushed my lips across his stubbly face.

"I started eating — hope you don't mind," Josh told me. "I've got to get ready."

I nodded and began to eat. I considered the fact that, so far, I'd escaped morning sickness, but the time had arrived to let Josh know.

He ate with gusto. The sun made its grand entrance and shone through the gauze curtain and lit up his hair.

"I'm pregnant," I blurted out. "At least, I think I am."

Josh dropped a piece of toast on his plate, took a slug of coffee, and swallowed quickly. "How do you know?" His eyes never left mine.

"I skipped my period last month," I continued. "And I feel bloated. And then there's the moodiness. Those are the only signs so far."

Josh jumped out of his seat, speechless. He pulled me from my chair and crushed me to himself.

"Honey, it's not a definite — don't get too excited," I warned, alarmed that I'd jumped the gun.

"On the way home from the clinic we'll pick up a home pregnancy test." He released me then held me for a moment at arms' distance.

"You better finish eating," I said. I couldn't hold back the smile that spread across my face. The room was filled with an electric excitement.

He nodded and sat down.

A feeling of nausea crept up inside me, more from nervousness than pregnancy. "Josh, if it turns out we're going to have a baby, will it affect your decision to be a donor?"

"I can't see why. Kathryn has to recover from her first surgery, but she should be ready for the transplant by the end of September." He chewed a last bite. "If that's the case, I'll be back in commission in a few weeks. Brian told us they'd harvest my kidney through a laparoscope, remember?"

"True. And that'd be long before my due date." Fragments of mirror chips from the kitchen's quartz countertop reflected dancing light on the walls.

"It'll work," Josh said. "Claire, if the home test's positive, you need to see an obstetrician right away. Your kidney doctor, too. I want you closely monitored."

"I'm so excited, Josh," I admitted. I touched my cheek and felt its warmth. "I don't want to set myself up for disappointment, but I can't control my happiness."

"What'll be, will be. But I sure hope . . ." Josh pushed away from the table and kissed the top of my head. "I gotta hurry."

***

We greeted Kathryn and Michael, who stood waiting outside the office building. The transplant team from the Bay Area — a tall silver-haired doctor and two women — entered the suite before us. When we walked into the waiting room, the nurse recognized me. A puzzled expression spread over her face.

"No, Elaine, I don't have an appointment," I reassured her. "I'm here with my friend." I pulled Kathryn forward. "Elaine, this is Kathryn Scott. I don't know if you met before; Kathryn was my donor — now it's her turn."

Elaine paled as I explained Kathryn's situation.

"And you already know my husband, Josh. He's here for testing, to see if he can be Kathryn's donor."

Elaine emerged from the receptionist's area and embraced us. "I've never heard of anything like this before," she stammered. A strand of long black hair fell forward into her face. She brushed it back with her hand and wiped her eyes with the same sweeping movement. "Take a seat — it'll only be a few minutes."

Ecru walls enclosed the cramped waiting room, creating the effect of a prison. Green plastic chairs resisted the curves of our bodies. Magazines lay scattered in disarray on an oak coffee table.

Elaine came for Kathryn. "I'll be back for you soon," she told Michael, who'd risen to follow. Kathryn trailed behind the nurse, then looked over her shoulder at her husband.

"You want me to explain how the whole thing works?" I asked Michael. Without waiting for his response, I dug into my own memories of the experience. "First of all, Kathryn meets with the pre-transplant nurse who'll draw her blood. Then, the transplant center doctor will examine her."

"What kind of blood test?" Michael asked.

"Blood type and antigens, the proteins that the immune system builds up against foreign invaders. The same test they'll do on Josh to evaluate their compatibility."

Michael fixed his gaze on me, soaking in every word.

"While Kathryn's waiting for surgery, they'll draw her blood every month and mail it to San Francisco — sometimes things change."

"How long before we know if I'm a match?" Josh asked.

"I don't remember." I plumbed the archives of my recollection. "It seemed like forever."

"I think Kathryn had to go through all kinds of poking and prodding," Josh said.

"You're right; there was a ton of procedures. Didn't she have to go to San Francisco for some of them?"

"I'd forgotten about that," Michael said. "Anything else?"

"Yeah," I squirmed in the uncomfortable chair. "She'll meet with a social worker today. I remember it well — I was so afraid something would happen to Kathryn, but the counselor reminded me to trust, to leave it to them to keep her safe."

Michael spoke up again. "Kathryn had a psychological work-up, too, didn't she?"

I nodded and glanced at a couple entering with a teenage son, a boy the color of yellow chalk. "You bet. They'll make sure Josh is stable and that there's no financial incentive."

The three of us watched as the young patient's father helped him into a chair, then went to sign in at the receptionist's desk. A smile broke across the child's face. He nodded in my direction and gave me a thumb's up.

I signaled back before turning to Michael and Josh. "I think he's telling us to be hopeful."

Josh nodded, while Michael's gaze drifted off into the distance.

"Do you think I'll pass the shrink's test?" Josh asked with a chuckle, pulling Michael and me back into the huddle.

"Now, that could be a problem," I said.

We fell back into silence and waited. Tiny beads of sweat formed on Michael's upper lip and he shifted position frequently.

Almost five hours later, when we'd jumped through all the hoops, the four of us left the office, energy depleted.

"Let's get lunch at Moxie's," Michael suggested. "I need a beer."

For a couple of hours, it seemed like old times. Almost.

***

"Let's not tell anyone until the doctor confirms the pregnancy test," I said to Josh as I propped my feet on rim of the worn coffee table and scratched Murphy behind the ears.

"Okay by me. Right now, everyone's preoccupied anyway, waiting to find out if I'm a match." I watched Josh pour fizzing liquid into two champagne flutes and we toasted.

"Who would've thought we'd make a baby so quickly? It usually takes a while." I sipped sparkling cider and pretended that it tasted and felt as good as the real thing.

Josh shook his head. "How accurate are these home tests?"

"They're reliable enough, but not definitive."

"I want you to see an obstetrician," Josh told me. "Soon." He gave me his wise-sage look — lips pursed and brows drawn together, not quite in a frown.

"I'll call tomorrow," I said in agreement.

Twenty-Seven

"*Josh gets the first call — that's how I remember it, anyway,*" I told Kathryn a few days later, while the two of us sat in the Scott's backyard.

Summer held sway and perspiration had formed on my upper lip. "They didn't let me know you matched, in case you changed your mind."

"Yeah, you're right," Kathryn said. "I called you at home, didn't I?"

I studied Kathryn, who lay shivering, stretched out on a lounge chair. She'd lost weight and energy, and sharpened cheekbones jutted from beneath her sunken eyes. She had stopped coming in to help me at the office.

"I don't know if I have the courage to go on like this, Claire. How do people live on dialysis for years on end?"

I didn't know how to answer. Instead, I stood up and took Kathryn's empty glass from her freezing hand and helped her to a standing position. "I'll drop by after work tomorrow, but we'll call if Josh hears anything before that."

I looked back as I drove away and saw Kathryn standing in the doorway with a blanket draped around her. The gauge on my dashboard read 92 degrees.

Twenty-Eight

Wednesday afternoon I waited on the porch for Josh to pick me up for our first OB appointment. A Gypsy King CD filled the car as he drove up to the curb.

"You'd drive to the beat if I let you, wouldn't you?" I said.

"I'm antsy!"

"No kidding — me too. I'm so tired of visiting doctor's offices."

"But this is different," he reminded me. "I was useless today at work, so I decided to reschedule patients for tomorrow. I'll be really busy, but I was afraid to take on anything too complex. I have zero concentration."

"I know what you mean, honey — we've got the cleanest kitchen in Reno. I scrubbed and cleaned out cupboards."

When Josh reached over and put his hand on my thigh, I felt a tiny pulse beating in the crook of his thumb. The energy of his excitement poured through me, too. We pulled in to Dr. Meredith Jansen's parking lot.

"Have you worked with her before?" Josh removed the key from the ignition and faced me.

"In med school. She's known for managing high-risk pregnancies, and even did an extra year of residency in Internal Medicine so she could handle patients like me."

"I'm impressed," Josh said. "Sounds like the perfect match."

"If I'm pregnant — don't forget — the home test isn't the final word."

The ambiance of Dr. Jansen's office was feminine, but not frilly. Tones of robin's egg blue and celadon green contrasted with dusky rose fabric and golden pillows. The well-cushioned chairs sat high, and provided arms to assist pregnant women to stand. Meredith had carefully chosen impressionistic watercolors, not prints. The subjects spoke of hearth and home — and motherhood.

Josh was the only man in the waiting room. I watched him fidget before finally settling on a Cooking Light magazine. I placed my head on his shoulder and he took my hand.

A woman across the room looked ready to pop at any moment. "I was due three days ago," she told me when she caught my stare.

I nodded and gave her a smile and a few words of encouragement, but I hoped the soon-to-be-mom wouldn't go into labor until I had my chance at the doctor.

A young nurse, wearing scrubs that matched the décor, called us back.

"I know you from somewhere," I told her.

She nodded in recognition and we shared an awkward moment. "You're a doctor, aren't you? I remember now — I worked with you in hospice for a few weeks several years ago. Oh, Dr. Bergano, I don't know how you do it! I just couldn't."

I didn't have time to respond. Meredith flew into the room and gave me a bear hug.

"My God, Claire Tressaint! How long has it been?"

"It's Claire Bergano, now, Meredith." I embraced her in return. "Meet Josh, my husband."

The physician shook his hand. "Your wife's one heck of a doctor."

"She's one heck of a wife, too." Josh flashed a smile.

"I heard about your transplant, Claire. How are you? And Kathryn? Word went around that she donated a kidney to you."

I told the doctor about Kathryn's cancer and saw horror transfigure her expression. "Josh was just tested to be her donor," I continued, with a subdued pride. "We're still waiting for results."

Meredith reached out and put her hand on Josh's shoulder, then turned to me and said, "Let's get down to business."

"They cut my position at hospice and we decided, if there's a chance I could get pregnant, this would be the time to do it." I beamed and handed Meredith a fistful of printouts. "These cover pregnancy in transplant survivors — have you worked with this before?"

"Twice, during my residency at UCSF, and it went well both times. One baby came a little early, but both women stayed healthy and went through normal deliveries."

"The transplant center gave the okay," I added. "Jeff Forrest is my kidney doctor here in Reno — he promised he'd work with us."

"If you're pregnant," Meredith reminded me.

"The home test was positive," I said, looking at Josh, who nodded in confirmation.

"Well let's find out!" Meredith drew labs and did a thorough exam.

Josh held my hand. His felt cold and clammy.

"See what you guys get out of," I said.

"I know — don't forget I'm a nurse. Besides, my mother reminds me of what she went through to have me every time she has a chance."

"Okay, I'm done," Meredith said. "Josh, come with me to my office. Claire, it's the room to the right as you exit. Get dressed and I'll join you in a few minutes."

Moments later, Josh and I sat together, our fingers interlaced. "We haven't talked to your parents in a while, Josh."

"Not since I told them about wanting to be a donor for Kathryn. That's a few weeks ago. They'll be excited if we're pregnant."

Meredith interrupted. Her Nordic eyes flashed and she bit her lip, as if to suppress a grin. "You did it!" she told us. "The blood test will be the absolute validation, but I can attest with 99% accuracy that you're going to have a baby!"

Josh jumped up and hugged Meredith, then leaned over and kissed me on the top of my head. I remained planted in my chair while tears trickled down my cheeks.

"Call the transplant team," Meredith cautioned, "and make an appointment with Jeff Forrest. I'll work closely with them — we're going to make this work for you."

"I don't want to tell anyone tonight," Josh said to me, on the way home.

"Me neither." I didn't want to dispel the magic of the moment.

Josh fell asleep after we'd made love, but I lay awake for a long while with my hand placed on my lower abdomen. Energy pulsed through my body.

That night I dreamt about Kathryn. She handed me a red tulip.

Twenty-Nine

When I left the office early Thursday afternoon, I called Kathryn. "Can I pick you up in about fifteen minutes? We need some quality girl time. Let's go to the Tea Spot."

"I'm strong enough to drive today, so I'll meet you there in twenty," Kathryn agreed after a moment's hesitation.

On the drive over, I tried to catalogue the feelings vying for my attention. The hours of anxious waiting for results from Josh's test had crept by in inches. No matter what the outcome, I faced uncertainty. If he matched, what would be the risk to him, to all we were building as a family? If he couldn't be a donor, could I bear to stand back and watch my best friend, the woman who'd saved my life, continue to decline and perhaps face death? An acrid taste seeped into the back of my throat — the taste of loss. Somehow, it was a familiar taste.

Then there was joy: images of stuffed animals, wide-awake eyes on Christmas Eve and first steps. Holding a bundle of warmth close to my center and feeling a heart beating counterpoint to mine.

Kathryn needed to know about these things, too. She deserved a break from the dreary tedium of days filled with exhausting treatments, restless nights, and doubts about the future. That was why I had invited her — to share these promises with my friend.

We chose a table by the window and ordered herbal tea. I peeked at Kathryn, who studied the décor.

"Josh still hasn't heard anything from the transplant center." I reached for a piece of bone china and fingered the delicate, hand-painted pink roses and gold filigree. The smooth coolness of the cup shocked my hand.

"I'm not surprised." Kathryn looked at me and smiled, but her eyes didn't follow her lips. "Life's about waiting, isn't it?"

The room was filled with chatter and the clinking of fine china and silver spoons. Women gathered across the tables and whispered. Words of gossip, perhaps, jostled with rills of laughter. Nowhere did I see a face etched in sadness, except for the face that gaped back at me.

The waitress arrived, carrying steaming teapots, each cuddled in a quilted tea cozy. Colors, patterns, and fabrics clashed in abandon. Everything was awash with warmth and color. A heady scent and steam spewing from the spout filled me with momentary contentment. Pouring tea through fine mesh strainers, I watched a few loose leaves slip through.

"Do you read tea leaves?" Kathryn swirled her cup, waiting for them to settle in a haphazard configuration.

"I don't think I want to," I confided.

"You haven't mentioned your mother for a long time. Is she doing all right?" Kathryn asked.

I squirmed in the plaid cushioned chair. "You don't need more to preoccupy you."

"Actually, I'm looking for distraction. Tell me."

I spoke rapidly, pummeling Kathryn with details of the past month. "André's sure she's drinking again and I feel like it's my fault," I said, in conclusion.

"You're not forcing her. If she's keeping a secret or something's gnawing at her, how's that your fault?"

Quiet enveloped us. I fumbled through my purse, not knowing what I was looking for. Finally I looked at Kathryn and asked, "Why do we have such obsessions with our past?"

"Because it's who we've become in the present," Kathryn said to me.

"And who we are affects everyone we love, huh?" I pushed aside my tea and leaned into the table. "I've got something else to tell you."

"I already know." Kathryn smiled, this time with her whole being.

"How can you?"

"I'm no dummy, girlfriend." Kathryn reached across the table and placed her hand on mine. "It's written all over you, from the inside out. Have you been to the obstetrician?"

"Yeah, I have."

We finally joined in the banter that surrounded us and blended in with the rest of the friends enjoying an afternoon together.

Thirty

riday morning, I waited for Josh in the family room as he fetched his cell phone to call his parents. I stacked magazines in neat piles on the coffee table and picked strands of dog hair off the couch. "What do you think they'll say?" I asked when he plopped down beside me.

"We'll surprise the hell out of 'em, honey. Years ago, I explained why we couldn't have children. I never told you this but it broke their hearts."

He hit the speaker button, and after three rings his mother, Elizabeth, answered.

"Hey, Mom, it's Josh and Claire."

I heard my mother-in-law gasp. "Are you all right? Are you a match?" Elizabeth's voice quivered. "Joe, pick up the phone — it's the kids."

A line on the other end crackled. "Hey, guys. You don't usually call on a weekday — what's going on?" Joe spoke in deep tones, like the radio announcer who did the morning traffic report.

"We've got news for you," Josh said. His words tripped out in staccato beats.

"You're a match for Kathryn," Joe stated.

"That we don't know yet — we're still waiting." I spoke up for the first time.

"Well?" Elizabeth asked.

"Well, you're going to become grandparents again," Josh found his voice and blurted out the news. "But this time it's your youngest son and his wife who're doing the honors!"

Silence answered him.

"But you can't!" Elizabeth pleaded. "Claire, your health."

"It's okay, Mom," Josh said.

"I called the transplant clinic and they gave us their blessing," I added.

"But you told us you couldn't," Joe stuttered. "Josh?"

"I did — I was afraid to risk it. But Claire did the research and she's the doctor."

I heard my mother-in-law crying. "Oh Joe, come here. I'm so happy — happy for you two, and for us. But you'll be okay, won't you? We don't want anything to happen to you, Claire. It was too close a call last time."

Elizabeth's reaction touched me and I couldn't help but wonder how my own mother would respond. I figured I'd find out soon enough.

After Josh left for work, I dragged the vacuum out of the hall closet — my call to Helene could wait for a while.

Around ten o'clock I climbed the stairs to my office and began to prowl websites for baby clothes and accessories. Soft colors painted the screen: pinks, blues, yellows, and lavenders. I wanted to reach out and touch the softness of the fabrics, smell the scent of skin care products. In my mind, I began to plan the nursery. I wouldn't need my office for a while, and it was right next to our bedroom. I could go to Home Depot on the way to meet Josh for dinner and pick up color swatches. Scenes of carousels, clowns, birds, and angels I'd paint in watercolor took form in my imagination — scenes of whimsy and joy.

The phone rang when I began to sketch some flowers.

"Claire?" The voice sounded tentative. It was Mother.

"I didn't expect you to call today." I put down my sketchpad and sank into the rocking chair.

"I've been so worried — I haven't been able to concentrate on a thing all week. I expected to hear about the results of Josh's testing. Why haven't you called?"

"We don't know anything yet, Mom. It does seem like a long time, doesn't it? Do you remember how long it took for Kathryn?"

"I thought it was only a couple of days, but I can't be sure." Helene replied.

My mouth went dry. "Can you take some more news?"

"You've taken another job? You don't need to — you'll be well cared for once we've sold the business. I thought you wanted to rest awhile."

"Well, it's not a job, in the traditional sense of the word." The cotton in my mouth expanded.

"I'm waiting," my mother prompted.

"Josh and I are having a baby." Outside my window, a tiny finch's nest snuggled in the crook of our ornamental pear tree, and I realized her reaction really didn't matter. I felt safe.

At the other end of the line stillness boomed. When my mother recovered she gasped, "Oh, ma petite fille, est-ce que c'est possible? Can it be?" She spoke so softly that I could barely hear her. "Is it safe? Oh, mon Dieu, est-ce que c'est vrai? Are you telling me the truth? "

"Yes, Mom — it's true. Josh and I went to the doctor yesterday and she confirmed it." I heard sniffling, followed by the rustling of a tissue. "Are you all right?"

"All right? I'm ecstatic!" she answered quickly. "As long as you stay healthy. Am I really going to become a grandmother?"

"I've sent you some articles to read. Trust me, Mom — I wouldn't have gone ahead with this if I had any doubt or if my doctors discouraged me. Do you know what I'm doing now? I'm planning the nursery."

"Can I come and help?" she mewled like a little girl.

"Of course, but not right away. If Josh is going to be Kathryn's donor, we'll wait till he's better before we start the project. I had no idea I'd get pregnant so quickly when I went off the pill."

"I know I told you to wait," Mother said, "but I've been lighting a candle every morning. I'll pray, my dear."

"But, you, Mom — how are you? André's been concerned."

"I'll do better now, I promise. It's just that . . ." she fell back into silence. "Oh, never mind. It's not important right now — we'll talk another time."

When? I wondered. And about what?

Dressed and ready to go, I picked up Josh's call.

"I'm leaving my last patient's home. I'm gonna drop off my paperwork, then I'll meet you for dinner. Where're we going?"

"Let's try 4th Street Bistro," I answered without hesitation. "We've got another excuse to celebrate — my mother's elated."

When we returned home later in the evening, the light on the answering machine blinked. A woman's voice stated blandly, "Mr. Bergano, this is the transplant center. We have the results of your tests to be a donor for Kathryn Scott. Please call so we can discuss them with you." She gave a number.

It was seven thirty on a Friday evening.

"Shit," Josh said.

Thirty-One

"Can't you call before you leave for work?" I asked first thing Monday morning.

I'd spent a restless night, dragging myself out of bed for a cup of warm milk at two-twenty. Warning voices tore through my mind: images of Kathryn and Josh faded into an unknown future. Anger simmered just beneath my consciousness, but the reason behind it remained beyond my reach. I fell asleep shortly before the alarm buzzed and shocked me back into wakefulness. A dull pain fanned out between my shoulders and up the back of my scalp.

Josh checked the clock and shook his head. "They won't be in the office before eight."

"It can't hurt to try."

"Let me go for a jog and shower first." He pulled a Wolf Pack tee shirt over his head and ran a comb through his wavy hair.

I snuck up from behind and put my arms around his torso, but couldn't find the strength to hold in my fear. "I'm scared, honey," I admitted. "I want you to be a match for Kathryn's sake — I can't bear to think of what'll happen if you aren't. But a little piece of me is ripped apart by worry. I don't know what I'd do if . . ."

Josh turned and held me in his arms but he remained silent. After a few moments, he released me and called the dogs.

I stood in the window and watched my husband set off at a slow trot toward the river walk.

Why didn't he say something? Can't he see how scared I am?

After his run, I sat beside Josh as he dialed the clinic. When a smile broke across his face, I knew that Kathryn had a donor. My hopes and fears clashed in a tangle of feelings. I looked into my husband's eyes and tried to match his joy with a smile of my own.

Thirty-Two

Almost *three months later, I walked into the drab* outpatient dialysis unit and spotted Kathryn reclining in a beige lounger by the window. The familiar sounds of machines and the odor of cleansing chemicals took me back to a place and time I wanted to forget.

Kathryn looked up, untangled her arm from under a fleece coverlet and reached for me, and I took her hand in both of mine.

A nurse who'd cared for me during my dialysis days wheeled over a black vinyl stool on casters. "Here, Dr. Bergano — have a seat. It's always so good to see you; we love it when our graduates visit."

I gave the nurse a quick hug and sat down next to Kathryn. "Your hands are frozen. God, I remember what that felt like." I shivered. "It's like a fridge in here."

Scanning the room, I saw the familiar sight of people covered in their own throws, rummaging through totes filled with projects to occupy the time: knitting, books, CD's, and even a laptop or two. Many just succumbed to napping, constantly interrupted by loud outbursts from staff or buzzers going off on the machines to alert the nurses that the blood had stopped its journey in and out of a patient. I shuddered at the thought.

"I'm surprised to see you, girlfriend. Didn't you have to work today?" Kathryn asked in a weary voice.

"I finished early, so I thought I'd come over. I've got news for you, and for Jeff Forrest, if I can catch him." I swallowed. My mouth had turned as dry as the Nevada desert at the end of summer.

"He's due to make rounds anytime now," Kathryn said. "How's Josh doing with his testing? I've got to admit, if there was any deterrent to giving you a kidney it was the needles and x-rays and God knows what else they did to me." Kathryn's eyes looked shallow; dark bags shaded her brown skin.

"He's fine with it, Kathryn. We got a call from San Francisco this morning."

Kathryn pulled herself into an upright position, fighting her weariness and coiled tubing that held her captive.

"There's only one more hurdle to jump," I continued. "The transplant coordinator asked him to drive to the Bay Area next Tuesday to have a renal arteriogram — the final test they have to do to make sure both of his kidney's are in good shape. They want to do it themselves and give Josh a final once-over." I choked on the words as I spoke them — words that gave flesh to reality.

"Is Josh all right? Does he still want to go through with this?" Kathryn asked me. Her hands shook in a fine tremor that soon overtook her body.

"He wants to do it as soon as possible so he'll be fully recovered before the holidays and before my due date." I caught myself stroking my abdomen.

Kathryn smiled. "Then I can go back to work and you two can focus on parenthood."

"The transplant doctor wants your team to let him know when you'll be ready, so they can schedule the surgery. I thought maybe I'd run into Jeff today and be able to tell you at the same time."

I resisted a glance at my watch. Instead, I began to describe plans for the nursery when Kathryn pointed to Jeff striding across the room to our station.

"I got a call today, ladies. I presume that's why you're here, Claire," the older Dr. Forrest told us. Unlike his son, his red hair was streaked with white. Jeff studied Kathryn over the rims of reading glasses.

"You're right." I stood, motioning the physician to the seat I'd abandoned.

"I talked to Brian before I came over." Jeff reached for his stethoscope and cupped it in the palm of his hand, a gesture I knew well: to warm it. "He says you'll be ready in two or three weeks, Kathryn. Claire?"

"Wow! Well, okay," I spurted out. "I'll leave you two to talk while I go call Josh."

When I backed away to give Kathryn privacy for her visit with Jeff, my heart thumped like a marathon runner. I exited the unit and glanced over my shoulder where I saw Jeff lean in toward Kathryn, with an open chart. I watched them peruse what I knew to be a lab report and recalled my own anxiety, how I'd felt blood pounding through my arteries and wondered if the machine was doing its job and clearing toxins from my body.

Outside the building I welcomed the warmth of sunshine. I sat on a bench and inhaled slowly, trying to rein in the nervousness that galloped through my body. After a few moments, I plucked my cell phone from my purse and hit speed dial for Josh.

"Joshua Bergano," he answered.

"It's me."

"Did you talk to Kathryn yet?"

"Yes, and to Jeff. They're together right now. Looks like she'll be ready the beginning of October."

"Good. I'll give my boss the heads up." Josh laughed. "Ha! Guess who gets to finish harvesting the tomatoes!"

"You won't stay in the hospital very long, just a couple of days — tomatoes don't weigh much, and a little exercise will do you good. Besides, I'm pregnant."

"We'll see. I'm on my way home, now." Josh changed the subject. "Stay with Kathryn as long as you want, then let's play nine holes at Wildcreek."

"My mother wants to visit after your parents leave," I told Josh. "She planned on coming for the surgery, but I told her to wait."

"She can have the guest room if she wants to come earlier — Mom and Dad will drive up in their RV, I suppose." Josh swung his eight iron and pitched the ball onto the edge of the ninth green.

"Says she wants to be here for you." Putter in hand, I walked beside Josh. As soon as I squatted to line up my shot, the sun slipped behind the mountain and the sky blushed.

"That's what she says," Josh laughed, after my ball zipped past the hole. "But I bet she wants to check up on her daughter and grandchild."

"And take me shopping for the nursery," I added. "I can't believe how delighted she sounded — I talked to her this morning."

"Did she have anything else to say?" he asked.

"They're supposed to close escrow on the business this week. She told me to expect a nice hunk of change. And André's in heaven — he'll be free to start classes in January."

We holed our balls, jumped in the cart, and headed to the clubhouse.

In bed that evening, I felt peace for the first time in weeks. "I can't explain it," I told Josh. "It's been a long, confusing day."

"It was good for us, being out together, playing our late afternoon golf, like we used to." Josh traced my lips with his finger.

"Do you think we'll ever know 'normal' again?" I lifted my hand to his cheek.

Josh slid his hands around my bare body. "I can tell you — right now I'm feeling 'normal.' Let's concentrate on that for a while." He kissed me, parting my lips with his tongue.

Passion infused our lovemaking and we came together as if for the first time.

Thirty-Three

"What color do you like for the walls?" Josh held an assortment of swatches next to the wallpaper border we'd selected.

Chaos reigned in my office that was in the early stages of its transformation into a nursery. Fabric samples, crown molding, and cleaning supplies were strewn about on every available surface.

I turned from my easel by the window and pondered shades of yellow and green before pointing to the one named Goldenrod. Behind me, a watercolor of a carousel had begun to take shape.

Nodding his agreement, Josh said, "We can stop at Home Depot after our appointment."

At the mention of my upcoming ultrasound, excitement raced through my veins.

"I better finish getting ready." I rinsed my paintbrush in a plastic container full of water and twisted the bristles into a fine point between my thumb and index finger. "God, honey; in a few hours, we'll be able to narrow down our search for a name."

"I've already decided. It's gonna be a girl and we'll name her Elizabeth Claire." Josh shoved the paint sample in the back pocket of his jeans and followed me down the hallway.

The bones in my hand crunched as Josh tightened his grip. Our eyes followed the doctor, who traced on the monitor, outlining evidence that our child was not a girl.

I raised my hand to Josh's dimple, deepened by the smile that spread across his face. "I don't think Elizabeth's a good name, do you?"

"I won't argue that one."

"I want him to be Joshua — after you. You can choose the middle name."

"We've got time to think it over. Just promise me you won't nickname him Junior, okay?"

Meredith swabbed gel off of my abdomen and grinned. "You're doing well, Claire, but be sure to keep your appointment with the transplant center next month."

"Too bad you can't come over the hill when I go next week," Josh said, as he helped me into a sitting position.

"Maybe I can call and see if they can fit me in," I said.

"No, Claire." Meredith turned to exit the room. "I don't want you taking that long of a car trip if you don't have to, and I'd like them to see you next month — that's what we've already scheduled at the outreach clinic. Better to keep your appointment there." She stepped into the hallway and leaned back into the room before closing the door. "I'll see you in three weeks, okay? Good luck with your test, Josh. Keep me posted."

Josh lifted me from the exam table. "A boy. We made a boy, honey." He waltzed me around the small room. "I'm gonna be a little league coach."

While I dressed, I entertained a vision of Josh and our son tossing a baseball in the cul-de-sac at the end of our street. A tingling feeling engulfed me when Josh threw his arm around my shoulder and walked beside me to the check out. I felt the warmth of his energy enclose me like a mantle.

"I'm taking tomorrow off of work," Josh announced Sunday evening, as he flipped off the TV. "I got a plan."

"Are you going to help me clean out the closet in the nursery? Let's get everything ready before your surgery then we can paint it before you have to return to work." I rummaged in the pantry for bedtime snacks for Murphy and Benisse.

"The closet can wait — we've been too busy. You, helping Kathryn and filling in at hospice, and me, with work. We need a little quality time together, don't you think?" He cornered me by the treat jar.

The dogs nabbed milk bones from the floor as I released control and eased into my husband's embrace. "What do you have planned?"

"I'll tell you in the morning. Just get a good night's rest, okay? Come on, dogs; last call to go outside."

Thirty-Four

*I*n the morning, I awakened to the sound of brewing coffee. Downstairs, I heard the banging of a fry pan and smelled breakfast in the making. "When did you get up?" I asked, leaning over the banister.

"Not too long ago," Josh called up the stairs. "Wear jeans and bring a heavy jacket."

"A jacket? It's still warm during the day," I said.

"Yeah, but we had a freeze last night, like I predicted. And wear your walking shoes."

When I came down, clothed as instructed, I noticed that Josh was busy making sandwiches. Our wicker picnic basket sat open, on the kitchen counter. "What, exactly, do you have in mind?"

"What's it look like, sweet stuff?" Josh handed me a glass of juice, kissed me, then cracked two eggs in the sizzling skillet. "We're going to have a picnic up at the Lake."

"We haven't been to Tahoe all summer, have we?" I said.

"We haven't been since our ski outing on Mt. Rose."

"I hope you don't have anything too adventurous planned this time." My thoughts shifted to Josh's sprained ankle and my stomach churned. "That seems like years ago."

Josh handed me my plate. "It does — wasn't that the start of the week that turned our lives upside down?"

Josh drove up Mt. Rose Highway, while I soaked in the beauty of junipers, conifers, and wild bursts of early fall color splashing the sides of the highway. When we crested the mountain, crystalline splendor greeted us. Lake Tahoe splayed like a sheet of glass on the horizon. A late-season boater cut through the stillness, sending ripples of contentment across the surface of the water and into my spirit. I wanted to hold on to the moment and never let go.

"Did you ever ask your mother anything more about your dream?"

Josh's question jolted me out of my reverie. I blew out a lungful of air. "Nope. I'm waiting to see her face-to-face."

"I think it's gonna be important to get a grasp on whatever happened." Josh signaled a right turn and eased onto the road circling the lake and headed toward North Shore.

"Why do you say that?" A gnawing feeling stirred in my gut. I stared straight ahead at the winding road.

"No special reason — but something weighs on you and I think you need to figure it out."

"Weighs on me? What the hell do you mean by that?" I turned to face Josh. He'd thrown a stone onto the surface of my peacefulness, casting waves that spread into the center of my being.

"Easy, honey," Josh patted me on the knee as though I were a little child. "You're the one who keeps bringing up some elusive memory — it's like you're possessed by fear."

"Don't you think there's reason for fear?" I looked straight ahead again, my eyes following the broken white line that separated us from on-coming traffic. Anger began to build up inside me.

Josh reached over and laid his hand on my thigh and I tensed.

"I could lose everything that's precious to me. You. Kathryn."

"That's it," Josh said.

"That's it?" I tilted my head and studied his profile.

"Loss. Whatever happened to you that you have such fear? I've seen it, Claire. Remember when your brother and Lauren flew to Europe? You were sure something would happen."

I settled back in my seat and the pressure escaped in a deep sigh. "You've got a point, honey. I don't know where it comes from, though." I pressed my fingers to my temples. "But I see what you're saying."

"It's nothing you have to deal with today. I'm sorry — I didn't need to bring it up now, did I? Come on; let's find the perfect place to settle." Josh hung a U-turn and parked in a spot where we could access the beach.

I followed him down the path to empty picnic tables. I smiled, pretending to bury the question Josh had raised. As he spread an old quilt in the pristine sand, I pulled my jacket tighter. A cool breeze hovered around us even as bright sunshine reflected from the lake.

Thirty-Five

I stood by, feeling useless, as Josh tossed a pair of boxer shorts and his razor into a small duffel bag. "I'm glad you decided to stay overnight in San Francisco, honey. It'll be a long, tiring day and I want you to feel alert for the drive back to Reno."

I perched on the edge of the unmade bed and nursed a cup of coffee. Murphy dozed, belly up, on his cushion. Benisse planted her head on the bed beside my leg, waiting for her morning scratch behind the ears, seeking assurance that no one would abandon her. Her liquid, brown eyes darted about the room and followed Josh as he gathered the necessities for his trip. Finally the dog crashed back on her cushion.

"I'll get an early start home tomorrow." Josh zipped his luggage. "Thank God it's not winter yet — at least I won't have to deal with snow when I cross the summit. That reminds me: listen to the weather tonight, and if it says that we're going to have another freeze, cover the tomatoes, okay?"

"Sure." I stood. "You had the oil checked, didn't you? It's been a while since you drove the pickup that far."

"Yep. And the tires rotated." Josh crossed the room to my side of the bed and buried my head in his chest. "You worry about everything you can think of, don't you?"

"Sorry." He was right, of course. I'd formulated a list of every possible hazard that a drive over the pass could present.

"I want you to know this, honey. No matter what, I'll always be here for you. You believe that, don't you?" Josh stooped down to me, so that his eyes were on a level with mine.

"I've got to believe it — it's not just about me anymore. We've got our baby to think about, too." I looked into his eyes to discover the beginning of a tear forming on his lower lid. I raised my finger to catch it, then I stood on tiptoes and we kissed.

"I better hit the road," Josh said, releasing me from his arms. "My appointment's at one-thirty and you never know what you'll run into on the way across the mountain. They're still doing road construction, Michael told me." He gripped his bags and ruffled the dogs, who barely stirred, before heading downstairs.

I stood in the driveway while Josh backed out. Brisk air from the northwest tousled my hair. Cotton-ball clouds bounced around in the cobalt blue skies.

He stopped, threw the truck into park, and hopped out. "One more hug, okay?" Josh said as he gathered me into his arms and kissed my hair, my neck, and finally my lips. "Don't forget what I told you, darling. I'll always be here for you." Josh jumped back into the Dodge and eased out of the driveway. He waved out the open window until he disappeared out of sight.

Before entering the house, I wandered into the backyard. Early morning dew glistened on the grass, caught the sun's light, and shattered it into tiny prisms.

The dogs were still asleep upstairs, so I tiptoed into the family room and stood staring out the panes of the French door, alone with my thoughts.

A dull ache, in the deepest part of me, commanded my attention. I realized I was holding my breath. Why did sadness have to steal away the beauty of a perfect, early autumn day? Why was I in turmoil?

I thought about Kathryn. My love for her had forced me to journey once again, with my friend, on that pathway of weakness and wondering. Tethered to a machine, dependent upon it for one day, or two, or three days of existence — life eked out in a blur of fatigue. The feeling of uselessness: sitting by, watching others do and become all you wanted to do and be. The doubt — questioning how long you could wait, and if the waiting would be in vain.

Next, concern for my mother captured my attention. Was she drinking again? She had promised to stay sober once before, but then succumbed. Promised again. Was my mother hiding something from us? What secret simmered beneath her need to drown her pain in gin?

And finally, there was Josh. It seemed now that every moment away from him heightened my fear that something could go wrong. My reason told me that he was strong, in perfect health. An ideal candidate to be a kidney donor. But what was the tightness I felt in my chest as the rhythm of my heart sprung into a gallop?

The irrationality of my feelings didn't console me. There they were — as sure as the neighbor's cat that slunk across the fence dividing our yards. The critter stood, staring at me. Taunting me. I opened the door, walked toward him and shooed him away with my hand. The Siamese arched his back and, for one ugly moment, I thought he was going to pounce on me. Instead, he scampered the length of the garden and landed with a thud on his own turf on the other side of the fence.

When I retreated to the house, I saw the dogs waiting at the door, tails wagging in synchrony. When I let them out, Murphy jumped on me in greeting. The heaviness that swathed me began to disperse.

Back inside, Murphy swept our abode, room-by-room, like a member of the bomb squad.

"He's not here, is he?" I said aloud when he plopped on the floor beside me and whined.

Half an hour later, I descended the stairs to leave for work. Overcast skies crawled into the Truckee Meadows. Gray effaced the blue sky and rolled over the landscape like a heavy tarp. With the drop in barometric pressure, the sense of oppression resurfaced. Rain clouds threatened in the west.

It wasn't often that I dreaded making home visits to my patients. I felt as though I wanted to indulge my own gloominess, not deal with families who faced the inevitability of death.

The waap, waap, waap, of a helicopter caught my attention when I put the dogs in the run. My eyes followed the big metal bird as it headed east.

Just as I opened the door to the garage, the phone rang. I sprinted into the family room, grabbed the phone, and hit Talk.

A male voice I didn't recognize greeted me. "Mrs. Bergano. My name is Officer Nelson; I'm with the California Highway Patrol. I'm sorry — I'm afraid there's been an accident."

I barely missed the kid who charged out in front of me from between parked cars. The tail of his red jacket slapped my left fender as he whipped past. He turned and scowled, extending the middle finger of his right hand with a rough upward movement, then dribbled a basketball across the street.

I slowed and pulled the car to the side for a moment, leaned against the headrest, and forced myself to slow my breathing. I don't have time for this. I slipped the vehicle back into gear.

A mile in front of me, the helicopter I'd seen as I left the house hovered, then began its descent over the regional trauma center. I stepped on the accelerator and merged into fast-moving traffic, speeding in the direction of the hospital.

What awaited me there? I couldn't consider the answer to that question. I just had to drive.

The colors of early autumn surrounded me, swirled as I passed. Was dying always this brilliant, I wondered? I remembered husks of aged bodies who'd been my patients. Lives that had been lived. Worn out: brown and dry and brittle. This year the leaves had frozen prematurely. Was beauty a sign of early winter? Of early death?

My fingers curled around the steering wheel and outlined the weave of tendons and of bones. A numbing chill shrouded me. The swooshing of windshield wipers whispered Josh, Josh.

Why had he said that to me? I'll always be there for you. I took it as a sign of hope. He'd promised — he couldn't leave me now.

Once I pulled into the physician's parking lot, I reached into the outside pocket of my purse and found the photo. The slick texture soothed me. A grainy image of a fetus: our child. Our son. I studied it for a moment before pressing it against my heart, then I slipped it in the pocket of my slacks. I exited my car and ran through the emergency room entrance as the loud-speaker announced a code blue.

"Myrna, I need to go back there."

"Oh. Hi, Dr. Bergano. What're you doing here? We don't usually get hos-pice patients in ER."

"It's not a patient — it's my husband. I think he's the one they just brought in by Care Flight."

The receptionist turned white as I steadied myself against the counter of the nurses' station.

"Hold on a minute, let me call." Myrna motioned to a nurse who was running past, then pointed to me.

An old couple sat in the waiting room, watching. I saw the man grab his wife's hand in his. His rubbery veins, covered by thin, bruised skin, criss-crossed like highways on a roadmap. The woman looked at him with rheumy eyes, magnified in thick glasses. He patted her on the hand, like a parent reas-suring a scared child. I longed for such human contact.

Instead, a door swung open behind me and Dr. Burns appeared. The cor-ners of his mouth, usually turned up, arched downward. Black eyes peered out beneath bushy white eyebrows. Fluorescent light bounced off the shiny surface of his bald pate, textured only by a few scraggly hairs. Hunched shoulders dragged down the appearance of the man, known for his joviality. "Claire." He reached toward me with the strong hands of a trauma surgeon.

"Where is he? Where's Josh?" I pushed away from the counter that supported me and headed toward the physician who had been dean of the medical school when I was a student. A trill of fear spread through my body and sparked numbness in my fingertips.

The doctor motioned for me to follow him, but kept silent. He lumbered down the hall to a conference room, where I had endured hours of emergency patient care management lectures. All that seemed a lifetime ago, and so insignificant now.

From the other direction, Father Brady approached at a trot. A slight man, with a lisp, he wore sandals and the robe of a Franciscan. White, shoulder-length hair and a beard bordered his round face, punctuated with bright blue eyes. Father Santa we used to call him, and that's how I'd introduced him to our guests after he'd celebrated our marriage, mine and Josh's.

When he arrived I flung myself into his arms and let him accept the pain I'd bottled in for the last half hour.

"Should I call Kathryn?" he asked.

I shook my head as I pulled away and looked to the physician for answers.

"Come on in and sit down." Dr. Burns dragged a chair across the linoleum and motioned to me.

"Where's Josh? I want to be with him." I hesitated before entering the room.

"He's stable for the moment, Claire. Sit down and let's talk." The doctor sat with a plunk, while Father Brady stood behind me, his hands on my shoulders.

"What happened? Please, somebody, tell me what happened."

"Your husband, as you know, was in an accident," Dr. Burns began. "He was driving west on I-80. I don't know the details, but it seems someone crossed the divider and hit him head-on." He spoke slowly, like he used to when outlining a complex case.

I listened.

"He sustained head injuries, Claire. He was in respiratory arrest when they brought him in. The paramedics kept him breathing during transport. Right now he's on life support and we're arranging for a bed in ICU."

The scenario unfolded in slow motion as I took it in, word-by-word. On the bookcase behind Dr. Burns sat a stack of textbooks. I straightened them in my mind, then arranged them in alphabetical order by author.

"Claire, are you with me?" The doctor stood and leaned toward me.

"Should I get some help?" Father Brady asked.

I sat up and forced myself back into my body. "Go on," I said. "Tell me what's next."

Dr. Burns fell back into the chair, while the priest took the seat beside me and reached for my hand.

"I've called Dr. Ahmad," the physician continued. "You remember him, the neurosurgeon?"

"Yeah. Him we used to call Dr. Do-Death. He was the one neuro doc who would discuss the hopelessness of a patient's condition with the family." As I spoke, I still felt detached from my body. My voice seemed to come from someone else.

Dr. Burns tented his hands over his mouth. "That's him — but he's also the most skilled neurosurgeon we have in Reno. He's the one I'd want if . . ." He left the sentence unfinished.

"Are you sure I can't call someone to come and be here with you, Claire?" the chaplain asked again.

"No, Father. Kathryn's the only one who's nearby, and she's sick herself. I can't risk putting her through this right now."

A knock on the door caused my heart to skip a beat. Myrna popped her head in. "Officer Nelson from the California Highway Patrol is here. Do you want me to show him in?"

"You want to talk to him?" Fr. Brady asked me.

I nodded my head. "I need to hear what he has to say."

The young man entered, holding his hat in front of him, head bowed. Sweat beaded on his upper lip. After his account of the accident he stood and took my hand. "Before your husband lost consciousness he said something to me, Ma'am. He told me I should remind his wife of what he said to her this morning. That's all he said. I don't know what he was talking about, but he said you'd know. I'm sorry I can't give you more, Mrs. Bergano, but it seemed important to him that I remind you."

The officer turned to leave. As he walked out of my life he left me with a shred of hope and a great emptiness.

Dr. Burns led the way into the intensive care unit where a cacophony of noises greeted us. Fr. Brady walked along side me, a purple stole draped around his neck. In his hand he held a tattered green book and a small vial of consecrated oils. The words of the ritual of the anointing of the sick played in the back of my memory.

Josh lay three beds down from the nurses' station.

Standing in the doorway, I caught a glimpse of him, buried beneath a cooling blanket and entangled in a web of cords and tubes. A ventilator hissed in the air like a deadly snake threatening everything I held precious. A monitor flashed streaks of green lines across its screen, indicating life still flowed through his body. My own observation told me he was non-responsive — probably comatose.

His palm lay extended, open and icy. I wove my fingers between his. Memories of Josh's strong hands poured in: the way his veins bulged when he worked hard; gentle touches that calmed me when I couldn't relax; the fist he'd make when, in teasing, he'd threaten to send me to the moon.

Already his lips were cracked and dry, while flakes of crusted blood formed in the corners of his mouth. Half-opened eyes focused on nothing, and his swollen black lids erased what I recognized as distinctly Josh — the twinkle of dancing eyes.

Fr. Brady touched me on the shoulder. "Claire, does your husband still have his parents? Is there anyone else who needs to know?"

"Oh, my God — I should have called right away."

"It hasn't even been a half hour; don't you think you needed to see him first?" the priest responded.

I needed to see how bad it was before I could believe this is really happening.

"Do you have numbers? I'll call for you." Fr. Brady placed his hand over mine.

"You anoint him, Father — I'll call." I let go of Josh and walked outside the room, but stood and stared back through the glass enclosure. I watched the priest's lips move while he traced small crosses on Josh's forehead, eyes, lips, and hands.

The doors to the unit wheezed open and a tall black man rushed down the hallway toward me. I looked up and Michael came into view.

"How'd you know?" I asked.

"One of the nurses in ER knows you and called for Kathryn." Michael reached out to me.

"I didn't want Kathryn to know, Michael."

"She doesn't — she's at dialysis. How's he doing?" Michael hovered beside me, glancing rapidly into Josh's room. He grabbed a handkerchief from his pocket and wiped sweat from his face.

When I opened my mouth to answer, nothing but air blew out. I shook my head and closed my eyes, willing the scene unfolding around me to be a nightmare, an illusion. Something I could chase away in the morning.

"Do me a favor," I asked and handed Michael my cell phone, removed a sticky note from my purse and began writing. "Here're two phone numbers. This one belongs to Josh's parents, Elizabeth and Joe. Call them and tell them there's been an accident. They live in the Bay Area. Ask them to get here quickly, but don't tell them how bad it is."

Michael nodded. "Whose number is this?"

"It's my mother's. Call her, too, and tell her I need her. Tell her I need her as soon as she can get here."

He took the phone and exited the Intensive Care Unit.

For a moment, I leaned against the counter of the nurses' station and covered my eyes with my hands. When I looked up again, Dr. Burns stood in front of me.

"Will you come back in the room? Dr. Ahmad has just arrived."

At Josh's bedside, hours later, I waited. My head leaned against the arm that had held me. I brushed my lips over unmoving fingers.

A woman's voice, fragile and tentative, startled me. "What happened, Claire?"

I stood and faced Elizabeth and Joe. My mother-in-law tottered toward me.

Without a word, I stepped into Elizabeth's outstretched arms while Joe walked over and encircled us both.

"He's in a coma. I asked the neurosurgeon to wait for you." I peeked at my watch. "He said he'd stop by when he finishes visiting his other patients — that should be soon."

"It's not good, is it?" Joe walked over and rested his hand on his son's shoulder.

"When will they operate?" Elizabeth asked, as I helped her into the chair I'd just abandoned.

I shook my head. "I don't know if that's an option."

Dr. Ahmad met with us in a small conference room. Indirect lighting cast shadows on pale walls, creating a sense of gloom. Josh's parents hunched together on one side of the table before Joe stood, put his arm around me, and helped me into the empty chair beside him.

Across a laminate table cluttered with pamphlets, the physician addressed me. "As you know, your husband's in a deep coma." He looked at Josh's parents, then back at me.

Elizabeth grasped Joe's hand.

"What do you mean by 'deep'?" I asked. I already knew the answer, since I'd reviewed the reports with the physician, but knew Josh's parents would need to hear the words for themselves.

After explaining that Josh's coma was irreversible, Dr. Ahmad asked, "Did he ever inform you of his wishes?" His eyes traveled from one of us to the other.

"We talked about it," I answered. "I'm a hospice physician. He doesn't want . . ." I choked on the words. "He wouldn't want to go on living if he's going to remain like he is right now."

I looked at Josh's parents, who nodded in agreement.

"When he got his first driver's license," Elizabeth said, "he became an organ donor and made sure Joe and I knew about it."

"It's all in his Advance Directives," I added. "I had our lawyer fax over a copy — it's on his chart." I bit my lip in anguish. "I can't believe it's come to this." I searched for the courage I'd known before, but any stoicism I once claimed had evaporated. The full burden of every death I'd ever witnessed, every hand I'd held, fell on me now and crushed me. The silence in the room covered us like a silk shroud.

Dr. Ahmad continued. "It's hard for me to bring this up now, but Josh is a young, healthy man. Do you think his wishes would be the same as they were when he was a teenager? Do you want him to be a donor?"

That was when I thought of Kathryn.

Josh's parents stood alone at his bedside, clenching one another's hand, stroking the head of their youngest son.

I watched them through the glass wall. Elizabeth seemed old all of a sudden; her body had caved in on itself. She reminded me of my fourth grade teacher: wispy and frail. Strands of silver hair fell from the clasp that held it at the nape of her neck. Glasses perched on the end of a slightly hooked nose.

Behind her, Joe braced the woman with his hands on her upper arms. His large body sheltered Elizabeth, but he bowed his head in a gesture that I had seen before from a man whose wife had been my patient. That other man was tall, blue-black, and spoke with a Caribbean accent. He'd clung to hope, all the while watching his wife waste into a waiflike being. As she'd shrunken, he'd wilted. Day-by-day it had happened until she'd withered away, leeching all promise from his stature. In the end he'd given up, too.

With Josh it was happening all at once — death was having its way, and left no time for hope or promises.

My turn to say goodbye would come next. Somewhere deep inside, a small tendril of comfort wrapped around my heart. Josh and I would always be together — he'd told me so. I cleaved to those last words and felt his energy stir in my womb.

"We've never held anything back from one another," I'd reported to Mother a few hours previously. "I haven't left anything unsaid."

"I'll be there first thing in the morning," she promised.

I shuddered. By then I'd be a widow.

My hand shook as I signed papers allowing the doctor to remove life support. I wanted to wail, but trembling fingers spoke my pain instead.

Josh would want to be a donor — I knew that beyond doubt. He would choose to save others, to'live on in them, and in some way, to be present to me. I scrawled my signature on a second set of papers to release his organs and thought of our son, growing inside me. Besides our child and Kathryn, how many others would benefit from Josh's gift of life?

"It's what he'd do," Joe had told me earlier when they gave me their blessing. "It's what he existed for — bringing good things to others and sharing himself."

When I handed the paperwork to the physician, I clasped it for a moment. Rain pelted the window of the empty room where, an hour earlier, a social worker walked me, step-by-step, through the process of harvesting Josh's organs and flying them to San Francisco. They'd already alerted recipients and many were en route to the medical center.

Right now, Michael was driving Kathryn across the same mountain pass that had claimed Josh's life. Kathryn, most likely rejoicing in the belief that an unknown cadaver was a match; Michael, having to pretend to share her joy in order to protect her, for now, from the truth.

Dark clouds enclosed the Truckee Meadows. I wasn't sure what time it was, if it were night or another storm.

Dr. Ahmad stood beside me, his hand extended, waiting.

I can't do this, I thought, but released my grip on the documents and on my husband.

"Take some time with him, Claire," the physician said. "I'll be back in a while."

Moments later, Elizabeth emerged from Josh's room, followed by Joe. "You go on in; we'll wait down the hall until the doctor comes back," Joe said in a broken voice.

I watched the older couple shuffle down the corridor. At the end of the hall, by a window, they clutched one another. As I walked to Josh's bedside, I heard my mother-in-law groan.

When the whooshing of the ventilator stopped, the nurses cleared the area of machines and gear. In one corner of the room, a half-empty bag of fluids hung, sagging like a balloon that had lost its air. In another, Josh's parents held on to one another. Alone, by his bed, I heard the breath escape from

Josh's body. I crawled onto the bed and held the lifeless form that had been my husband until they came to take him to operating room to harvest his organs.

It was only then that I gave myself permission to lose consciousness.

Thirty-Six

The garage door creaked open and emptiness yawned in front of me. Joe pulled his vehicle into the spot beside mine, the spot that should have held Josh's pickup truck.

When I opened the entry to the house, a chill slapped me in the face. Two shaking dogs stood and waited at the door. I sank to my knees and buried my face in their fur.

Dragging a rolling suitcase behind him, Joe stopped and helped me to my feet.

I wandered through the darkness and let the dogs into the yard, then put a pot of water on the stove.

"Have you eaten anything?" Elizabeth asked me.

"I didn't even think of it."

"We can't let anything happen to you and the baby," the older woman said and began to scavenge in the refrigerator. "What'll it be — dinner or breakfast?"

The clock above the stove told me that it was after five in the morning. "Breakfast, I suppose."

An intermittent beep announced a phone message. Kathryn's voice filled the room when I hit play. "I tried to get you, girlfriend, but you didn't answer your cell phone. Oh, Claire, it's a miracle. I'm on the way to San Francisco. They found me a kidney from a young man, it seems, who was killed in an accident. They're flying his organs in from somewhere. Tell Josh he doesn't have to go through surgery. I'm scheduled for seven o'clock tomorrow morning and have to be there at five. I'm going for another dialysis late tonight, so don't try to call. I'll talk to you when it's all over. Love you and give a hug to Josh, okay?"

A scream took shape in the depths of my gut and crawled up my body before it escaped in a low moan. I hunched over the counter until Joe gripped me by the shoulders and guided me into the family room.

He sat beside me on the couch. "The doctor in ER said you need to take it easy — it's no wonder you fainted. Why don't you stretch out while Elizabeth and I get things settled?"

From the kitchen, the smell of toast drew me back into reality. When Joe let the dogs back into the house, Murphy flew onto the couch and burrowed into the coverlet my father-in-law had spread across me. Benisse nuzzled her furry head into the crook of my arm.

Moments later, Elizabeth plodded into the room, carrying a tray with the toast and bowls of steaming oatmeal.

I swung myself into a sitting position, then swallowed the food rapidly in an effort to fight off the urge to vomit. How could I enjoy a meal when my husband lay cold in the basement of the hospital's morgue?

When I looked up, I caught a glimpse of my mother-in-law.

The woman stood, staring out the window into darkness. Deep lines crevassed her face, wrinkles I'd never noticed. Beneath Elizabeth's eyes, black half-moons rested on sagging cheeks.

"Sit down," I invited, patting the empty space beside me. "You're exhausted."

Elizabeth dropped onto the cushion beside me and I put an arm around her and drew her close. This was the woman who had given life to Josh, and who, today, had seen that life ebb away.

She needs me; we need each other. An image of the man I loved formed in my mind. He stood between me and Elizabeth: comforting and protecting. In a heartbeat, I understood I could get through this day if I pretended that I was fulfilling Josh's request. He would be the first to ask me to be there for his parents.

The three of us who loved Josh the most ate in silence.

When Elizabeth stood to clear dishes, I rose and gently eased her back onto the couch. "Let me get rid of these, then we need to talk about what to do next."

"You're going to San Francisco, aren't you?" Joe asked when I returned.

"I don't know; I need to make arrangements for Josh," I said. I hadn't even thought about going to be with Kathryn.

"But you should go for your friend," my father-in-law answered. "It's what Josh would want, don't you think?"

I nodded. "That's how we planned it — that I'd be there for Kathryn and Michael. And for him. Oh, sweet Jesus."

"Go," Elizabeth said in a low voice, patting my knee. "Go — we'll stay here and take care of whatever needs doing."

Hair on the back of my neck stood on end. The thought of telling Kathryn what had happened caused my throat to constrict. "Michael can handle it."

"No, Claire. You know you want to be with them," Joe said.

"My mother's coming." I glanced at my wrist and saw that it was only a few hours before Mother's plane would touch down.

"I'll pick her up," Joe offered. "You get yourself upstairs and catch some sleep, then we can decide what's best."

Mid-afternoon, I backed out of the driveway and eased the car down the street leading out of our neighborhood. Beside me, in silence, my mother extended her hand and reached for mine — a gesture so uncharacteristic of her. In the rearview mirror, I saw Josh's parents disappear from sight.

Silence hung between us as I headed down West Fourth Street toward I-80. Along the side of the road, sage blossoms burst into yellow flames. To our left, the Truckee spilled lazily over rocks, signaling the end of a dry season.

When I merged onto the highway, Mother cleared her throat. "Are you okay? You look haggard."

"I'm numb — on automatic pilot," I admitted.

"Are you up to this drive? We could still get a flight out."

"No — I rested a little. By the time we get to the airport and go through security we'll be there." I blinked back tears. "This is good — it gives me time to think. I have no idea how to tell Kathryn what happened."

"It'll come to you, don't you think?" my mother said. "How many times have you had to give people bad news? Do you plan it out?"

"I guess not, but I'm so confused right now, and I feel so empty. I can't imagine what my life will be like without Josh."

"Josh will always be a part of you, Claire."

I sucked in a deep breath. Those words had resounded through my head the last twenty-four hours and had begun to sound like an empty promise. "How do you know?" I asked.

"You're carrying his child within you. He'll live on, in Kathryn and who knows how many other people. Besides, you believe in more than this life. At least, I hope you do — that's how I raised you."

Do I? I shuddered. "I always have, before — but right now, I'm not sure. What if this is all there is?"

Mother's head fell back on the seat. "That's a question I'm not willing to consider, Claire."

"I had a dream last night." I reached over and took my mother's hand. "This morning, I guess it was. A young woman, a girl, was trying to talk to me, but I couldn't hear what she was saying. I've dreamt of her before. I tried to ask you about her a little while ago, remember? There's a picture . . ."

"I remember."

I glanced at her.

My mother squeezed her eyes shut and drew her lips into a pucker.

"When this is over," I said, "before you leave, I need you to talk to me."

"I know," she answered. "It's time."

Thirty-Seven

Michael and I sat together in the ICU waiting room. It was the afternoon of Kathryn's surgery, the day after Josh died.

"Did you sleep at all, Claire?" Michael asked me. His brows creased above his deep-set eyes.

"My mother and I got in late yesterday, then I lay awake most of the night because I couldn't stop thinking about Josh and our years together. I begged God to make this all a huge mistake, a nightmare." I buried my face in my hands before continuing. "Michael, I can't imagine life without him. What about our plans for the future? Our baby? It isn't supposed to be like this."

Across the room, Mother sat, buried in a chair too large for her.

I caught her staring. Wide-open eyes, fixed on me, the woman's face twisted into an expression of concern and helplessness.

Behind her, I saw myself, mirrored in the reflection of a window. My complexion was chalk-white; redness circled my eyes. I felt tears sitting on the rims of my lower lids, posed to trickle down my cheeks. Any pretense of strength had abandoned me and grief coiled in the pit of my stomach like a viper waiting to strike.

"Did you speak to Josh's parents this morning?" Michael asked.

I nodded. "They went to the funeral home last evening. I decided to leave the details up to them and gave them the phone numbers they'll need. Has Kathryn asked any questions?"

"She's still out of it." Michael took my hand and held it in both of his.

"What'll we tell her?" I asked.

"God, I don't know. Do you think it'll impact her recovery?" Michael's voice broke. He handed me a tissue and grabbed one for himself.

"We can't let it." I shifted my attention to concern for Kathryn, and tried to shove my own sense of loss and emptiness deep inside me. "Kathryn won't forget that she's responsible for Josh's kidney — that's how I've always felt about the one she gave me. She's got to realize that what happened to Josh isn't her fault."

"Josh wouldn't have been driving to San Francisco if it weren't for Kathryn."

"She can't look at it like that — none of us can." I almost added, "Things happen for a reason," but couldn't bring myself to form the words or embrace the belief.

I reached for the cup of bitter hospital coffee Michael offered, tasted it, and puckered my lips.

"Nasty stuff, isn't it?" Michael said. He took a gulp of Coke and shifted in his chair. Discomfort stole across his features. "What do we do now?"

"We can plan as much as we want," I said, my eyes surveying the door to Kathryn's room, "but it just happens. Come on — let's go see if she's awake."

When we stood, Mother rose to follow, but I signaled her to wait.

Abandoning the tepid beverage, I rubbed my face with the sleeve of my sweater. I asked God for strength and entered Kathryn's room with Michael in tow.

The nurses' aide had just finished taking Kathryn's blood pressure. My eyes darted to the catheter bag, filled with straw colored urine, lots of it. I smiled and a breeze kissed my body. For the moment, I felt like Josh was really here — his kidney infusing life into my best friend. Are there others in nearby rooms who are alive because of him? I wondered.

Kathryn set aside the wet washcloth she'd used to wipe her face and hands. "Nothing to drink yet — maybe later today." She grinned at me and her husband, who stooped to kiss her. "Is Josh still in San Francisco?"

He's here. He promised he'd be here, I thought, but only smiled. My heart pounded so hard I could feel it shake my chest. I clasped my frigid hands together and took a deep breath.

"Take a seat, Claire," Kathryn pointed to a chair. "Here, Michael, sit on the corner of the bed. Don't bounce, though — it hurts."

I stared out the window at some invisible vanishing point and when I turned back toward Kathryn, I saw horror etched on my friend's features.

"I had a dream last night," Kathryn murmured. "I think that Josh was in it, but I don't remember anything about it. When I awakened, I felt sad."

Taking in a quick breath, I understood that Kathryn had some sense of premonition.

Kathryn brushed hair out of her face and began to cry. "Claire, tell me!" Her face scrunched and her eyes opened wide open. "Something's wrong, isn't it?"

I wept freely now, while Michael imprisoned a sob in answer to Kathryn's question.

"Oh God, Claire — I'm so sorry." Kathryn's shoulders shook the bed as she held her wounded body and poured out grief. The only sounds filling the room were stifled weeping and the beep of a monitor in the alcove by the door. "This is his kidney, isn't it?"

I didn't answer with words, but drew my chair next to the bed and laid my head beside Kathryn's extended arm.

"What happened?" Kathryn ran long fingers through my hair.

Michael stood behind me. He was the one to recount the events of the past twenty-four hours, while Kathryn listened with her eyes closed.

When he'd finished, she just looked at me and held my hand so tight that my fingers blanched. After a while, she let go and closed her eyes.

"This isn't how any of us thought it would be, Kathryn," I said. "But right now, it's what Josh would have wanted."

"How can you stand being here with me?" Kathryn asked.

"This is where I am able to feel his presence. He's here in a different way. I don't know how many, but other people right here in this hospital are receiving his organs. I just hold on to this — that in his own way he'll live on. All I ask of you is to take care of yourself. For him. For all of us who love you. Okay?"

A slight smile formed at the corners of Kathryn's lips and she nodded.

"I'll stay with Kathryn, Michael," I told him. "You grab a bite to eat. On the way, ask my mother to come in — we'll leave when you get back. We've got to get ready to go back over the hill."

I released Kathryn and whispered, "Get some rest now — you need it."

Kathryn nodded in compliance. As she closed her eyes, tears escaped from beneath her lids.

Mother joined me and we remained at Kathryn's side until she dozed off into a restless sleep.

It was then that, for the first time, the baby inside me, Josh's baby, began to move. I grabbed my abdomen and jumped straight out of the chair.

"Mon Dieu, Claire! Are you okay?" Mother asked. "There's nothing wrong, is there?"

Early mountain snow marred the drive back to Reno. A light dusting of powder swirled above slick asphalt like chalk from a blackboard.

Tense silence prevailed between the two of us as I leaned forward over the steering wheel, focused on the two small tail lights of the car in front of us that flickered on and off. Pain seared in the muscles of my upper back.

What I'd hoped for now was a chance to talk to Mother. To uncover whatever secret from the past marred my ability to deal with all this loss and kept me stuck in fear. To reveal the unknown force that kept my mother from sobriety.

Near the summit, traffic slowed to a halt. I relaxed back into the seat and looked at her. She sat, spine erect, eyes closed. Old hands lay in her lap; her gnarly veins distended when she clenched her intertwined fingers together, then relaxed. I hadn't noticed her disfigured joints before. Once more, she squeezed, then released.

"Are you okay, Mother?"

She shook her head. "No."

"Can I help?" I shifted the car into drive and began to edge forward, slowly.

"It should be the other way around — I should be the one to help you, but I'm worried. You saw how I overreacted when the baby startled you."

"Well, it scared me, too; I'd almost forgotten he was there." I recoiled at the sound of the words I'd just spoken. A dull aching throbbed in the center of my body, the place that cradled my emotions. Anxiety for our baby collided with grief. I hadn't even thought about the fact that Meredith wouldn't have wanted me to drive to San Francisco. Besides, how could I go on like this? How could I go on without Josh?

After more edgy moments of silence I asked, "When are we going to talk? I need to know — I need to know what happened."

"André's flying in tomorrow morning. We'll talk when the three of us are together, after the funeral."

Thirty-Eight

I shrank into a tiny folding chair at the rim of a deep hole. An earthy smell permeated my senses. Just behind me, Mother and André stood like sheltering trees, as though trying to protect me from reality. To my right, Josh's parents held on to one another, their faces creased with pain. Michael pushed Kathryn in a royal blue wheelchair with chrome casters glinting in the bright sun that filled the blue sky of Indian summer.

The crowd was large and, for a funeral, young. They clustered like flocks of birds: friends from work, from our wine-tasting club, some nursing colleagues, and a few of Josh's college buddies. A gaggle of doctors who'd worked with me gathered, dressed in business suits, anxious to get back to patients scheduled for early afternoon appointments, I'm sure. Brian Forrest stood off to the side with his father, Jeff, my kidney doctor.

At the edge of the gaping chasm stood Father Brady. Stooped, he waited for the casket to arrive. I hadn't spoken to him since the day Josh died, that final day of our life together.

Six pallbearers made their way across the lawn. I touched the smooth wooden box as they slid it onto supports stretched over the yawning grave.

The priest began the ancient rites commending the spirit of my husband to the care of angels, and his earthly remains to the dirt from which he came. Father Brady's words floated by on a puff of air but I didn't really hear them. All I could hear was Josh telling me, "I'll always be here for you."

At the end of the service, well-wishers passed by and mumbled words of sympathy to me and the rest of the family. "Thank you, thank you," I repeated to each one, not able to say much more.

When the last person walked away, I noticed an elderly woman in the distance, standing alone under a spreading oak tree. I excused myself and went to embrace Emily Hardin. It'd been over five months since I'd seen her — Josh had been with me then — that day of therapeutic garage sales.

"Emily, we were going to meet for tea," I said. "When was it? April? May?"

"Has it been that long? When I saw you at the garage sale, I promised I'd call but I never did — I was afraid to disturb you. I'm so sorry."

I hugged the fragile woman. "I'm not working full time right now, so we should be able to get together soon."

"May I ask you something, Dr. Bergano? This is just a guess, but are you pregnant?" Emily's eyes were fixed on my normally flat abdomen, and I realized that a telling bulge pushed against my seamless black skirt.

I nodded.

"You'll always know your husband is with you, my dear."

Emily's phrase stunned me and I reached for the woman's wrinkled hands. She'd spoken Josh's words. Somehow, there he was, reminding me again.

"You'll be a wonderful mother, Dr. Bergano."

"Please call me Claire."

"All right, Claire. This time I promise I'll telephone soon — I still have your number."

I hugged the old lady again and felt like Josh had nudged me once more. He'd told me that I should make friends with Emily back then.

The long stretch limo crept back to our home. Michael hopped out first and extracted the wheel chair from the trunk, then scurried to the front, where Kathryn rode with the driver.

"It's a feat to get out of this thing," Joe mumbled, as he unfolded lanky legs and reached in to extricate Elizabeth. Mother and I followed Josh's parents as André lumbered behind.

I unlocked the entrance and found Murphy and Benisse stretched out, waiting. They'd been moping, hanging out at the back door, anticipating Josh's return. The dogs slept with me now, perhaps sensing my need to feel weight on the other side of the bed.

Memories of Josh sounded among us as everyone shared their recollections, one-by-one. For my part, I sat in silence and absorbed the words like notes of a fugue. The theme was life. The range of emotions covered octaves. Notes of joy, sorrow, revelry, and humor played a concert in my mind.

After an hour of rest, Kathryn joined us. She walked gingerly, holding the left side of her lower abdomen. Michael stood and gave her his seat and stretched out on the floor beside her.

When he'd returned to Reno the previous day, the day he'd driven his wife back home, Michael told me about Kathryn. During her hospitalization, reality had set in. Kathryn sobbed, he explained, and then retreated into herself. Today she cowered in a corner as though she bore the guilt for all of our loss.

I dragged myself from beneath a blanket of sadness, and crossed the room to Kathryn. I leaned in and gave her a squeeze, but felt no response.

Finally, I knelt beside her and took her hand in my own, touching skin that was cold and clammy. "You should go home and rest — it's too soon for you to be so active."

Kathryn nodded her assent.

"I need you," I told her. "I need you to be here for me and to remind me of him."

The corners of Kathryn's lips curved upward, barely. A spark of light returned to her deep brown eyes. "I have his kidney, Claire, and you have his baby." Kathryn ran the tips of her fingers down my cheek. "I wish you had him."

"I do, too," I whispered, as Michael stood to help Kathryn to her feet.

After they drove away, I returned to the family room. Elizabeth and Joe were preparing for the trip back to the Bay Area. In a few moments, I'd be alone with Mother and André.

"Elizabeth and I are leaving tomorrow," Joe told André, "but we'll be back soon to check up on Claire and our grandbaby." He smiled. "We can't let anything happen to them."

Mother nodded in approval.

Elizabeth smiled. Her hand flew across the row of knitting; a baby blanket in variegated pastel tones unfolded before our eyes. She packed up her work and looked at Joe. "We better get back to the hotel, get packed and ready for the trip across the mountain."

Joe stood and stretched. "Claire, we'll be by before we leave in the morning, okay with you?"

I rose and hugged my father-in-law. He patted me on the head and planted a kiss on my cheek.

Walking over to Elizabeth, I felt hot tears rising again. "I didn't think I had a drop left in me," I said, feeling embarrassed. We hugged again, and over her shoulder I saw a broad smile on Mother's face. I couldn't help but recall the day that Mother told me, "They're not good enough for you." I suspected that she would recant those words if asked for an opinion today.

When we'd said goodbye, I returned with Mother and André to the family room. "It's the first time we've been alone," I sighed.

"You've been so strong, Claire. I'm so very proud of you." Mother began to pick up empty bottles and glasses, hauling them to the kitchen.

"Leave them for now, okay? Let's sit together for a while," I said and collapsed into the couch next to my brother. "You've been so quiet, André. Thanks for flying up."

His wistful smile answered me. "I liked Josh, Claire — he always took time to listen to me. One time we spoke about our marriages — I don't know if you realize how much he loved you."

"What'd he say to you?" I wanted to taste, touch, feel, or hear anything I could of Josh. Anything I could add to the archives of our life together.

"I don't know that I recall his exact words. It was everything about him, as though he existed to care for you." André pressed his fingers to his forehead.

I nodded, then turned my attention to him. "You can find love now, André. You're free to find someone who wants you for the person you are." I tucked my arm inside his. "Some girl would be lucky to claim you."

He shook his head.

I wasn't sure if he were denying the possibility of love in his future, or regretting the choices he'd made.

Mother cleared her throat.

My eyes darted to my mother, whose head bowed forward, eyes staring at the floor where the dogs lay sleeping.

André caught my eye and hunched his shoulders as if to ask, "What's up?"

"André, when we were driving to San Francisco last week," Mother began, "I told Claire I needed to have a talk with the two of you." She hesitated and took a gulp of air, then looked at me. "Is this all right, Claire? Will it be too much if we do this now?"

"I've been waiting," I answered. "The day before Josh died he told me I needed answers. I wasn't sure what he meant — I thought he was alluding to the fact that I'll be a mother soon." I settled back on the couch and rested my hands on my abdomen where the baby was jogging in place. "He told me I needed to work through whatever it is that keeps me in a place of fear and worry, and that I need to have answers which I haven't had before. Maybe he had a sense of what was to come."

"Is this about your dream, Claire?" André asked. "The one you told me about?"

I answered with silence and gazed back at my mother, waiting for her to respond.

"Yes, André." The words came from Mother. "That's exactly what she's referring to, although this is the first time I've admitted it."

I pulled myself up, went and sat beside Mother, and took her arthritic hand in my own.

André scooted over on the couch so that he was adjacent to us. He reached for the other hand, which Mother offered.

"I've lived so many years with the guilt of what I'm about to tell you, I don't know where to begin." Mother's eyes flitted to me, then back to my brother.

"It happened when you were four or five, Claire. André, you were just beginning to toddle all over the house."

A sense of panic began to curl at the base of my spine. I wanted to scream, to stop my mother from uttering another word. I swallowed hard and squeezed her hand while I waited to hear the truth that had festered under a layer of deceit for so many years, the truth that I knew I'd recognize when the lie was finally lanced.

"You had an older sister," Mother said with hesitation. "Her name was Stephanie — she was fifteen years old at the time it happened."

What happened? What happened? I dove into the murky waters of my memory. Just below the surface swam something I couldn't face, didn't want to face. I reached for the glass of water my mother had nursed throughout the afternoon and took a sip before handing it back to her.

"Stephanie was a beautiful child," Mother went on. "She had the palest blue eyes and the voice of an angel. She was intelligent — no, brilliant. I encouraged her; so did your father." She halted in the middle of her narrative and shuddered. "No, it wasn't encouragement; we pushed her."

An image surfaced from the depths of my mind. I pictured the young woman of my dream, the girl in the blurry photo. Dishwater blond hair hung down the middle of Stephanie's back in a ponytail. The girl sat at a desk in the guest bedroom, the room that must have, at one time, been hers. Tears flowed down her cheeks as she tore a composition into tiny pieces and threw it on the floor. "I hate it," Stephanie had shouted. "I can't do this anymore." She stood and ran from the house.

I remembered the scolding Stephanie had received from our parents, who wouldn't allow her to join us at the dinner table until the composition had been rewritten and read aloud to the entire family. How could I have buried this? I wondered. How could we have erased her so completely from our lives? Bile rose in the back of my throat.

"What happened, Mother?" André asked, in a whisper.

"It was the end of her sophomore year. She had been a straight A student — she had always been a straight A student. When the report cards were sent out, she'd received a B+ in civics." Mother opened her mouth, but nothing came out.

"Go on," I encouraged.

"We were enraged, your father and I. We scolded her for not working up to her potential." Mother crumpled in dry sobs. "I wouldn't let her go to her best friend's party to celebrate the beginning of summer. The next morning . . ."

She didn't need to continue. It was then that I remembered it in minute detail. I remembered the blood.

For a long moment, deafening silence hung between us.

André leaned back in the couch and stared straight ahead. His usual ruddiness drained from his face and left him the color of paste. He let out a deep sigh.

A rush of nausea overpowered me and I jumped from my seat and fled to the bathroom. Leaning over the basin, I retched gulps of air from the empty pit of my stomach. The images raced into my mind, one after the other. I'd been the one to find my sister the next morning. Blood spatter from the girl's severed artery had decorated the tile floors and walls like a monochromatic canvas of some obscure abstract expressionist. The sounds of my mother's screams and father's curses echoed in my head. Within moments, someone had hustled us kids to the home of our Aunt Beatrice. Days later, when we returned home, no evidence of our sister remained. Over the years, all re-membrance of Stephanie had dissipated. But, similar to the effects of a vivid nightmare, the impression of the moment lingered like a heavy fog. That was when I understood what Josh had wanted me to know — that the mystery of Stephanie's life and death had affected me profoundly.

At the sound of approaching footsteps, I stood up and splashed water on my face. In the mirror I saw my mother stumble toward me, hugging the wall of the hallway.

André followed, hands outstretched, prepared to catch her.

I turned and reached for her.

Mother's shoulders heaved under the weight of silent sobs as she released the burden of years of secrecy and slumped into my arms with a loud moan.

We supported her back to the family room and eased her onto the couch. I handed her a damp washcloth, then went and sat beside my brother, taking his hand in mine.

"Why?" André asked.

Mother answered him with a vacant look.

"Why did you hide it?" The question escaped my lips like a roar.

"We were afraid it would affect you," Mother answered in a small voice.

"It has," André and I answered in unison.

"I know — it was a horrible mistake. I'm so sorry." Our mother doubled over on herself and squeezed her arms around her body while she convulsed in noiseless weeping.

I buried my head in André's shoulder. I wanted him to be Josh, to have Josh as the one who'd help me sort it all out.

"I've lived with guilt for so many years," Mother continued in a muffled tone. "I ask you both to forgive me. If you can't, I'll understand." She stopped short, trying to regain control. "But the only thing I want now is your happiness. Can you believe me?"

"I don't know," I answered.

André stood and walked to the door leading out to the garden. Raking his fingers through his hair, he shook his head, as though in disbelief. He turned, looked at me, and opened his mouth to speak, but remained silent. Then he opened the door and walked out. The door remained ajar. An autumn breeze blew in, adding to the chill already pervading my thoughts.

Mother sat in silence, eyes closed. The expression of her face reminded me of the Pieta as it should have been — not serene acceptance, like that of Michelangelo's Madonna, but the utter anguish that accompanies the greatest loss.

I watched from the opposite end of the couch. Part of me wanted to go to her, to take her hand, and tell her it was okay. That part of me wanted to respond as I wish she had so many times when I was growing up, but I didn't move.

We sat like that, the two of us, without speaking. Through the half-drawn blinds I watched my brother, standing in front of what was left of the tomatoes. I wondered what thoughts played in his mind. Regret, no doubt. Anger. And sadness.

These I recognized, because they were my thoughts. If only Josh were here to hold me sort them out.

When André reentered he sat beside Mother, but fixed his eyes on me. "It never should have been like this, but we can't go back," he said.

Mother stared straight ahead.

"I want to start a new life," André continued. "I want to put all the crap that's been a part of my every day behind me. I can't hang on to it anymore. And, Claire, I don't want you to have any more pain than you already have."

I closed my eyes and visualized Josh saying something along the same lines.

André reached for Mother's hand. "I'll never understand what drove you and father to keep the truth from us. I don't see how you couldn't recognize the effect it would have. But I have to believe that in your own way, for whatever reason, you thought it was the best thing for us."

I got it then. It was all so wrong, but their intention wasn't.

"I'd like us all to move forward on our own paths," André said. "Claire, you have a baby to bear and a husband to grieve. It's going to take all the energy you have to get through the next few months — maybe even years."

I pulled my sweater tighter around my body. Murphy hopped up on the couch just then, and curled into a little ball, snuggling up against me.

André took Mother by the shoulders. "You need to stay sober. To find something to enjoy that doesn't have anything to do with business. And soon enough, you'll be a grandmother."

Mother and I looked at each other and the beginnings of a smile tugged at my lips.

"As for myself, by God, I'm going back to school and do what I've wanted to do for so long."

He looked at me. "What do you say, big sister?"

I hesitated before moving over to sit on the couch, on the other side of Mother.

"I don't know that it will be a one-step deal, Mother, but I'll try. Your son already sounds like a professor — he makes some good points. A few minutes ago, you said that all you and father wanted was our well-being. I guess I'll choose to believe you. I forgive you. I confess, I don't feel it yet, but I mean it as much as I can right now."

Mother pulled us in to her and held us like she never did when we were growing up. "That's all I want that for the three of us. It can be a new beginning."

Can it? I wondered. Do I have the courage to begin again?

Thirty-Nine

hree days after the funeral, I returned to an empty house.

When we said farewell at the airport, my mother had begged to stay for a while. The temptation to hold on to someone who loved me was alluring, but I declined the offer. I had to hasten the inevitability of being alone, and I needed time away from her to work through my feelings about what she'd told us.

André had stood back, awkward in his attempt to console. He'd dragged the heavy bags to the Skycap and handled details as Mother and I stood silently. Fluffy clouds in the luminous blue sky mocked our grief.

"Call me when you get home," I told her as I backed away toward the car idling at the curb. I threw another kiss to André, then buried myself in the Lexus and pulled into traffic without looking back.

On the drive home, the dialogue between André and me replayed in my mind.

"I don't remember a thing, Claire," he'd admitted. "Nothing. But still it's haunted me — probably because of what it did to Mom and you."

"What'd you feel?" I asked.

"Probably something of what our sister must've felt. Expectations. I never could live up to what they wanted of me. Maybe that's why I stuck with a job I hated for so long, and why I married a woman I didn't love and who certainly never loved me. I wanted to prove myself, I guess. How about you, Claire? How has it affected you?"

I had folded my hands and leaned my head into tented fingers as I considered the question that had hounded me for hours. "Expectations? Yeah, I know what you mean, but somewhere along the line, I broke out from under them. Mostly."

"Probably when you moved away."

"That helped, but sometimes, I still find myself wanting to cave in under the pressure of what I think Mother wants."

"Anything else?" André had asked me.

"Josh used to ask me why I was afraid of loss. Why I was afraid, period." I remember stopping to look out the window. A wind from the southwest battered a tree that scrapped the side of the house, begging for attention. "You know, little brother, I'd managed to wipe out every memory I had of Stephanie, but when Mom spoke to us the other day, everything came flooding back in. And here, it's happened just when I'm dealing with the worst loss I could imagine."

"Do you think that knowing the truth will help you any?"

"That remains to be seen, doesn't it? But the questions, the dreams, and above all, the fear — Josh wanting me to get to the bottom of things — all that seems like more than coincidence, doesn't it?" I took my brother by the hand and looked into his sad, hound-dog eyes. "We'll talk soon, won't we?"

In answer, he'd put his arms around me.

As I pulled into the driveway, I took in a deep breath. I've lost my husband, I thought, and in the process recovered my mother and brother. Why couldn't I have had all three at once?

When I let the dogs in through the doors leading from the garden, I viewed wilted plants and spent flowers in abundance; scraggly grass begged for the lawn mower.

Benisse and Murphy tore through the house and went straight to the door leading from the garage, still waiting for Josh. I sank down beside them and curled up onto the rug outside the mudroom, pulling the two critters into my arms.

The ringing phone propelled me into action. I jumped up and answered, "Dr. Bergano."

Kathryn's soothing voice responded. "Good, you're home. Did everyone leave?"

"I'm alone." The words hung around me like stale air. "I just dropped off my mother and André at the airport. How about you, Kathryn? Do you feel okay?"

"Still a little sore, but getting stronger. How do lay people figure out all these meds?"

I stood up, stretched, and headed into the family room. Snuggling into Josh's space on the couch, I pulled his throw blanket close to me and smelled the lingering fragrance of his aftershave.

"I felt muddled," I agreed. "How many pills do you take? About forty-some a day, I bet. It never ends, but it does get simpler — I'm down to half that amount now."

"That's comforting," Kathryn said with a laugh that didn't sound sincere.

"I worried about you the day of the funeral," I interrupted. "You seemed crushed, almost as if you carried the weight of everything that's happened. Did they give you something for depression?" I asked.

"I didn't think to ask — let me give it a while," Kathryn answered. "When I start to bottom out, I think about what Josh would say to me. Deep down, I know it's not my fault."

I didn't tell Kathryn that I wouldn't take antidepressants either because I feared what it could do to our baby. When sadness intruded I would soak in Josh's words: I'll always be here for you.

"If I'm not asking too much," Kathryn said, "could you take me to Brian's tomorrow for a follow-up appointment? I'm too weak for lunch, but we could come back here for a while — I want to spend some time with you."

"Of course I will." Relief spilled through me. "It'll do me good. I don't go to back to work till Monday, and that's too many days alone."

"Is there anything Michael or I can do to help?" Kathryn asked. "Do you want to come for dinner tonight?"

"I've got leftovers, and it's time to face this first night alone. But thanks — I'll pick you up tomorrow."

"Two o'clock, okay?" Kathryn asked before disconnecting.

From nowhere a reminder struck me. I jumped up, stepped out onto the deck, and retrieved my gloves from the wooden storage box in the corner. I slipped them on, along with my gardening clogs.

"Ha!" he'd told me. "You get to finish harvesting the tomatoes." I'd better get started, so I crossed the yard to the vegetable garden where the last of deep red and golden globes waited for me to pick them. The ones in the front row had shriveled from the frost, but from the rows behind, I filled two baskets with heirlooms. I seemed to hear Josh speaking to me in the work of his hands.

I'll dry the seeds and he'll live on through them, too, I thought, popping a yellow cherry tomato in my mouth. A burst of late-season sweetness rewarded me and I savored the comfort that my husband continued to provide.

Murphy flew across the yard and deposited a saliva-lathered tennis ball at my feet. I reached down and tossed the sticky sphere, then wiped my hand on my jeans. The dog bounded away full speed and skittered to a sudden halt, looking side-to-side for his prize. I had to smile when I recalled the games of keep-away Josh and I used to play with him.

Back in the house, I stroked the taut skins of the tomatoes, then filled paper bags with an assortment of fruit. In the morning I would leave them on neighbors' porches after they left for work. I wasn't quite ready to face anyone yet, and knew I'd crumble if someone offered sympathy.

Later, I reheated remains of a pot roast Mother had made and sat in front of the TV to eat. I watched reruns of Law and Order to wash away memories of the ritual Josh made of our meals.

Exhaustion overtook me and I finally crawled into bed. The dogs leapt up and filled the empty space to my left. I fell asleep immediately for the first time in days, once I shooed away the loneliness tapping on the door to my mind.

Forty

The scent of incense from Benediction lingered in the near-empty chapel. Broken shafts of light cast an ethereal ambience that sucked the air from Helene's lungs. The Carmelite nuns, hidden behind a grill, chanted Evening Prayer.

Helene slipped into the last pew. She ran her hand over the hard oak, smoothed by years of sweaty palms that grasped it in supplication or penitence. After a moment on her knees, she eased back into the seat and closed her eyes.

The assurances she'd received from her children brought some measure of peace. Helene had seen them shed years of questioning and uncertainty. The weight of deceit crushed her a little less, now that she'd unloaded her secret, but complete serenity still evaded her.

There was more forgiveness to be sought. Where would she find it? To whom would she confess?

God understood — she was sure of that. Time and again she'd brought her burden of guilt to the Sacrament of Reconciliation, but relief still eluded her. She waited in quiet, waited for a message, an insight.

The clear words intoned by a young nun sounded the opening verse of Psalm 139: Oh Lord, you search me and you know me . . . Older voices joined in. You know my resting and my rising. You discern my purpose from afar. All my ways lie open to you.

Immediately, Helene knew. Asking forgiveness of God and of her two surviving children wasn't enough. She needed to ask forgiveness of Stephanie. Stephanie, whom she had pushed to the brink with all her demands.

But she also needed to absolve her oldest daughter. Her child had taken something from her, as well.

In the background the nuns continued to chant the words of the psalm: For it was you who created my being, knit me together in my mother's womb. Even there your hand would lead me, your right hand would hold me fast.

How could her daughter have so easily destroyed the gift of life that her parents had brought into being? How could she have killed herself?

Only silence answered her. Total darkness seeped into the chapel, except for a candle flickering inside a blue glass container beside the tabernacle.

He rescued us from the power of darkness, and filled us . . . The choir sang words from the New Testament.

Why wouldn't the emptiness inside her be filled? Was there more to be forgiven, to forgive?

At that instant, light flooded the chapel and the ancient extern, Sister Consolata, shuffled down the aisle from the cloister entry behind the altar.

"Mrs. Tressaint, we haven't seen you for weeks. You haven't been sick have you?" The sister reached out her withered hands to Helene. "I hope you're taking care of yourself. It's dangerous, the change of seasons, even here in California. The flu's making it way around."

While Sister Consolata chattered on, offering news of her community, Helene clung to the woman's words of greeting: I hope you're taking care of yourself. That was when she realized that she hadn't forgiven herself.

It was almost nine-thirty when Helene opened the back door.

André rushed out of the den to greet her. "My God, Mom. Are you okay? I've been worried sick."

"I'm better than I've been in years."

Sister Consolata had proven worthy of her name. She'd listened like a mother confessor as Helene had poured out years of self-hatred and shame. The fact that the nun was a bit senile hadn't mattered at all. Helene was the one who needed to hear her own admission. She was the one who had to give pardon, and to let go of her own sins.

When Helene smiled at her son, she felt that her insides followed suit. "I bet you thought I was out drinking, didn't you?"

A blush rose up André's face, informing Helene that her suspicions were right on target.

"I was at the Carmelites. I had some more work to do."

André let out the breath he'd been holding.

"Come on, son. Let's call Claire — this is her first night alone."

Forty-One

*K*athryn, *now almost two weeks post-op, stood straighter* and walked taller. She greeted me, and I hugged her gently and helped her into the car.

Chopin poured out of the speakers. Autumn held court along the route, boasting color. Flaming maples and yellow aspens lined the streets of the older neighborhood we drove through.

"I spent some time clearing out Josh's garden last evening," I told her. "There's a bag of tomatoes for you and Michael in the back seat — don't let me forget to give them to you." I spoke with a certain sense of calm. Working the earth had grounded me.

Kathryn nodded approval.

"I discovered Josh's recipe for canning tomatoes and pasta sauce on the window sill in the kitchen," I continued. "I guess he planned to keep busy during his recovery, so I'm going to try it myself — he'd want me to."

"He'd be proud of you." Kathryn reached over and squeezed my arm.

I flashed a quick smile. "It's not only about me anymore, is it?"

When I saw Kathryn peek at my belly, I cradled my body with one hand in a gesture that had become habitual, my way of holding my husband's presence. I felt a blush creep up my face.

A dozen patients filled Brian's waiting room. "Looks like we're going to be here a while," Kathryn noted. "Tell me, when's your next appointment with your OB?"

"In two weeks — I wonder if she knows about Josh."

"Don't you think you should get in sooner? What you've been through could affect you and the baby."

A danger signal sounded, and I felt the blood rush from my head and dizziness overtook me. "I'll call right now."

I reached into my purse, extracted my cell phone, and hit the speed dial I'd assigned to Meredith at the time of my first visit.

"This is Dr. Bergano; is Dr. Jansen available?" I didn't want to waste time trying to explain Josh's loss to a receptionist, so I pulled my "doctor" status.

"Claire?" Meredith answered immediately in a taut voice. "I heard about your husband. I'm so sorry. I planned to be at the funeral — I'd even cleared my calendar, but ended up with an emergency C-section."

I struggled to keep my voice steady, relieved that I didn't need to tell the story again. I took in a deep breath and asked, "Do you think I should see you sooner? Do you have any openings this week?"

"You're psychic — I just left a message on your answering machine — can you come in tomorrow? I had a three o'clock cancellation."

"I'll be there. Thanks, Meredith." I disconnected quickly to avoid questions. There'd be time for talking tomorrow.

Kathryn looked at me with a question written on her face. "Well?"

"Tomorrow afternoon," I responded, as I slipped the phone back into my bag.

"I'm coming with you."

"No, Kathryn. You're not ready to run all over town," I insisted.

"Let me see how I feel by the end of today — I won't be foolish, I promise."

Kathryn's name rang out in the waiting room and interrupted my objections. In the examination room, I helped Kathryn into a gown and stared at the long, comma-shaped scar that curved on her lower abdomen. I saw a mirror image of my own scar, reached over and laid my hand gently on the small protuberance made by Josh's kidney. With my other hand I felt Kathryn's kidney inside my body. I had to pull the sleeves of my sweater down to cover the goose bumps on my arms.

Brian entered the room, greeted his patient, then crossed the room to me. His green eyes reflected my pain as he gave me a brotherly hug.

Then I watched him probe Kathryn's brooding expression while his face registered concern for both of us. Brian assisted Kathryn onto the examination table, pulled up a stool, and sat while I sank into an empty chair nearby. The surgeon reached out and grasped her hand, then mine.

"I don't know what to say — I'm so sorry. This should be a time of celebration, Kathryn. You've been given another chance at life, but what a price! I can't imagine the sadness you both must feel."

His strong handclasp spread a sense of comfort throughout me. Brian reminded me of all I'd lost when I lost Josh. I held my breath, lest the pain I felt should explode in a sob.

Brian released his grip and pivoted toward Kathryn. "How does this affect you, Kathryn? You can't blame yourself, you know."

Kathryn turned her head to the wall.

"In all my years of practice, I've never seen anything like this. Someone preparing to be a living donor. . ." Brian's words trailed off.

I blurted out, "It wasn't because of Kathryn."

"No, it wasn't," Brian said. "But, does she believe that? Kathryn, do you?" He reached out and touched Kathryn's shoulder to catch her attention. "Do you?"

"In my heart, I know it's not my fault." Kathryn pulled herself upright. "But in my gut, I hurt so much. If Josh hadn't been on his way to San Francisco, he might still be alive."

"I was afraid you'd feel that way, but don't forget — Josh was doing what he felt called to do. He was a fine man." Brian brushed his hair back off his forehead in the same careless manner that reminded me of my husband. "I respected him for what he was ready to do for you, Kathryn. To me, this is a personal loss."

I watched the surgeon lean forward in a pensive posture.

"I'd never discourage anyone from becoming a donor," Brian said. "It's safe and gives new meaning to one's life — I'd offer an organ myself." He stood and approached Kathryn, then glanced over his shoulder at me. "I'm so glad I got to meet Josh, Claire. He was an extraordinary man."

"Are you too tired to stop for ice cream?" I asked Kathryn, as I helped her into the car.

"Oh, God, that sounds so good. My appetite's getting better, and the sound of a hot fudge sundae is yummy. Let's do it."

"You wait in the car, and I'll bring it to you." I helped Kathryn recline the backrest a bit and left the motor running so the heated seat could help take the chill off the day that had begun to remind us more of winter than autumn.

"You never did tell me how it went with your mother and André after the funeral," Kathryn said, as we dug into our treats. "They stayed a couple of days, didn't they?"

I swirled the hot fudge into my vanilla yogurt, allowing it to melt into a creamy consistency. Eventually, I would tell Kathryn the story of Stephanie and all the drama that surrounded it. I needed to. She was my best friend and now, my only confidant. But I hesitated. I couldn't help notice the fatigue that had dulled her eyes, nor the way she still guarded her surgical site when she moved, or when the car had hit a pothole.

When I turned to face her, her expression was one of concern.

"There's something you're holding back, isn't there?" Kathryn said.

"It was a good visit," I answered. "We talked about things that needed to be talked about. Hard things, from years ago. But all that will wait. I won't hold anything back from you, I promise."

"Tell me now," Kathryn said.

I looked at her for a few moments, trying to decide if it was fair for me to burden her with my story.

"Go ahead, Claire. Is your mother supporting you in all that you're going through?"

"She does the best she can. Yes, I guess so. I have so many conflicting feelings about her, Kathryn."

"Has she ever answered your questions about that dream you had. That one with the girl in the photo."

"Yes. Yes, she has. She chose now, of all times to tell me about it."

"And…"

"Are you sure you're up to this, Kathryn? It's a soap opera. No. More than a soap opera."

"Please tell me," Kathryn said.

So I did.

By the time I'd finished the account with all its details, I was in tears. The pain and anger that I still nurtured combined with grief, and my body was trembling. Kathryn's ice cream remained untouched, a puddle in the bottom of the cardboard container. The pink plastic spoon floated on the viscous surface like a toy boat.

"What did you say to her? What did André do? Did she ask you to forgive her?"

I nodded. "We both said the words and, I guess, in a way, I meant them. I tried to focus on the fact that my parents' intentions were for our good. I feel forgiveness sometimes. I try to let go, but at other times, I struggle. That huge, horrible secret has affected all of us. Mother drank. André's been miserable most of his life. And I...the fear that has haunted me for so long has just simmered in my core for as long as I can remember."

"But look at yourself, Claire. Look how you've dealt with the absolute worse thing that could happen to you. Does knowing what was behind that fear help you to face it? Has it helped you to confront what you've been up against so often?"

I guess it has, I thought, but couldn't say so. Not yet.

The afternoon's outing had visibly exhausted Kathryn. I helped her recline the passenger seat again and she dozed on the trip up the hill to Caughlin Ranch.

When we pulled into the Scott's driveway I reached over to awaken my friend. "I'll walk you to the door, but I can't stay. You need to take a nap, and I don't want you to even think of coming with me tomorrow."

Kathryn eased out of the car with my assistance.

"I'm so grateful that you got a good report in spite of everything."

"Brian's a caring person," Kathryn didn't respond directly. "He tried to help us both."

"He is a good man — I hope his wife appreciates him," I agreed.

"You didn't know, Claire? Brian's wife died from a ruptured aneurysm a few years ago."

I took in a short breath as Kathryn headed toward the entrance of her home and inserted her key into the sturdy lock. I lagged behind, toting the sack of tomatoes.

"He lost Joanne about the time you were out of commission." She entered the house, turned, and added, "I'll call you in the morning."

I stopped to study the vista of Reno from Kathryn's driveway. The growing city sprawled before me. Behind me, the Sierra Nevada embraced the valley. A breeze swept across my face, but I noticed that the trees in Kathryn's yard remained perfectly still.

I stood in the empty kitchen with my hands on my hips. One of Josh's chef aprons covered my clothing and an open cookbook on the counter presented menus under a sub-title "Cooking for Two."

No wonder people who live alone don't eat balanced meals, I thought. I recalled my elderly patients who often subsisted on TV dinners and leftovers from restaurant meals as I struggled to separate a frozen chicken breast from its mate. Josh used to bargain hunt, and carefully divided his spoils into portions for the two of us. He'd wrap and store servings in small Ziploc bags marked with the contents and date.

The two stiff slabs of meat taunted me. They were a pair — they belonged together, like I belonged with Josh. I threw the chicken back into the bag, sealed it, and flung it into the bottom drawer of the freezer, then I filled a cereal bowl with Cheerios, poured on some fat free milk and ate it at the counter. It tasted bland and left me hungry. If Josh had been there, the kitchen would be filled with scents of spices and the hustle of activity that surrounded his preparations for dinner. Tonight all I savored was emptiness.

I can't do this — I can't eat this way while I'm pregnant. I finished the scant supper, picked up the cookbook and a pad of paper. I sat at the kitchen table to plan a menu for the week, nibbling on an overripe banana to assuage the guilt I felt from the meal I hadn't prepared. I promised myself I'd cook every other day, using both portions. Just what I used to tell my patients, I realized.

The shopping list I wrote blurred before my eyes. The dogs were jumpy. I felt confused, and wandered around the room, picking things up, touching the memories they evoked before putting them back where they belonged. I refuse to succumb to the trap of television or computer games. I won't give in to my grief. Armed with the strength of my resolution, I opened the door to the garden and let the dogs out into the yard so they could release pent-up energy. I stood on the deck and watched Murphy and Benisse play tug of war

with their nylon pull toy. The ring of the phone, once an annoyance, presented a welcome interruption. I yearned for human contact, even a telemarketer.

"Dr. Bergano, this is Emily Hardin. Did I catch you at a bad time?"

"It's perfect, Emily." I felt a smile tug at the edges of my lips. I honestly
hadn't expected to hear from the elderly woman so soon.

"I remember the first few days after my husband's funeral, once every-
body had left. I never felt so alone, so abandoned." Emily cleared her voice.

"It's hard — I ate cereal tonight," I confessed. "I'm not sure what to do
with myself." I felt conflicted in revealing this to a former client. But now, I
reminded myself, I've got to build up a support system.

"Could we have tea tomorrow?" Emily asked.

"I wish I could, but I've got an appointment with my OB doctor."

"Do you need someone to go with you? I'm free in the afternoon," Emily
offered.

I hesitated for a moment. Kathryn had told me that she would accompany me, but I visualized my friend's fatigue just that afternoon and the thought
of going alone, sitting in a cheery waiting room filled with happy couples,
overwhelmed me.

"I know I'm a lot older than you, Claire, but I've been through it before,"
Emily said. "I had babies — that's not something you forget. And I've lost my
husband. You helped me then — please let me help you now."

Weighing my options, I relented. "You're a godsend, Emily. Yes, and we
can stop for tea after I'm finished with the doctor. Can I pick you up about
two-thirty? I remember where you live, but give me the street number, just
in case."

Emily's suggestion sparked my determination. I jumped up and grabbed
the loose end of the pull toy Benisse had abandoned. I twirled around as
Murphy hurtled through the grass, and I promised myself that I would re-
claim my life, for the dogs and my baby, but above all for myself.

That's what Josh would expect of me.

Forty-Two

athryn sounded relieved when I called in the morning and related Emily's offer. "I have to admit I'm still exhausted," Kathryn told me. "I planned to lie to you."

"And you don't think I would have known it?"

"I didn't want you to go alone. I even thought about asking Michael to take a couple of hours off work."

"That'd get them talking. You should've seen me last night trying to fix my own dinner." I was able to laugh about it now, so I recounted the drama in detail. "But, don't worry — I've got a strategy. This morning I'm hitting the grocery store. I'll get a handle on it — it took me by surprise." Vigor infused me as I faced this small hurdle, a challenge that I knew would be the first of many.

"Plan on having dinner with us on Saturday night, Claire. Michael suggested it this morning before he left for work."

"That'll be a relief," I admitted. "Ask Michael to make enough to send me home with a care package, okay?"

Before hanging up, Kathryn told me to give her a report on the OB appointment. "I need to know everything's all right."

I bit at a hangnail on my ring finger. What if it isn't?

During the short drive to Emily's, I ruminated on the last time I'd visited the older woman's house — the garage sale Josh dragged me to, to ease the pain of my job loss. The thriller book by some unknown author Josh finally rescued from the deep cardboard box still lay on his bedside table. I wondered if he'd read it.

When I pulled the car to the curb, I pictured myself holding on to my husband, walking up that same path. Emily breezed out the front door and met me halfway.

The petite older woman stood on tiptoe and touched weathered lips to my cheek. Emily stood back and observed. "You've lost weight, Dr. Bergano. I'll have to monitor you." Laughter rippled from Emily's upturned mouth as she hopped into the passenger seat with all the suppleness of a teenager.

When I circled around the rear of the car and slipped behind the wheel, I picked up the faint fresh scent of Yardley's lavender. I reached over, squeezed Emily's perfectly groomed hand, and said, "Thanks for coming with me."

Emily leaned back into the plush seat and announced, "I thought I'd adopt you for awhile. Your mother won't mind, will she?"

I smiled. "I don't think so, not anymore. She knows I love her and there's enough to go around." I decided call Mother tonight, to keep her involved with my progress and tell her about my new friend.

Emily pored over a Woman's Day while I followed the nurse back into the examining room.

I put on a pale pink gown and waited for Meredith. Anxiety snuck in from nowhere. My imagination ran amok as I considered what could go wrong given the tragedy that had visited me these last two weeks. I was a little less than five months pregnant, in the middle of my second trimester. What could happen to our baby when I had been assaulted with so much trauma, so many changes?

When Meredith entered, I stood and let the large woman enfold me. My obstetrician stood a head taller than I; she was full-bodied with straight blond hair worn back in a ponytail. Circular framed glasses accentuated the physician's no-nonsense expression, but her hug exuded confidence and warmth. I felt secure under her care.

"Are you aware of any problems, Claire?"

"Not really, except that I'm not eating well, but I'll deal with that," I admitted.

"Good. I want you to add a prenatal vitamin, okay?"

"Josh got some for me — I just haven't started them yet." As I spoke his name, I swallowed hard.

Meredith waited a moment before she continued. "Are you sleeping through the night?" she asked as she helped me recline on the firm table.

"Last night, for the first time."

"How about depression?" Meredith fixed hazel eyes on me.

"I won't deny it, but I'm moving through it. It's lonely, empty. I see and hear Josh everywhere. I open a drawer, and there's something of his that I didn't expect to find. I uncover a pair of dirty socks tucked behind a chair, and I lose it. I used to nag him about those things. He's in every room and assails every sense. I smell his aftershave; I tasted the tomatoes he grew before he left for San Francisco."

Meredith sat quietly and listened.

I felt able to unload little things, things I hadn't even shared with Kathryn or my mother. When Meredith began to examine me, I continued to ramble.

"You've got to have a support group, Claire. Not necessarily a formal one, but a network of friends who'll be there for you."

"I have Kathryn, but she's recovering. And my mother. Then yesterday the wife of a former patient reached out to me — that's who's here with me today."

"Talk things out with someone. If you do, you shouldn't need extra medications." Meredith took a business card out of the pocket of her lab coat and wrote on the back. "Here's my cell number; call anytime."

Continuing the exam, Meredith pulled out her stethoscope and placed it on my abdomen.

Its coldness startled me.

Meredith smiled. "Sorry, but the good news is that I hear a strong fetal heart beat." She covered me with the soft white sheet and helped me back into a sitting position. "The baby's fine, but I want to see you every two weeks for a while, until you're past these critical stages. Do you want an amnio to make sure everything is okay with the baby?

"No. I'm having our son no matter what," I answered firmly.

Meredith chuckled.

"Thanks for the time you've taken with me — and for working me in right away." A smile found its way back to my heart.

"You'll do fine, Claire. You're a strong woman, and you've got Josh's baby to keep you going." Meredith waved before she closed the door to the examination room behind her.

Promise suffused me as I pulled on my slacks and ran a comb through my disheveled hair. When I reentered the waiting room, I winked at Emily, who mimed hand clapping and grinned back. We walked off arm-in-arm, like mother and daughter.

Emily stood aside and motioned me into her dark, cool home.

A yellow painted wall of books caught my attention. I strode over and soaked in titles: classics, mysteries, literary fiction, and recent best sellers.

Emily burst into laughter. "You do the same thing I do. Libraries draw me like a magnet draws iron filings."

"You have so many kinds of books," I exclaimed, as I continued to scan the collection.

"You can tell a lot about people by what they read," Emily noted. "I devour everything — I'm an addict."

I stroked the covers of ancient leather bound tomes, smelled the musty odor of moldy bindings, and caressed spines of shiny covers — some books I'd already enjoyed and many I'd never heard of.

Emily had insisted that we return to her home for tea. "I've baked some scones," she said. "I'll go get the water boiling."

I listened to the woman bustling in the kitchen while I studied pictures hanging on the wall above the fireplace. A young couple, circa the early 1940's, stood arm-in-arm. He wore a military uniform. The bride ducked as a child heaved a handful of rice. Below it, the same couple drove off in a vintage convertible with a homemade "Just Married" sign affixed to the rear.

I moved on. A very pregnant Emily sat alone in the next picture, on the stoop of a front porch. She showed off a wooden model of a WWII bomber.

"Those are my stories," Emily interrupted, entering the room softly. "I won't bore you with them, not all at once." Breaking into a wistful smile, the older woman set a silver tray on the coffee table.

I folded into a lavender wingback chair as Emily poured her tea. "You were a war bride?"

"Yes — and a war widow."

"Tom wasn't your first husband?" My eyes widened with surprise.

"No, we married in 1945, soon after the war."

"You were pregnant, Emily." A shudder crept up my spine.

"Yes. I was five months along when Arthur was shot down. Like you. That's one of the reasons I knew I needed to reach out to you."

"Oh, Emily."

I saw that tears had formed in my elderly friend's eyes. She came and sat beside me. A sense of peace came over me — I knew that there was someone who understood what I was going through — someone who had walked along the same lonely path and had kept on going until she caught up with love again. She read my thoughts.

"It never goes away, Claire," Emily admitted to me. "But love comes back in if you keep your heart open. And I needed to — I had a baby to care for."

We sipped tea in silent companionship, both of us deep in thoughts of love and loss, I guess.

Josh, you brought this lady back into my life, didn't you? How could he have known?

I felt smug that the chicken Caesar salad turned out so well, and set aside the second piece of meat for tomorrow's fajitas with Spanish rice and refried beans.

I checked off my To-Do list. I'd called Kathryn and Mother. Both were thrilled that the baby and I were healthy.

"I hope to visit next month, Claire," my mother promised.

I grinned — I'd just told Mother about Emily.

"What'd you fix for dinner?" Kathryn asked me. I remembered the smell of chicken grilling on the barbecue, and reported the outcome to another one of my self-appointed food monitors.

Things went a little better today, honey. I watched the dogs chase each other across the lawn from the French doors. The days were shortening and I'd have to bring them inside before long. I closed my eyes and visualized Josh beside me. Our baby's fine. Meredith listened to me blather on about you. Oh! And I've made a new friend. Remember Emily from the garage sale? She went with me to the doctor's. She was widowed, too. When she was five month's pregnant.

I stroked the smooth oak door that Josh had sanded and finished the previous summer, and continued to speak in my heart to the man I loved, the father of my child. He didn't answer, but I believed he heard me anyway.

I dreamt of Josh that night. He drove by in a convertible as I sat on our front porch. He laughed and blew me a kiss then went on his way. I ran into the street and chased after him. Running as fast as I could in spite of cramping in my legs, I couldn't catch up.

Forty-Three

In the first few weeks after Josh's death, I submerged myself in work — Kathryn's work, really. The distraction, along with my commitment to our child and to my own life, redeemed me from loneliness. Emily continued to join me for my OB appointments.

The visits to Meredith increased in frequency, and my friendship with the older woman deepened in intensity until we met at least once a week, sometimes more often, for lunch or tea.

Little-by-little, I gleaned morsels of the rest of her story — a story of survival and hope.

"I can't tell you how terrified I was when I was waiting for Tom to pick me up for our first date," Emily told me at lunch one day. "Here I am, leaving my baby with a babysitter for the first time. He was just a few months old, as I remember, and I'm fussing about making myself attractive for some man I didn't know." Emily took a bite of her salad, and chewed for a moment. She scrunched her face at the thought of the elusive memory, then laughed.

I waited in silence.

"I felt guilty, like I was being unfaithful to Arthur. Plus, it seemed wrong to leave my baby. Oh, Claire, I was a mess. I didn't want to answer the door when Tom came, right on time. But my sister, who was my babysitter, pushed me to the entryway and unlocked the deadbolt. I didn't have much choice then, did I?"

"Did Tom know you had a baby?" I asked.

"Yes. My friend who'd set us up had told him. That would have meant something to me, but she didn't say anything about it." Emily shook her head. "Do you know, he introduced himself and right away asked to see Eddie? When he did that, all the resistance bottled inside me just melted away. That's all I wanted in a man: someone who would respect and love me and care about children. It was a fun romance. He gave as much attention to Eddie as to me. We'll talk about it more, later. But now, enough about me. Tell me something I don't know about you. Tell me about your family."

By the time I'd finished my narrative, we had become close friends.

I watched the diminutive elderly lady study me one morning in mid-December. Dull skies threatened to pour dreariness into a day that had begun with a hint of sunshine. Deciduous trees clung tenaciously to the few leaves spared by a brittle wind, which penetrated layers of clothing and pierced the spirit. Lawns had gone dormant. The landscape was boring, in tones of brown and beige.

"Are you eating well, Claire?" Emily quizzed. This was the first question Emily posed every time I came for her.

I nodded.

"And sleeping?" the inquisitor continued.

"Not so well. It's lonely, Emily," I admitted

The older lady patted my hand but said nothing.

"You're doing really well, Claire, from my perspective," Meredith told me. "You're seeing your nephrologist, right?"

"Monthly," I responded. "My kidney function's holding steady. He's pleased, but he wants me to start coming every three weeks now."

Emily treated me to lunch that day. As always, we spoke of our husbands to keep their memories alive.

"Even after I married Tom, I mourned Arthur," Emily confided. "The past lingers; you don't want to lose those moments. My love for one husband never interfered with my relationship with the other. They were two precious gifts in my life. Some women go through life without knowing a special love. Me, I've had two. How blessed I am."

"I can't imagine wanting anyone but Josh," I said. A lump rose in the back of my throat. To the west, a light frosting of snow covered the foothills. Steel gray clouds hung over the peaks, covering the mountains in a shroud of gloom.

"Claire, you need to think about your future, too." Emily looked stern, like a fifth-grade schoolteacher counseling a recalcitrant student.

"What do you mean?"

"This bullshit about mourning for a suitable length of time — I advise you to ignore it." Emily leaned forward and whispered loudly. "If you can, find someone quickly. You need a man to help you raise your child, and it would be nice to have one to care about you as well. Just listen to me. I was alone only eight months after Arthur's death when Tom and I began dating. He welcomed a widow with a baby. Do you think I waited around for the sake of propriety? No way! We became engaged before my baby's first birthday."

"I don't know, Emily. I'm hardly in a condition to start dating." I pointed at my belly.

"Just be open to whatever comes your way — that's all I'm saying. It's what Josh would want for you. I've always believed Arthur watched out for me after he died and he still does. When he left for England he told me he'd never leave me alone, and I believed him. He sent Tom, I'm sure of it."

I gazed out the window. A young couple passed, pushing a stroller. Emily had a point — a child does need both parents. "I'll always be there for you," Josh had said. As if in reminder, Josh, Jr. gave me a lively kick inside my womb.

Forty-Four

ay by day, I witnessed brightness returning to Kathryn's eyes, a healthy glow to her complexion. When I arrived to accompany her to appointments with Brian, Kathryn's step bounced as she descended the stairs of her front porch and slid into the seat beside me.

"I'm getting stronger," she announced about six weeks after her surgery. "I want to ask Brian if I can start back to work part time. You're six months pregnant, girlfriend. It's time for you to start cutting back, don't you think?"

A drizzle of rain on the windshield blurred my vision. I hit the lever for one swipe of the windshield wiper that cleared the path before us. I had to agree with Kathryn, but the thought of my future paralyzed me. What would I do with the extra hours that would fall into my lap, and how would it be without the distraction of visiting patients, of having others need me? What would I do all day, alone?

"Work's important to you, isn't it?" Kathryn asked.

"Right now, yes. But I'll be okay once the baby's born."

Discomfort flooded the car. Kathryn sighed and folded her arms around her body. It seemed to me as if she were trying to shelter herself, not only from the blustery day, but also from the reality of my loss.

"Kathryn, I know it's time. You need to get back to your job, and I've got to create my future." I reached over and placed my hand on her forearm. "Think of what it would've been like for me if I didn't have these past few months to acclimate. I'm grateful you asked me to help, but by the time you're able to work full time, I'll welcome it. I have to prepare the nursery — and myself. Really, I'm ready."

"Thanks, Claire."

When we pulled into the doctor's parking lot, the rain had stopped. Through the wisps of clouds that veiled the sun, prisms of color formed an arc across the sky.

While Kathryn was dressing, Brian approached me. "How's everything going with your pregnancy?" A blush fanned up his neck till it reached his face. "I hope I'm not being too nosy."

"It's good, Brian. My labs are fine and the baby's healthy. Your dad and Meredith Jansen take good care of me."

"But you? How're you doing now that . . ." He left the sentence unfinished.

"Now that I'm alone?" The bluntness of my statement startled me. "Oh, Brian, I'm sorry. Reality's settling in, but I don't need to explain that to you, do I?"

"No, Claire, you don't. But loss affects each of us differently. I just thought maybe I could help."

I looked into those clear green eyes of his and found that I wanted him to say more.

"That we could help each other," he added. "I'd like to call you."

I smiled and hunched my shoulders.

"Is it too soon?" he asked.

"I'm not sure," was all I could say.

He looked off down the shadowy hallway, as if seeking approval from someone unseen, then locked his eyes on mine. "Josh will never be far from your thoughts or out of your mind, but I don't believe that you, or I for that matter, have hearts so tiny we can't open up to something new. I've always believed my wife would want me to move on."

It would just be for companionship, I reminded myself. It won't ever become more than that.

Brian handed me one of his business cards. "My home number's on the back. Take your time, Claire."

Without hesitation I reached into my purse and pulled out my own card and handed it to him. He held my hand for a bare moment, squeezing it before he let go, then entered another examining room, leaving me alone with a potpourri of emotions.

"How about if I start next Monday, four hours a day?" Kathryn said as we headed to the car. "You can update me on our patients, then cut back your hours gradually as I regain strength. We'll job-share for a while." This time, she helped me into the car then slid into the driver's seat.

"Whatever works for you and hospice," I agreed, suddenly detached from the need to stay busy. A new sensation, new possibilities buzzed inside me, but I wasn't ready to talk about it — not until I had something to say. "I'll have plenty to do at home."

Kathryn smiled. "You're getting excited, aren't you? I'd like to give you a shower next month."

I smiled. Pregnancy gave me a warm radiance that overcame the pallor left by Josh's death. "I'd like that, but can we plan it a little later? December's too busy. My mother's coming for a stay in mid-January and I bet Josh's mother would drive up too." When we pulled into the driveway, I added, "Let's keep it small, okay, but don't forget Emily."

After I changed clothes, I pulled our wedding album from the shelf in the library and carried it to the rocking chair in the soon-to-be nursery. I stroked it with trembling hands. This was the first time I'd touched the book since Josh's death. I opened the leather-bound tome at random and happened upon a portrait taken in the church. We faced away from the camera, looking together into the future. Rays of sunshine streamed through stained glass windows, symbolic of blessings we would share. Josh's arm wove around me, cupping my hand in his, and gestured toward an unknown future. It seemed soon to move on, but at that instant I understood what Josh would want me to do. I wasn't sure about the timing, though.

Forty-Five

November and December hurtled by in a whirlwind of activities. André and Mother came up to Reno for Thanksgiving while Joe and Elizabeth joined me for Christmas, along with Emily and the Scott's.

I tried to bury holiday nostalgia in a flurry of preparations for the baby. With family and friends I began new traditions, attending Midnight Mass with Emily.

By mid-January, I stepped out of my position as hospice medical director pro tem, and walked smack into the role of mother-to-be.

Thirteen women attended the baby shower. As guests departed, I reclined in a low chair, buried in piles of blue and yellow ribbons, torn wrapping paper, and presents. Melted ice cream puddled in china plates piled on a side table. The five of us who remained ignored the crumbs and disarray.

Elizabeth recounted stories of Josh's infancy with Helene and Emily listening on. "I couldn't get him to nap," she said. "He wanted to be in on everything. Joe and I took turns holding him, rocking and cooing. He'd stretch his little neck to see what was going on behind him."

"My Eddie was just the opposite," Emily added. "He was a dream baby. Only woke me up once a night for his feeding. The problem — he's still lazy. He'd sleep his life away, given the chance." Emily's laughter rolled through the room.

"Mom's dying to throw in her two bits," I whispered to Kathryn, who sat in the corner beside me. I'd abandoned my shoes and propped slightly swollen feet on an antique coffee table.

Kathryn leaned in and spoke in a hushed tone: "Your mother and Emily are both reaching out to Elizabeth."

"The two of them have already been down that path — losing a loved one — they're letting her talk it out."

I picked up the downy baby blanket Elizabeth had finished. Shades of pastel swirled in as I pressed the soft fuzz to my cheek. I recalled the picture of Josh as a baby, which held a place of honor on my mother-in-law's dresser. Soon I'd be able hold a very real reminder of my husband.

Forty-Six

The Wednesday after the shower, I stood in front of my full-length mirror. I'd just dressed to usher Kathryn to her final visit with Brian Forrest. Soft teal fabric draped my very pregnant form, making me feel feminine.

I thought of Brian's card, propped on my nightstand in front of Josh's picture. I smiled. I hadn't called yet because I wanted to wait for it to feel right. But today I would open the door an inch or two.

I crossed the room and picked up Josh's framed portrait. I gazed into his eyes and asked him for his blessing. His love-of-life filled me when our baby stretched inside of me. I kissed the photo, returned it to its place of honor, and pulled a coat from the hall closet before walking outside to wait for Kathryn.

"You look gorgeous, oh pregnant one," Kathryn lilted in greeting.

I folded into the warmth of the car, escaping the harsh winter day. "So how's everything, Dr. Scott?"

"It's so good to be back at work." Kathryn confided, lowering the visor to shield herself from bright sunshine that broke through a fast-moving cloud bank. "Nasty, cold day, isn't it?"

"Windy," I agreed.

We rode in silence for a while and I practiced my invitation in my head. I remembered inviting Daniel Healy to the Senior Prom at the Catholic girl's academy I'd attended. This time I didn't want to blurt it out all in one breath.

Back then I'd spoken so rapidly Daniel hadn't understood me and I'd had to go through the whole agonizing speech again, word-for-word. But the gawky boy had accepted and had even given me an orchid to wear on my wrist. Here I was, almost twenty years later, still grappling with the awkwardness of a seventeen year old.

"It's my last follow-up visit with Brian," Kathryn interrupted. "I wish you would have called him Claire — you're losing out."

"No, I'm not," I answered.

"When you don't have occasion to see someone on a regular basis, your chances slip away. Don't make me say 'I told you so.'" Kathryn shook her head like a mother scolding a child. "You'll be sorry, girlfriend."

"No, I won't." I turned toward Kathryn, adjusting the seatbelt woven tightly across my belly. "I'm asking him to dinner."

"Yesss!" Kathryn extended her hand to give a high five. "When you told me about Brian's interest, I was so excited. I'd about given up on you, Claire. How long's it been?"

"To be blunt, it feels like it's not long enough." I leaned my head back into the seat and closed my eyes. "But something is telling me to go for it." I looked out the window as we passed an empty field where horses grazed on the edge of urban sprawl. "But one thing I know for sure — I'll find no peace from you or Emily if I don't give it a try. That lady's relentless, Kathryn."

"I'm so glad she's become a part of your life," Kathryn said as she pulled into a parking place at Brian's office.

"It was a setup, I think, and I bet my Josh is behind it. I honestly believe he's watching out for me — for us." I struggled to extricate my lumbering body from the bucket seat. "But Kathryn, don't forget — it's just dinner, okay? I have absolutely no intention of anything more serious than friendship. Not for a few years, anyway."

Kathryn came around the car and gave me a hand. "Well, you've got to start somewhere."

I patted myself square on the abdomen. "If Brian accepts me like this —
it's a beginning."

"You've no idea how beautiful you look. You absolutely glow." Kathryn's
laughter, like wind chimes, filled the air.

When we entered the office, I wondered if I'd gone crazy. I'm only weeks
away from delivering a baby, I'm not much of a cook, and I'm planning on
inviting a man into my life. Over for dinner, I appended.

I studied Brian while he examined Kathryn, and listened to the timber
of his voice while he gave her final instructions. He spoke in soothing tones,
deep and gentle. I liked it. Josh sometimes talked too quickly, mumbled. I'd
have to make him repeat what he'd said. But still, the sounds of his words
lingered in my heart. A twinge of regret caused my body to tingle. If I gave
into my instinct at that very moment, I would bolt out the door and run till I
was home safe. Instead, I followed Brian into the hallway while Kathryn got
dressed. I took in a gulp of air.

He turned abruptly and met me face-to-face. "Well?"

"This weekend?" I straightened up and grinned. "I'm learning to cook —
want to let me practice on you?"

"You don't understand." His chuckle escaped from deep down inside.

I felt hotness fan out over my face and creep into my body. I'd waited too
long and he must have given up on me — or found someone else.

Brian continued. "I think of myself as a gourmet chef, you see — cooking's one of my passions. Would you allow me to show off for you?" A mischievous grin covered his face. "I like to garden, too."

"Sounds like someone's been telling stories," I said, as we walked into his
office.

Feigning innocence, Brian raised his hands as though to ward off the
accusation.

"I'll pick you up," he offered.

I nodded and reached for a pad of paper sitting on the edge of his desk, the offering of some pharmaceutical rep.

He took the paper from me and touched my hand lightly, explaining, "I won't need directions, Claire. Kathryn gave them to me when she debriefed me a few weeks ago. Five o'clock, okay?"

He hugged me like a brother.

That evening, I snuggled on the couch like a sandwich, between two dogs. I'd had to help Benisse up onto the couch and I suspected that it wouldn't be that long before I'd have to deal with yet another loss. I recalled a conversation Josh and I had had not long ago about bringing in another dog soon, so that Murphy would have a chance to get used to him and we wouldn't notice the emptiness so much.

Josh had wanted another Golden Retriever but I'd campaigned for a different breed. "I don't want to risk comparison," I'd told him. "Any Golden we get will fall short of our expectations. We'd want her to be just like Benisse, don't you think?"

"It's not something we need to deal with yet, honey," he'd reminded me. "We'll know what to do when the time comes."

My thoughts turned naturally to Brian. He wasn't like Josh, as far as I could tell, even if he could cook. His appearance wasn't as athletic and I'd make book that if he was into sports at all it was as an observer, or perhaps, an occasional golfer. For all I knew, he might not even care about the same things Josh did.

"He's not bad looking," I said to Murphy, who turned his head and glanced at me, then snuggled back into a ball. I'd seen just a touch of silver in Brian's auburn hair and, instead of Josh's carefree expression, Brian almost always had an air of concern about him. But then, look what my contact with him had been — dealing with Kathryn's life-threatening condition.

I reminded myself that I wasn't really looking for a replacement. No one could replace my Josh. So maybe I am right about finding a new breed of dog. Go for someone different, Claire. Don't put yourself in the position of having to compare.

I tossed aside the romance novel I'd been pretending to read, and felt a bit of excitement stirring deep inside, in that old, familiar place reserved for love.

If Brian is going to become someone important in my life, it will be for who he is. Not just a replacement.

Forty-Seven

That night, after our first dinner, I lay awake for hours. I rewound the tape of my memory and played the events of the evening, frame-by-frame, on the screen of my mind.

Brian's gold turtleneck sweater contrasted with his hair, presenting a palette of autumn colors. When he rang the doorbell, unlike Emily, I had rushed to answer. He greeted me with a broad smile that deepened dimples I'd barely noticed before.

"Your chauffer awaits, my lady," he'd said with a sweeping bow. In the same motion, he presented me with a yellow rose he had hidden behind his back.

Josh always gave me pink roses, until the day he proposed to me. On that day it was white. "Why white?" I'd asked. "Because white reflects all colors, like you reflect everything I want in life."

It didn't take the dogs long to bound toward the stranger. Murphy's tail wagged like a metronome, measuring out the beat of a piece of music, written in allegro. Benisse jumped up and slopped a kiss on Brian's cheek.

If he can tolerate this, he'll pass one test, I thought as I took the flower from him. When I retreated to the kitchen to put it in water, I glanced at our wedding picture that sat on a bookcase in the formal living room. Josh's eyes seemed to catch mine in his own. His look was one of hope — his smile, one of encouragement. I sucked in a breath, then walked back to Brian, who awaited my return.

"Your home is beautiful, Claire," Brian said. "And your dogs are almost as bad as my Eskie — I mean that in a good way."

I smiled and accepted his help with my coat. Okay, buddy, you've aced this one, I thought, and followed Brian into the shadows of evening.

He lived just over a mile from me. When he unlocked the front door and ushered me in, an American Eskimo greeted us. Long white hair, perfectly groomed, flowed from the dog's small body.

"Meet Molli," Brian said, leaning over to scratch the animal behind the ears. "She's my current girlfriend."

I squatted as best as I could and came face-to-face with large black eyes. Molli nuzzled me, then trotted off to the kitchen.

The evening passed in slow motion. Brian's cooking almost rivaled Josh's and I savored every bite. When we cleared the dishes, I noticed that he did surpass Josh when it came to cleaning up after himself. Guilt smoldered in the pit of my stomach for having picked up on that.

I sipped a cup of herbal tea as Brian rolled a brandy snifter in the palms of his hands. Our conversation lingered. I listened as he told a story of his father: "Whatever you do, Brian," Jeff had told his son, "Whatever you do, don't become a doctor. You won't have any time to yourself, except Wednesday afternoon when you might go golfing if you're not held up in surgery."

"But you love medicine, Dad," Brian had answered.

"Don't do it, boy. It's hard and you're not a good enough student — you'll never make it."

Predictably, Brian had ignored his father's advice. It was only at his graduation that, puffed up with pride, his dad confessed that his greatest wish had been to see Brian follow in his footsteps.

I could picture the elder Dr. Forrest, my nephrologist. He'd probably worn a bow tie and a vest for graduation. His wry sense of humor had amused me through many difficult days — his skill had saved my life. The day he'd told me I would need a transplant I'd sprinted from his office in a rage. He had followed me to the car. Goddamn it, Claire, I remembered him hollering. You've always been a fighter — this is a hell of a time to quit. The words had served me as lifeline on the days when it all seemed too much to bear.

"Dad knew I'd do the very thing he admonished me not to," Brian said. "The old bastard fooled me again."

When Brian dropped me off at home, he walked me to the front door. A simple goodnight was all he said in response to my thanks.

Does he know how scared I am? I wondered.

I closed the door behind me and watched Brian drive away. Later, when I climbed the stairs to the bedroom, the dogs stayed at the front door, waiting like they always waited for Josh. Maybe I'm not the only one who'd like a male companion, I thought.

Forty-Eight

It wasn't until the third week of our friendship that Brian sat beside me on the couch in the family room of my home and took my hand in both of his. Benisse lay splayed at our feet, snoring gently, while Murphy snuggled on the seat beside Brian and forced him to move closer to me.

"I told my dad we've been spending some time together."

"What'd he say?"

"Not much. He peered at me over those bifocals he wears, then after what seemed like forever, Dad smiled. 'I'm glad,' he said. That was about the sum of it."

"He's a good man."

"Just a bit rough around the edges, Claire. He likes you a lot, I know — said you had balls."

I snorted. "That's supposed to be a compliment?"

"From him, yeah. A couple of days later, he told me you were a keeper. We weren't even talking about you. Just out of nowhere he says, 'Claire Bergano, she's quite a woman. She's a keeper.'" Brian laughed, then reached over and scratched Murphy behind the ears. The terrier turned over on his back, spread eagle, and purred. "Think our dogs will get along?" Brian asked.

"Yep, I do."

In the fireplace, the flames began to falter. Brian let go of my hand and rose to add a couple of logs. Sparks flew and crackled.

When he returned to my side, Brian put his arm around my shoulder and eased me toward him. "You're getting close to your due date, aren't you?"

"Just two or three more weeks."

"How are you doing? Are you scared?"

"No, not really — I'm in good hands. I just wish that Josh was here to share it, to help me."

Brian didn't answer.

I saw his even features outlined by the glow of the fire. A slight smile curved his lips. I felt the warmth of his body next to me. My eyes traveled to his hands — the hands of a surgeon. Finely tapered fingers interlaced with mine. He was a good friend, and I felt safe with him. For now, I was afraid to feel anything else.

The cold night air slapped me in the face as we exited the Pioneer Center. It had been years since I'd been able to attend a symphony, and powerful chords of Tchaikovsky still thundered in my core. The Reno Phil had acquitted themselves well under the direction of the new conductor — a woman.

Brian pulled me closer as we tagged along behind Kathryn and Michael. "I say we all go get a hot drink," he said.

"Sounds good to us," Michael agreed, answering for both of them. "A hot brandy would work for me."

In the small café/bar Michael and Brian huddled together, talking politics while Kathryn and I listened in without comment.

"It looks like they could be good friends," Kathryn said.

"Looks like they already are."

"Michael likes Brian."

"So do I — a lot."

My thoughts turned to the conflicting emotions that used me as a battleground. I knew I had barely begun to grieve, but couldn't deny the strong attraction I felt for Brian. It felt so right. And it felt so wrong.

"I'm feeling a bit crazy, Kathryn, and it's more than just the hormones that are a part of being pregnant."

"I can imagine," Kathryn said. "But don't forget how we counsel our hospice families, that it's okay to move on."

"But I haven't begun to process all that's happened."

"And how we tell them that there's no such thing as closure. That grief is a forever-process that just gets more manageable with time."

"But it's only been a few months."

"And that the timing is different for everyone," Kathryn said, outlining the hospice playbook.

"I know everyone tells me to get on with my life, that Josh would want me to move ahead, that our baby needs a father." I lowered my voice. "I have no problem with that; it's the feelings I have for Brian that confuse me. I want him for that, but more than that."

"You want him for you. Isn't that okay, Claire?"

Before I could respond, Brian turned to me. "So what do you think, Claire?"

I had no idea what they'd been discussing. My thoughts were searching for an answer to Kathryn's question.

Forty-Nine

It seemed counterintuitive that I could experience joy in the midst of so much sadness and loss. Josh's absence still touched raw nerve endings, and at times the pain was unbearable.

The emptiness would happen in those moments when I'd look for Josh to show him a rainbow, or the early morning sun hitting Peavine Mountain just so — so that it shone like highly polished brass or a burning ember.

I would taste it when I'd walk into our empty bedroom on a dark night and catch a sky full of stars shining through the window — a sky meant to be shared with someone you love.

But interludes of happiness invaded those gloomy winter days as well.

Sometimes in the evening, I'd stretch out on the couch with a good book and a CD of Schumann or Bach playing softly in the background. Wind could be howling outside or snow gently layering the railings around the deck — it didn't matter. The fireplace exuded warmth and then, out of nowhere, our baby stirred or even kicked, and Josh would be with me in some obscure way. In spite of my aloneness, I knew I was protected.

And then it happened that I didn't find myself alone so much.

Five days out of seven, the doorbell would ring and there I'd find Brian — never empty-handed. He'd offer a potted plant or a bouquet of fresh flowers, a loaf of freshly baked bread. One time, even, a spa basket. "Don't worry," he told me, "I don't expect to share it with you," he laughed and set it on the stairway that led to a place we both knew to be off-limits.

At times, I would be with Brian and forget he wasn't Josh.

That's what happened one Saturday in late January. That was the day I succumbed, once more, to fear.

For four days, snowstorms passed through in the early morning hours, dumping several feet of soft white stuff in the valley.

Brian made sure I didn't have to leave the house. An early morning phone call, another check midday, and in the evening he'd make his way down slick streets into my neighborhood, as yet untouched by the plowing crew. He shoveled and sanded and cared for me — and I liked it, had even grown to expect it, I guess.

When the cold front finally passed through, the snow began to melt and I watched the banks shrink in size and form rivulets in the streets of my neighborhood, leading to the Truckee. The sun scattered diamonds across the yard, and blue jays emerged from the spruce and junipers to gorge on seed in the feeder Josh had built not long ago.

Early Saturday afternoon, Brian arrived with a bag of classic films and a tub of popcorn. We settled in for a movie marathon with two dogs at our feet, who were on the watch for the occasional kernel we would toss their way.

The hours went by in a blur, along with images of Tracy and Hepburn, Wayne and O'Hara, Rogers and Astaire, and how many others, I don't remember. We laughed and cried, lost in a world of imagination and happy endings.

When it was over, it was night. Darkness had slithered in, and chill had settled once more. Temperatures plunged into single digits.

Brian took my hands in his as he stood to leave, and kissed me tenderly on the lips.

"Today was special, Claire. I want it to be like this forever."

So do I, I admitted to myself. So do I.

"Not yet, Brian," was what I said, though. "Someday, maybe."

He nodded, but the look in his eyes was one of sadness. As he walked out to his car, I wanted to run after him — but something held me back. I closed the door behind him and walked back into the room where the fire sputtered its dying breath and two dogs snored gently before it. I sank back into the couch and a sense of panic took hold of me, its icy fingers encircling my heart. I began to cry as I realized that I couldn't go back and yet I feared moving ahead. It was too soon. Brian was not Josh, as much as I wanted him to be, and it wasn't fair to him to lead him on, to use him to fill up that void so deep within the center of my being.

I reached for the phone. I hated to do it like this, but I was afraid that if we were together I would lose the courage to say what I knew needed to be said.

The message I left was long and rambling. I don't remember my exact words or the reasons I gave him but it must have been clear enough for him to understand that I needed some space.

Fifty

J.C. *Penney's buzzed. Kathryn and Emily flanked me* as we wandered through the store toward the baby department.

Emily sported a suit, navy with white trim. She carried a small handbag and wore sensible shoes. She led our brigade of shoppers, taking charge of hunting down last minute items to fully outfit the nursery.

I shuffled through the aisles. It was only ten days till my due date and I was ready. This has got to be my last foray, I thought, unless I want to induce an early labor.

"Just make sure we have the necessities," I told Kathryn. "I'm not up for much more of this."

We roamed about the baby department and caressed soft fabrics, choosing calming shades. Kathryn piled the counter high with cloth diapers and whimsical baby toys.

People stepped aside for me, allowing me to go first at the cashier. A middle-aged woman caught our attention. Sadness in the lady's eyes told a story of unfulfilled dreams.

A younger girl, not much more than high school age, checked us out. Her face was covered with acne scars and braces filled her mouth. I winced at the memory of awkward adolescence.

Mother came to mind. She would arrive the following day. I breathed a sigh of relief that I wouldn't need to repeat this safari with her.

"My doctor's pleased with me, Mom," I had reported during my weekly call the previous Saturday. "The baby's finally dropped, getting ready to enter our world. Meredith credits herself with the fact that I've carried him to term, without complications. She told me that when Josh died midway through my pregnancy, she worried I wouldn't make it. Good thing she kept that to herself."

My mother insisted on making travel arrangements. "I want to be there — I don't want you to be alone when you go into labor."

She had visited every month to take inventory of my needs, and then spent lavishly for the baby and for me. In November, she'd overseen the remodel of my old office and, finally, in January she'd hung my paintings. Brush strokes in bright primary hues filled the paper that Mother had framed in white with mats in colors complementary to the pictures, but in softer tones.

"It's like a nursery on HGTV," Mother boasted to me at her last visit. "And you're so talented, Claire," she repeated, pointing to the artwork like a docent leading a tour. "We'll need to convert another room into a studio."

I'd settled into Josh's office but kept it as he'd left it, carefully piling his paperwork into neat stacks — understanding that eventually I would need to organize it and research our investments myself. A while back, Brian told me he'd help, but that wasn't going to happen now, was it?

The office space seemed big enough for a studio, I admitted. I could sell Josh's free weights to create room for my art paraphernalia, but for now I was too busy with other things.

"Let's get some lunch." Kathryn took my arm and steered me toward a table in the mall's food court. "I'm starved, and you've been on your feet too long, Claire."

Emily nodded in assent, snaring a light package from my hand.

From an orange acrylic bucket seat, I accepted the attention of my two dear friends. I admitted my fatigue, leaned into the unforgiving chair, and tried to position myself to find comfort. I waited while my friends went in search of food.

I viewed Kathryn as she approached the table, juggling a chicken sandwich, mixed green salad, and two sodas on a small tray. "I thought we could split these," Kathryn offered, dishing up greens on an extra plate.

With caution, Emily walked across the open court, balancing a full bowl of vegetable soup and homemade French rolls. The scent of freshly baked bread tempted my senses.

We ate in silence for a few minutes, while listening to the buzz of conversation in the crowded area.

My mind wandered to Brian — the dinners we'd shared at his house, an occasional lunch taken on the run, and the phone calls every single evening after our first date. Those conversations had comforted me. He was funny, with a wry sense of humor like his father's, stubborn like Josh, and sensitive. He used to let me ramble on about the past and drew my hopes into the future.

Then there was that Saturday of movies.

I missed him.

"So, how are you and the young Dr. Forrest doing?" Kathryn asked in a nonchalant manner. Emily stopped eating, set her spoon at the side of her bowl, and focused attention on me.

I answered in a non-committal tone of voice. "He's a nice man, a good cook. He's easy to be with."

"And?" Emily encouraged.

"We're not seeing each other right now. It's been more than a week." I busied myself with picking onions out of the salad, but offered no further information.

"I ran into him at the hospital yesterday." Kathryn's brown eyes searched mine. "He seemed, well, tired — now that I think of it, even sad. What happened, Claire?"

I took a bite of my sandwich and chewed a long time.

"Come on, Claire," Emily insisted.

"Leave it alone, you two. Don't you think I've got enough going on at the moment? You both know I never had any intention of going beyond friendship. It's just too soon." Sweat formed on the palms of my hands. "It's way too soon, ladies — I'm not ready." I took another bite of my sandwich.

"Time's a human invention," Emily provoked. "Love transcends time." A suppressed chuckle escaped Emily's lips once she'd completed her philosophical treatise.

I had to fight off an urge to smile and agree. Embarrassment ran down my face, masked as tears.

"Emily wants you married before the year's out," Kathryn warned.

"Okay, ladies. Here's how it is," I began.

It seemed like the clamor in the vast eating space subsided and fellow shoppers were hanging on my words.

"I really enjoyed being with Brian and I wouldn't rule out seeing him again — even falling in love. But please, stop bugging me — at least until I have this baby." I folded my arms around my abdomen, locking eyes with Kathryn then with Emily. "I asked him to back off for a while."

"Now that he's entered the world of dating again, I bet he won't want to wait too long," Kathryn warned. "Now he remembers how good it is not to be alone. Don't be surprised if his timeframe is different than yours. Like I told you before, women are lined up waiting to get a hold of him. You're a fool."

Emily didn't say a word.

I felt miserable. "I don't think I can eke out the energy to shop anymore," I sighed, as we piled our dishes on the cafeteria tray. "Can we go home after this? The walking is getting to be too much."

A dull backache nagged at me.

"We're about finished up," Kathryn acknowledged. "Let your mother wrap up the rest. That'll be one way to get her out of the house in case you need a breather."

When we dropped Emily off at her home, she bent and kissed me on the forehead. "I bet the next time I see you, you'll be a mother, Claire."

Squeezing Emily, I agreed. "Could be."

In bed that night, my emotions roiled, keeping me awake.

When I'd start to fall asleep I'd think of Brian. Of the sound of disappointment in his voice, and what I imagined to be anger when he called back as soon as he'd played my message.

Then Emily's chiding voice would awaken me, and Kathryn's — and I thought I heard Josh telling me to get on with my life, but I'd jerk awake in the new-moon darkness and find myself alone.

Then I realized the date — February thirteenth. Josh had proposed to me on Valentine's Day.

I finally fell into a restless sleep and dreamed that Josh stood beside me, coaching me in the delivery room. I wanted to cling to the feeling of his presence and to allow him to hold me, so I resisted awakening. But finally a warm wetness between my legs, followed by a strong cramping pain that spread from my back and circled my abdomen, jolted me back into the real world. I reached for the phone and dialed Brian's number.

Fifty-One

Thirteen hours later, I surfaced from a muddled world of pain, noise, bright lights and confusion. People who I loved surrounded me — I was sure of that: Kathryn, Michael, and Josh. I held his hand, squeezed it, while my head whirled in a daze of medications. I remembered calling Josh's name, but it wasn't his voice that responded. It was a comforting voice, but it wasn't Josh.

A crying baby startled me. It was close by. The cry pierced the quiet again and I opened my eyes, and captured Meredith placing a bundle on my belly. Reality hit me as I reached out and welcomed Josh, Jr. into my arms.

A wrinkled little face, with scrunched-closed eyes and a bow-tie mouth made sucking noises in the air. Tiny fists wrapped tight around his thumbs, clinging to the known, unwilling to let go. I inserted a finger into the gripping vise and Josh, Jr. grasped me and pulled me toward his hungry mouth.

I looked around the room. Kathryn and Michael stood to my left. Meredith remained at the foot of the bed, and Brian held my right hand. It wasn't Josh — I knew that. Brian was the one who had driven me to the hospital, stayed with me, called Kathryn, and coached me through the contractions.

"You're fine, Claire," he said. "Your baby's perfect."

Kathryn approached and laid a hand on my shoulder. Tears magnified her brown eyes. "You did great, girlfriend."

"Everything's a blur. What time was he born?" I asked.

"Twelve fourteen," Meredith answered. "Lunch time."

I looked at Brian.

"Valentine's Day," he grinned.

Bittersweet joy brimmed over into my smile. "It's perfect."

Kathryn was patting my brow with a damp washcloth when Meredith stepped forward and addressed my companions. "I don't want to break the spell, but Claire needs to get some rest and we need to finish checking out this handsome boy."

Kathryn leaned over and brushed her lips across my forehead. "Michael and I are going to pick up the proud grandmother. Last Helene knew, you were still in labor. She'll be landing in about ten minutes.

"Did you call Emily?" I asked.

"We told her we'd pick her up on the way back with Helene — is that okay with you?"

Nodding, I watched Meredith in the background, examining my baby. A pang of sadness broke through my contentment like the wisp of a cloud crossing the sun on a clear day. Only one person would be missing, I realized.

Meredith made no move to evict Brian, who'd pulled up a chair and settled beside my bed. Nor did I.

"You're not at work?" I asked.

"Of course I am," he grinned. "I'm overseeing a high-risk delivery of one of my father's patients."

"Seriously, Brian." Apprehension sneaked its way into my thoughts. Here I was again, with everything happening so fast — but I had no inclination to stop it at the moment.

"I'm sorry, Brian — and grateful."

"I'm a patient man, Claire." He shifted in the chair and drew his brows together. "When you called last night, I didn't have to think twice. I guess I believed it would happen sooner or later."

"I haven't been fair to you."

"That's in the past. What do you want now, Claire?" He stood and walked to the window. "Wait; don't answer that. This is no time to get into this discussion. Just let me know when you're clear about what you're looking for. I'm willing to wait, but not forever. Okay?"

"I had this morning blocked out for a round of golf," he continued, "but I do need to leave soon. I have patients scheduled in about an hour. Thanks for including me — I'm so happy you asked me to be a part of this. I love you, you know."

When I opened my mouth, I found no words to answer Brian. Instead, I reached for his hand and squeezed it tightly, as though willing him to stay with me. To stay forever.

"We'll talk later," Brian said. "For now, enjoy your baby and your family. Josh's parents will be here this evening, too, but know I'm only a phone call away, okay?" Brian ran his fingers through my damp hair and brushed his lips across my cheek. "Why did you call me instead of Kathryn?" he asked.

"It just seemed the right thing to do." You were the first person I thought of, I didn't say. I felt my smile spread to my eyes. "Thank you."

I watched the comforting man stride across the room, remove his surgical gown, and dump it in a hamper. Brian blew me a kiss before he left.

Finally alone, I fell into a deep slumber. Josh took Brian's place in the chair and leaned his head on my shoulder. When I awakened, I was all alone.

Fifty-Two

Mother remained with me for three weeks following the birth of her grandson.

Two days before her scheduled departure, I relaxed in the nursery's rocking chair as she ironed a new pair of curtains she'd bought to complement the wooden shades. Josh, Jr. dozed in my arms.

"So tell me about Dr. Forrest," she asked point blank.

"He's a wonderful nephrologist. He and Meredith managed my pregnancy so well. Given all that could have happened, it went off without a hitch." I shifted in the chair gingerly, not wanting to awaken the baby. Sunlight streamed in through the half-opened shades, washing the room in gold.

"That's not the Dr. Forrest I'm talking about. Tell me about Brian." Mother unplugged the iron, placed the gingham curtains carefully across the crib, and pulled up a chair. A mischievous glint in her dark eyes teased me.

"He's Kathryn's urosurgeon and we went to medical school together," I began.

"And his wife died a few years ago," she continued.

"It sounds like you already know everything. Okay, I like him a lot. We've gone on a few dates — I guess you could call them that." I felt cotton form in my mouth, reminding me of the inquisitions I sat through when I was younger.

"And you called him to take you to the hospital," Helene probed.

"I did — he's a doctor. Okay, so's Kathryn. Mother, I don't know why I called Brian. I didn't think it through. But I'll confess — I'm glad I did."

Continuing to fix her stare on me, Mother added, "It makes sense to me — I'm glad you have someone like Brian. You're too young to have to go through life alone."

"Who told you all of this? Who've you been talking to?" I asked. My heart took off like a dog on an agility course.

"I have my sources," she responded with a wink.

"Emily. You two are scheming aren't you?" Part of me wanted to deny there was anything between Brian and me — the other wanted to talk about him till nightfall.

"Claire, he's called a few times and we've spoken. He seems so kind, and he cares about you."

"You didn't give me the calls?" I tilted my head, looking at Mother as she continued ironing.

"I told him to call back, so you could answer the phone yourself. I'd like to meet him, so I invited him for lunch tomorrow."

"My God!"

By then, I'd decided to leave the door open to a future with Brian. Something about it felt so right and the fog of fear had begun to lift. Oh, I wasn't ready to rush it, but I'd come to acknowledge that I didn't want to be alone, that it wouldn't be fair to my baby. And, even though I wasn't remembering my dreams right now, it seemed that Josh was in them and that he was encouraging me to go ahead. At least that's what I wanted to believe.

Mother's voice broke through my musings. "I know — I've got nerve. But it may be a couple of months before I get up here. I want to know who we're talking about when I call."

Laughter began to uncoil inside me. When I finally let it loose the baby woke up and began to cry. "Okay, you're the boss," I conceded, knowing I had little choice in the matter. Besides, I liked the idea of having my mother meet

Brian. I had to believe that she had learned valuable lessons in her previous judgments of Josh and Lauren and could offer input, when it was time. If it ever comes to that, I corrected myself.

"I hope it hasn't been too awful for you, Brian — being scrutinized by three women, that is." Emily's eyes twinkled from beneath scraggly brows. "Especially since two of us are old ladies."

"Speak for yourself, Emily." Mother carried a stack of empty plates from the table.

Brian stood to help her.

"You and Claire go on in the family room." Emily took the plate from his hand. "We'll join you in a minute. I've got to cut up my world-famous lemon bars and brew a fresh pot of coffee."

"Thank you, Mrs. Hardin."

"Emily," she corrected. "You might as well get used to me. I'm one of Claire's best friends and, quite frankly, if it weren't for me she would never have considered dating again."

"I told you so," I whispered. "The great conspiracy." I led Brian into the adjoining room where the baby dozed.

"Thank God for Emily," Brian said. He stopped and looked at the infant, then me. "It's true what she says, isn't it? That you were scared even at the beginning?"

I nodded. "I was — and, as much as I enjoyed being with you, that fear seemed to grow the closer we became."

"Is this still how you feel? I'm not pushing you, am I?"

"Not so much." I laced my fingers through his. "I want to move ahead, Brian."

His smile spread across his face. "I told you I'm a patient man. I'm willing to wait — and work for those things that are worth the trouble."

While we waited for Mother and Emily, I told Brian the story of Emily's second love.

"Do you believe her, Claire?" he asked me. "Do you believe there's room in our lives for new love?"

"I know there is. I've found it."

A crystal blue sky filled the view from the window. Pendulous drops of water hung from naked tree branches. A ray of sun broke through a prism and tiny rainbows reflected on the glass of the coffee table.

An hour later, Mother and I watched as Brian and Emily walked to his car.

Emily threaded her arm in his. Her left hand sliced the air, accenting her lively conversation, but she spoke in a tone so low that I couldn't catch a word.

Brian's expression left me wondering, and filled me with gratitude for the two special people who had stepped into my life.

Fifty-Three

The next day, after I dropped Mother off at the airport, I swung the car by St. Joe's.

"Hey, I'm ready for a break," Kathryn said. "How about lunch?"

I looked at Josh, Jr. who wiggled in my arms. "I don't know — where could we go? Our usual haunts aren't exactly baby-friendly."

"I know one that is. You drive," Kathryn said. She walked toward my car and opened the door.

After a drive through Wendy's, she directed me to Crissie Caughlin Park and we left the motor idling to stave off the February chill. "You look so healthy, Claire. Motherhood becomes you. I'm so happy for you."

"I love being a mother. God, Kathryn, it's not even a year since you tossed that idea my way."

"You know, Claire, I'm not sure I even meant it. I was just trying to get your mind off of your job loss."

"That seemed like such a big deal then," I admitted.

A woman bundled in a faux shearling coat ambled by, tugged by a massive black dog. Steam billowed from the dog's mouth as he pulled at his leash and dragged his mistress behind him.

"So, do you think you'll want to go back to work?" Kathryn asked.

"I don't know. Right now I just want to concentrate on my baby. And Brian."

Kathryn's head snapped around and a smile widened across her face. "You mean it, don't you?"

"I want to say I do, yes. What do you think? Am I completely crazy?"

At the far end of the park, the woman gave up her tug of war and released the dog from his leash. In a surge of energy, the dog bounded toward the river and splashed in the frigid water.

"Josh was all about life, Claire," Kathryn said. "Just being around him used to animate me. Right now, his kidney is doing its job, keeping me going. You know he'd want you to go for it."

"I know that in my head, but how long do you think it'll take the rest of me to catch up, Kathryn?"

"Don't over-think it, girlfriend. Trust yourself; you'll know what to do. But for heaven's sake, don't dillydally. Don't forget..."

"I know, I know. You personally know of a lot of women who'd like to be in my position." The huge dog raced up and down the bank, in and out of the Truckee, until he came and collapsed at the feet of his owner.

"Like I said," Kathryn reminded me again, "just follow your heart."

When we said goodbye, I watched Kathryn trot up the steps to her office. On the porch, she turned and waved.

Thank you, Josh. Because of you, I didn't have to lose her, too.

After settling the baby down for his afternoon nap, I dialed Brian's direct line and left a message.

Late in the afternoon, I sat alone in the family room. The fireplace filled the area with warmth and the scent of pinecones I'd collected in the fall. Cradled in my arms, protected from the chill, lay Josh, Jr. I hadn't heard a word from Brian.

I studied the delicate features of the baby's face, the perfect shape of tiny curved fingernails. He'd nursed greedily before slipping into sleep. The orbs of his eyes beneath delicate lids moved left and right. It was too early to determine whom he would favor, but my vote went to Josh.

The chime of the doorbell startled me. I rose cautiously, taking care not to awaken the baby. I peeked out the curtain beside the entryway and my eyes took in Brian.

He stood tall, with bags of groceries in both arms, and greeted me with a broad smile.

There was certain shyness in his expression and it dawned on me that perhaps, he, too, felt fear. Disarmed, I unfastened the lock, opening the door to allow him entrance. "What are you doing here?"

"I'm going to fix you dinner — I figured you have enough to do. I've joined your conniving support group to make sure you get adequate nutrition."

"Support group?'" Self-consciously, I ran my fingers through my hair and moistened my lips.

"Your entourage, of course: Kathryn, your mother, and Emily. Even Michael. They're all on our case. Come on, let me in and close that door. It's February!" Setting down his parcels, Brian removed his overcoat and hung it on the banister. Pulling aside the coverlet, he peered at Josh Jr., who didn't stir. Brian raised his eyes to mine.

"Pork chops okay," he asked, "with sweet potatoes and broccoli?"

I wrinkled my nose and answered, "Broccoli?"

"You'll like what I do with it — wait and see." Brian heaved the bags into his arms and headed straight for the kitchen. As though he owned the place, he settled in to prepare dinner.

The baby continued to doze as I dragged a chair to the counter and observed my new chef. "How'd you get out of the office so early?"

"Today's surgery day. My schedule was light enough to finish up, check on all my post-op patients, shop and make it here by four-thirty."

"I have an appointment with your dad tomorrow," I told him.

"He told me." Brian sorted through Josh's spices and pulled out what he wanted for the meat. "Josh and I could've opened a restaurant together — his collection's almost the same as mine."

"That's good — I won't have too many adjustments to make." I suspected he could see me blushing.

Brian interrupted his culinary adventure and stared at me. One corner of his mouth pulled into a slight smile.

I laughed. "That's not how I meant it," I defended myself. "Not exactly, anyway."

Josh Jr. began to cry, interrupting the confusing energy, which overpowered me at the moment.

"Got a diaper to change," I announced, grateful for the chance to make an escape. "See you in a few minutes."

Once in the nursery, I tended to Josh Jr., laid him in his crib, and fell into the rocking chair. "What am I doing?" I asked myself in a coarse whisper. "I love Brian, I do. But I'm still so scared."

I buried my head in my hands and prayed aloud. "Oh Josh, help me. Help me know what to do. You know I'll always love you."

Silence answered me. When I raised my head, the red button on the baby monitor announced that not only Josh, but also Brian had heard my prayer.

After I slipped into the bedroom to freshen up, I checked on my dozing baby and tiptoed back to the kitchen.

Brian looked up as I approached. He opened his arms and enfolded me. His lingering kiss aroused my desire for him.

"I'll always love Joanne, too, Claire." He held me with gentleness for a moment, then let me go and returned to his cooking.

Fifty-Four

The following afternoon in Jeff Forrest's office, I sat across from the man who'd brought me through so much.

Jeff studied my lab reports, then looked up at me. A pair of bifocals sat on the tip of his nose. The physician pushed them up with his index finger. "Damn specs," he said, then cleared his voice. "Remarkable. All of your tests are right in line. Remember that day, Claire. What was it, five or six years ago, when I told you to get on the transplant list?"

I nodded. Tears filled my eyes as I thought of all that had unfolded since then. Kathryn, Josh, Josh Jr., and now, Brian. I wondered how much Jeff knew about me and his son.

"You've come a long way; you've been through a lot, and survived. I knew you'd make it, Claire. Back then you were so angry. You said you wanted to give up, but I never saw anyone with so much will to fight."

"It's been hard, Jeff. I don't know if I could have faced it if I had known then what I know now — I might not have had the courage to go through it. If I'd refused Kathryn's kidney, life would be so different." I looked down and gazed upon my son, asleep in my arms — the baby born of the love I'd shared with Josh. I could never let go of life. Things were exactly as they should be, and I trusted they would continue that way.

"You're still young enough to have another baby, you know," Jeff quipped, "if you hurry up about it. I'd love to be a grandfather."

Winter is Past

Victoria C. Slotto

A Reader's Guide

Discussion Questions

1. In the opening of the story, Claire confesses that she is overwhelmed by fear. What do you believe she feared more than anything else? Why? In one word, what is your greatest fear?

2. Why do you believe Helene and Robert chose to keep their family tragedy hidden from their children? How did this secret affect Helene's life? Claire's? André's?

3. Are you (or would you consider becoming) an organ donor? To whom would you consider giving a kidney? A spouse? A child? Another relative? A friend or co-worker? A stranger? What might be the benefits to an organ donor as a result of their generosity?

4. The story addresses end-of-life issues. Do you have an Advance Directive in which you have designated someone to make medical decisions for you in the event you are unable to make them for yourself? How would it be for you to make these choices for someone who has no Advance Directive? What are the advantages of Advance Directives?

5. Claire and Kathryn were friends for many years. What qualities do you believe nurture and sustain such a friendship? How did they play out in their story?

6. Michael's anger compounded the crisis Kathryn was facing. If you were Kathryn, how would you deal with him? Do you believe the friendship between the two couples would have endured had Josh not offered to become Kathryn's donor?

7. Both Kathryn and Claire have a sense of Josh's presence. What are your thoughts about the afterlife — do you believe those who have gone before us are able to communicate to us in dreams or in other ways? Do dreams play any role in your spiritual or psychological life? Can you give examples?

8. Why was Emily such an influence on Claire? Do you believe God puts other people in our lives for a reason? How do you believe Claire would have reacted to her situation without Emily's support?

9. What factors played into Helene's downhill spiral into alcoholism? What was her moment of redemption?

10. At the end of the story, the author leaves it up to the reader to imagine what will happen next. How do you think a sequel would begin?

Interview with Victoria C. Slotto

What inspired you to write this novel?

As I writer, I often discover story lines by asking the question: what if? In 2001, when I learned I was in end-stage renal failure, a friend and co-worker, Paula Roukie-Dinkins, offered me a kidney. An obvious answer to the what if question is, "What if something happened to Paula?" The rest evolved from there.

Is your story autobiographical?

The only autobiographical aspects are related to the kidney transplant. All the other characters and events just came to me as the story unfolded. My 90-something year old mother was concerned that she inspired Helene. The only similarity is that Mom's home was in my mind as I wrote the story. However, I did draw from my own experience with dialysis and the surgery itself.

How else has your background impacted your writing?

I'm a Registered Nurse and worked most of my career in the field of death and dying. I've had a lot of experience with families who are dealing with grief. I was a nun for 28 years and you will find threads of Catholicism and spirituality woven throughout the book. And, of course, my first-hand experience as a kidney transplant survivor and my medical background helped me in understanding and explaining the clinical and practical aspects of kidney transplantation.

Why do you write?

I think most writers will answer because I have to. I've always been a creative person but my life decisions lead me to work with death and dying. For me, nursing is an art. Yes, my degrees are in the field of science and management, but there is much that is intuitive when it comes to helping others deal with life-threatening illness, impending death and bereavement. When I was "helped" into retirement—my position as Community Educator for a local hospice was eliminated—I came home and told my husband I wanted to write. He told me to do it! And within a couple of weeks I began the long, tedious process of writing *Winter is Past*.

How long did it take you? How did you go about it?

I'm almost embarrassed to say. I began it in the spring of 2003. I began writing by hand, without an outline. In fact, the entire plot emerged from the characters and went through many, many transformations. I participated in a number of writing critique groups and conferences, which included workshopping. At first I heeded every suggestion and made changes accordingly (big mistake). I sent out queries before it was ready. I signed a contract with an agent who was wonderful to work with, but who didn't really represent my genre. And, finally, I met my publisher at a friend's book-signing. In the meantime, I have another novel completed. I've also written and published articles, short stories and poetry. I spend a lot of time blogging now, mostly poetry.

What did you learn in the process? What did you change when you tackled your second novel?

The second time around I outlined the story, scene-by-scene and did worksheets on characters and setting—not that it turned out the exact way the story unfolded. Just as in *Winter is Past*, the characters drove the plot, so in *The Sin of My Father,* they led me down unexpected byways. I also used an expert as a consultant. This time, I did not show the manuscript to anyone until it was completed. Only one writer-friend has read it and I've yet to review her comments. It's gestating for now.

What are your plans?

Right now, the immediate focus is to work on promotion of *Winter is Past.* I would also like to self-publish some poetry.

My blog, http://liv2write2day.wordpress.com, keeps me busy and I contribute articles to a poetry community at http://dversepoets.com. By the way, the whole retirement thing is a huge myth. I'm as busy as ever.

Is your second novel a sequel?

No, it's a stand-alone. I woke up at 3 AM one day and jotted down the plot. I don't have any solid plans for a sequel to *Winter is Past*, but there are some ideas jiggling around in my head.

Tell us a little about the second novel.

It's called *The Sin of His Father.* It's about a young man who learns on his mother's deathbed that he was conceived in an act of rape. He must then go out and find redemption through forgiveness.

Who will want to read Winter is Past?

I see it as a novel that will appeal primarily to women. People who read inspirational or Christian fiction will enjoy it. It will be helpful to those who have experience with organ transplantation, or who are facing that surgery or the prospect of becoming a donor. I'd like to think health care professionals, especially those in areas such as hospice, would find it useful. People who like authors such a Jodi Picoult or Nicolas Sparks will find that it is along similar veins as their novels. To me, perhaps the most significant audience for this book is book clubs. There are issues that bear discussion, such as transplantation and Advance Directives. To that end, I have included questions for their consideration.

Acknowledgments

I have so many people who have helped me through this process. My husband, David, you've often wondered what I was doing, spending so many hours at the computer, but you've always given me your support, your delicious cooking and the beautiful photo we chose for the cover of this book, taken in the garden you nourish.

Over the past few years, I've belonged to a number of writing groups and received much good advice. My dear friend and "Sis," Judy Haar, you've read this book so many times and made many valuable suggestions. Jeanne Jacob's critique group, the two smaller groups that burgeoned out of workshops at the TMCC writer's conference: I'd love to mention each of you by name, but I'm so afraid I'll miss someone as people drifted in and out over the years. Just know you each made a difference.

Paul Roukie Dinkins – without your gift of life, I don't know if I would be here to pursue these dreams of writing. You never hesitated to take the risk of giving me a kidney.

Mom, you've always believed in me throughout all the ups and downs of life. You are such an inspiration to me. You're the one who showed me how to survive loss. If you resemble anyone in this book, it's Emily.

Thank you to those of you at Lucky Bat Books who have helped bring this to publication: Judith Harlan, Colleen Kuehne and Theresa Rose. You've made it a pleasant process.

And to the Divine Creative Spirit. In *The Artist's Way*, Julia Cameron mentioned a mantra that reads, "As I create and listen, I will be led." Those words creep across my monitor in the screensaver mode to remind me of the Source.

Read More

Read more about Victoria C. Slotto's fiction, poetry and writing on her Website, http://VictoriaCSlotto.com

And follow her blog, http://liv2write2day.wordpress.com, for up-to-date reports on her next book.

www.ingramcontent.com/pod-product-compliance
Lightning Source LLC
Chambersburg PA
CBHW031451260626
47154CB00016B/726